THE PRESIDENT'S MEN

By
C T Mitchell

Wood Duck Media
PO Box 2138
Ashgrove West Qld 4060 AUSTRALIA

First published in Australia by Wood Duck Media in 2023

www.WoodDuckMedia.com

A legal document copy of this book is available from National Library, Canberra

Paperback 978-0-6484605-8-9

Printed and bound by Ingram Spark

Wood Duck Media is committed to a sustainable future for our business, our readers and our planet.

TABLE OF CONTENTS

Chapter 1.. 1

Chapter 2.. 5

Chapter 3.. 8

Chapter 4.. 12

Chapter 5.. 16

Chapter 6.. 20

Chapter 7.. 23

Chapter 8.. 29

Chapter 9.. 33

Chapter 10.. 38

Chapter 11.. 43

Chapter 12.. 49

Chapter 13.. 56

Chapter 14.. 60

Chapter 15.. 64

Chapter 16.. 71

Chapter 17.. 77

Chapter 18.. 82

Chapter 19 86

Chapter 20 92

Chapter 21 99

Chapter 22 105

Chapter 23 111

Chapter 24 118

Chapter 25 124

Chapter 26 129

Chapter 27 136

Chapter 28 144

Chapter 29 149

Chapter 30 154

Chapter 31 162

Chapter 32 169

Chapter 33 175

Chapter 34 181

Chapter 35 187

Chapter 36 193

Chapter 37 198

Chapter 38 204

Chapter 39 211

Chapter 40 218

Chapter 41 224

Chapter 42..232

Chapter 43..239

Chapter 44..246

Chapter 45..253

Chapter 46..261

Chapter 47..269

Chapter 48..277

Chapter 49..285

Chapter 50..293

Chapter 51..301

Chapter 52..308

Chapter 53..316

Chapter 54..324

Chapter 55..332

Chapter 56..340

Chapter 57..347

Chapter 58..355

Chapter 59..363

Chapter 60..371

Chapter 61..380

Chapter 62..388

About the Author...392

DEDICATION

To all those who have lived in an abusive relationship, whether at home or at work, there is a better world out there for you.

Leave the narcissist

CHAPTER 1

"Your father worries me." Sally Barton leaned back in her deck chair and closed her eyes behind her over-sized sunglasses. "I know we are supposed to be relaxing, enjoying some mother-daughter time, but I can't relax when I'm forever thinking about your dad. What if he does something while we're away?"

It was a stay vacation close to home, but still felt like miles away from the city that never slept.

"He'll be fine Mum. We're enjoying ourselves on vacation. What else is there to do?" Beth Barton tugged the wide brim of her sun hat further down on her forehead. "Dad isn't a child, Mum. He's at work."

"You know that's not what I mean." Sally bit down so hard on her bottom lip that she tasted blood. "What if he has one of his episodes?"

"Why don't you check his YouTube channel? That's the only way any of us can keep track of his comings and goings anymore."

"Great idea!"

Sally picked up her phone and tapped on the YouTube app. She knew Warren's channel address by heart now. Warren-Rants. They'd watched and re-watched every single video he posted to try to make sense of the dark turn his life had taken since starting at the financial firm seven years ago on Wall Street.

Warren grew up wanting for nothing. Doors were instantly opened for him. But in the past twelve months, the lights dimmed. The psychologists said the notoriety made him feel entitled and out of touch with reality. He was used to getting what he wanted. And when that didn't happen with the people around him, he had a furious reaction.

He posted nasty things about them online.

First, it was Facebook, and then he started a YouTube channel with his video blog 'Warren Rants'. It turned out Warren says a lot of things and none of them were flattering about his co-workers, especially his immediate bosses.

"Maybe you're just a little too sensitive," Sally remembered telling him after he uploaded his first video. "Bullying happens. Just brush it off. I'm sure that will do the trick."

But it didn't do the trick that time. It seemed every one of Warren's colleagues had it in for him. A jibe here. A smart remark there.

To Warren, it was always personal. Most times they apologized, but it wasn't as easy for Warren to put the constant rejection behind him. And he didn't accept the behaviour of the President and his executive team.

"Oh, look, Mum, Dad's uploaded a brand-new video."

Sally clicked the play button and held out her phone so they could watch it together. Warren's face filled most of the frame. He didn't look dangerous with his 'Brad Pitt' looks and perfect smile. He certainly didn't look like the sort of guy anyone would tease.

The only thing that seemed even the slightest bit off about Warren was his eyes. They shifted back and forth like an over-wound metronome, particularly when he started ruminating on screen.

"Is he drunk?" Beth muttered. "He looks out of it."

"Hush, darling, so we can hear what he has to say."

"Hi everyone, this is Warren. Today on Warren Rants is 'payback a prick day.' I'd like to dedicate this very special episode to Nick, Jack, and Michael. I've tried to be nice. I tried to do my job well. But you continue to bully me. You deny it. But you're lying. You're lying through your pearly whitened teeth, Nick. You have defrauded accounts, and now it's payback time. And you Jack, 'Mr. Three Month Married Man' still touching the asses of every little 25-year-old girl you can lay your grubby fingers on. And Michael, you cocaine snorting, unemployed for the past five years; you are a grovelling ass. See you in Hell, pricks!"

Warren jostled the camera around so he was no longer the focus. Instead, it showed the front of the financial headquarters on Wall Street.

Sally and Beth heard a round of pop-pop-pops that sounded like firecrackers going off. But it wasn't. Screaming, running, and swearing was happening as someone big and burl dressed all in dark navy tackled Warren.

They realized their worst fears were coming true.

Those weren't firecrackers going off.

Those were gunshots.

CHAPTER 2

With taking down an offender, Detective Jack Creed was always taught to react first and think later.

"I need backup in Central Park!" he shouted to a passer-by, who was standing around with his mouth hanging open. What was he trying to do, catch flies?

"Just hold him a little while longer, Jack." Detective Danielle Rodrigues hit the ground like she was sliding into home plate and cuffed Warren.

Danielle was the complete opposite of Creed. She could play both sides of the card as needed, rough and tumble cop or undercover veteran.

Today she was both.

"Danielle to the rescue," he joked.

Jack knew being transferred to the States was going to be a huge adjustment. His wife was pissed, but she understood this was something he needed to do. It was a change for the better. He had burnt his bridges back home.

But he was experienced with a good record for catching crims and that's what the yanks wanted.

His family was going to join him after he settled in. The market was slow, but they had some prospects checking out the property.

"As usual," she replied with a grin and brushed her dark Latin hair out of her face.

Creed sat up and dragged the offender with him. "I just wish we had gotten here two minutes earlier."

"It is what it is," Danielle said.

"Tell that to the families of the staff he shot."

"Who is talking to the press? You or me?" She stood and dusted off the knees of her jeans. "Cause if it's me, I need to put on something that's more we-are-deeply saddened-and-in-shock instead of I-just-woke-up-after-an-all-night-bender."

"You're the camera-ready one, Danielle, not me. Besides, the media prefer a good-looking hot girl with curves over a wrinkly, gray-haired fifty-something-year-old," Creed said with a smirk, knowing full well it would rile her up.

Danielle didn't bite. "Why wouldn't they? Not bad for 37. And you? Fifty? Ha, closer to sixty, I'd say." She mocked with a smirk.

Creed shook the offender, who howled for his lawyer.

"Good call. Besides, I have this prick to deal with."

*****

"For the last time, I told you I'm not saying anything until you get me a lawyer," Warren insisted. "Call my wife. She'll give you the number of the guy we used to buy our house. Not sure if he'll be much fucking use here, though," Warren huffed.

"Oh, you've said plenty already," Creed remarked. "We've had you on our radar for months. Your videos speak louder than anything you could think to say right here and now."

"What videos?" Warren squirmed in the metal chair. "I don't know what you're talking about."

"Don't play dumb with me," Creed snapped. "You know exactly what videos I'm talking about."

"Why did you shoot those three guys today?" Creed questioned.

The interrogation had begun. Maybe Warren would slip up and give away some details about the crime.

He'd shut up faster than a politician in the middle of a scandal

"You had an office full of people. You could take aim at anyone. Why them?" He slapped three pictures down on the table in front of Warren. The three victims. "Why Nick, Jack, and Michael?"

"Why not?"

"What did they ever do to you?"

He shrugged. "Plenty. I was a joke to them. Now the jokes on them."

CHAPTER 3

"How long did you have him going till he clammed up?" Danielle asked.

Rodrigues arrived back from the press coverage and stood next to Creed behind the two-way mirror. They could see into the interrogation room, but Warren couldn't see out.

"He can't deny the shooting. He's the one that posted the video online." Creed sipped at his steaming cup of black coffee. "We can stick that on him, maybe more. We're gunning for the hate speech. Those videos he posted..." Creed shook his head. "Those videos are our most damning evidence if we can find them."

Danielle frowned. "What do you mean, if we can find them? They're up on his YouTube page. The guy is obsessed with documenting his every thought and move."

"Was obsessed with documenting his every thought and move," Creed corrected. "He's deleted them from his account and the guys in IT can't find a cache. We'll need to get a warrant to search his home to see if we can find the original copies."

"So, he's smarter than he looks, huh?"

"Seems so." Creed took another long draw from his coffee cup. "His wife and daughter are on their way to the station. I think we should separate them and question them to see what they knew while the boys work on getting that warrant approved."

Danielle nodded while palming a locket around her neck. "Count me in."

*****

Beth Barton looked up when the door to the tiny interrogation room opened.

"Miss Barton, I'm Detective Creed." Instead of offering to shake her hand, Creed set a folder of crime scene photos in front of her. Old blokes don't shake young girl's hands. Kind of weird. "I'm in charge of your father's case."

"Do you think my Mom or I had anything to do with this event?" Beth asked. "We're in as much shock as anyone else." Creed glared back at her with a look that showed he had heard it all before.

"He's lost his way." She looked at anything and everything but the crime scene photos.

Creed didn't really blame her. Three families lost their husbands today and her dad caused it. Why would she want to be reminded of that? Denial was easier. Denial helped you sleep at night.

"What changes did you notice in your father within the last few months?" Creed asked.

"You mean when he started posting those horrible videos?" Beth looked up and held Creed's gaze.

"Three months ago, Dad started changing. He withdrew from us and refused to tell us where he was going or who he was seeing. He dropped all his old friends and only wanted to be alone." Beth frowned.

"At least that's what he said. Mum and I weren't so sure. We could hear him talking to someone late at night. More like arguing. They were planning for something, but when we confronted him about it, he said we were being paranoid and to leave him alone.

We were forced to subscribe to his YouTube channel if we wanted any hint of what he was up to. He never talked to us anymore. It was like living with a ghost. He was there, but not there. Mom and I are just as shocked as anyone else by today's events at the office. Believe me, Detective Creed, if we could have stopped it, we would have."

"When you say you heard him arguing with someone at night, did you ever question him about it?"

"We tried, but he always got upset and told us to mind our own business and stay out of his life." Beth spread her hand out in front of him in a hopeless gesture. "That's when we subscribed to his YouTube channel. Why would he tell the world what he was thinking, but not his own family? We didn't understand, though we wanted to."

"Could you hear this other person at all? Did Warren ever talk to them over Skype or Messenger?"

Beth shook her head.

"We're going to need to search your house," Creed said. "It's probably best if you're not there. With the media crawling around, you're going to thank us for that advice."

Beth nodded. "I understand. We were on vacation. We can just go back up there to the hotel. I can leave our number in case you need us for anything. Your parents alive, Detective Creed?"

Creed nodded.

"If your dad did something so horrible and so heinous that you couldn't wrap your head around it, what would you do?"

"I'd do the same thing you and your mother are doing," Creed assured her. "Sometimes people are just broken, but no matter how hard we try to fix them, it's really up to them to fix themselves." Creed looked at Beth with understanding.

CHAPTER 4

The Barton house was eerily quiet. Creed and Danielle led the team to Warren's office. "Dust for prints," Creed ordered. "Based on interviews with his family, we might look for a second person as well."

"Just what we need. Two men haters running loose." Danielle crouched and shined a flashlight under the desk. "This guy should have just accepted a joke or two and moved on. Instead, he goes out and kills three guys."

"Maybe it's not that they made jokes at him but how they said it," Detective Jenkins, one cop dusting for prints, said. "I mean, what makes snide remarks above the law?

"Oh, don't tell me you're standing up for this idiot!" Danielle pulled several boxes out from under the table. "He just needed to harden up and not be so sensitive."

Danielle was a tough bitch. You had to be growing up with four brothers. She had to fight for everything.

"So, you think calling somebody a black bastard is, okay?" Jenkins argued.

Nick was the biggest racist of them all. He hated blacks and expressed his views often. The others followed suit. They needed to save their jobs – spineless pricks.

Danielle shrugged. "Of course not. There's no place for racism."

"Danielle, can you turn on Warren's laptop? Perfect. No password to protect his stuff."

"Well, our shooter has left quite the video trail." Rodrigues double clicked on the video with the earliest one first.

"Hi, all. This is Warren, and you're watching Warren Rants. I know a lot of you are going to say 'so what's up with all this whining? Just suck it up and move on, buddy,' but I can't. How would you feel if you were being constantly bullied by your bosses? Nick, this is for you. You said my finance knowledge would be helpful when I joined the company. But then you turned into a total bastard. What gives? How can you use someone like that? Think it's okay because you are the President? Well, it's not, pal. I'm calling the shots and you're going to get what's coming to you. You heard it here first, Nick Reid."

"Sick" Creed commented.

Danielle clicked on the next video. Warren's face filled the screen again.

Society sickened her. She was becoming jaded. It didn't help she lost her soul mate on the job. That fateful night when they broke the news was still fresh after several months of mourning his loss. Being widowed was bad enough.

Her daughter Tina was a handful. She was hanging with the wrong crowd.

"Hi all. This is Warren from Warren Rants. Today's video is dedicated to Jack. I bet you thought I'd still be upset with Nick, right? Wrong. Jackson and Wright are just a boy's camp of failed real estate agents out to bash anybody they can while trying to sell the American dream.

Double standards. You make me feel like shit 'cause I dared challenge you. We're not all 'yes men', dumbass. Jack. You think you're hot. Working out the gym, flexing your muscles. Who fuckin' cares, dickwit.

Preaching morals to the team while you are trying to get into the panties of every young girl who crosses your path. And you've been married for just three months. Disgusting. Berate me in public... oh, you'll get what's coming to you."

"Jesus, this guy is troubled." Danielle combed through the box she pulled from under the desk.

It was like a treasure chest of racial propaganda.

Creed clicked on the next video. "I think the constant barrage pushed Warren over the edge."

"Not everyone goes to that extreme when they're pushed over the edge," Danielle reminded Creed.

She cringed at the memory of the bullet in the chamber sitting at her kitchen table with an empty bottle of vodka.

"Not everyone is Warren Barton."

"Yeah, thankfully."

Warren's face filled the screen again. "Hi, all. This is Warren from Warren Rants. Today's video blog is for Michael. You are as bad as any of them. But you think you are the only one with talent. Remember when you lost a two million dollar account and made me look like the one responsible?

"You're a racist asshole, Michael. I'm the last guy you'll ever treat with such disrespect."

"Those are the big ones," Creed said. "We can use the other video blog entries to show a pattern of how he felt repeatedly disrespected until he took matters into his own crazy hands."

"What about phone, text, and instant messenger records?" Danielle asked. "I know we'll have to put in a request for the phone and text message records, but what about IM? Did he save any of those logs on his computer?"

Danielle searched through all the files and folders till she found what they were hoping for. "Bingo. Let's see who Warren was talking to leading up to the crime."

CHAPTER 5

Creed crowded close to read the chat transcript over her shoulder. It started innocently enough.

Warren, under the internet handle Wsez, was talking to someone who went by the handle DynoMite. They exchanged, "Hey, how are you," and, "Good, man, you?" before it delved into more sinister territory.

Wsez: Did you get the guns?

DynoMite: I always get the guns. It's easy.

Wsez: We can't keep them here. I can't have anyone get suspicious that I'm planning more than just an internet rant.

DynoMite: I know a place. You can pick it up on your way to the office.

Wsez: Me? I thought we were in this together.

DynoMite: We are, but if someone tips the cops off, we need to finish the job. We can't go in together. Those bastards have probably already blabbed to the cops about how 'threatened' you make them feel. The cops will expect you to do something. They won't think twice about me.

Wsez: So, I go in first and then you follow?

DynoMite: Not the same day.

Wsez: But what's the point if we don't take care of all the assholes at once? We need to hit them while everyone is scared. There's more confusion that way. You'll be able to blend with the staff.

DynoMite: What we need is to keep the element of fear. If they know you didn't act alone, it will freak the bastards morning, noon, and night. That's payback till we bring the curtain down on the last act with a BANG.

Wsez: They'll pay.

DynoMite: Trust me, you'll be a legend.

Wsez: So, same time/place as we talked about?

DynoMite: Definitely. See you there.

"We're dealing with two offenders here. Detective Jenkins, call the real estate firm and let them know to be on high alert. Get a copy of Warren's phone records while you're at it. See if he's called or texted anyone more than usual. Rodrigues read through these chat transcripts and looked for any clues as to DynoMite's identity. Call me if you find anything. I'm going to the office."

Were they planning to take down the entire company? Danielle skimmed the transcript, looking for answers. She had a horrible feeling they were running out of time.

Wsez: It feels like 'Gang up on Warren' day.

DynoMite: Dumb bastards don't know they are marked. They'd be nicer if they knew not to mess with you. Pretty soon everyone will know not to mess with you.

Wsez: I'm tired of waiting.

DynoMite: Not long now. Pretty soon everyone will know your name.

Clearly, the second suspect shared Warren's opinions and goaded him on just as much–if not more–than the bosses at work. But who were they? Danielle needed to find more clues.

Wsez: So you know a lot about me, but you've never really told me much about you.

DynoMite: It's best this way.

Wsez: But how can we plan if I know nothing about you?

DynoMite: You know plenty about me. You just don't need to know everything.

Wsez: Is this a setup? Are you going to get me to do your dirty work and then back out?

DynoMite: Of course not.

Wsez: Then tell me who you are.

DynoMite: You know who I am. We work for the same company. I hate those guys just as much as you do. Don't back out on me now, Warren. We need to see this through. Now, do you remember the drop location?

Wsez: The storm drain next to the office entrance.

DynoMite: What you need will wait for you there.

Wsez: What about you?

DynoMite: I'll be ready for round two on Friday. Two 'events' in one week. Those assholes won't know what hit them.

Rodrigues punched Creed's number into her phone. "Jack, are you at the office yet?"

"Just got here."

"Good. The drop location is in the storm drain by the office entrance. The only other clues we've been able to find is that they work in the same company."

"I'll check the staff roster and see if anyone has been missing from work since the incident," Creed promised. "Send back up, please."

CHAPTER 6

Creed found the storm drain. He removed the manhole cover and peered down into the darkness. There was no telling what was down here. He was already thinking about scrubbing his skin raw and burning his clothes.

He climbed down before using the light on his phone to see. Someone had removed the metal grate from the maintenance tunnel. Jack focused his light and crept inside.

"Jesus," he muttered when his flashlight illuminated hate speech graffiti all over the walls.

Kill the bastards!

The only good boss is a dead boss.

Shotgun says... dead!

He captured those words on his phone. This was a chain of evidence.

He needed to check that staff roster list, and he needed to check it now.

*****

The clerk in the office chatted amiably as Creed waited for her to print out a copy of the official staff list.

"I really need that list of names, so if you can hurry it up, I'd appreciate it. Also, crosscheck it with any absences since Wednesday."

"That's not my job. You'll have to check with HR if you want staff attendances." The clerk handed over the list. "There you go. Hot off the press."

Creed looked down at the list.

Warren was one of only five guys in middle management. He'd bet big money that DynoMite was one of those guys. Should he find them or go talk to HR about attendance? There was no time to track down five guys with the clock ticking on another attack.

He needed to go straight to the source: the head of HR.

Creed walked quickly to Kellie Fletcher's office without looking panicked or suspicious. If the suspect knew they were on to him, would that bump the crime up? Creed didn't want to even think about how many people were in the building.

They were all in danger. No one was safe.

Creed took the stairs two at a time. A managerial meeting was set to begin in ten minutes. "Ms. Fletcher?" Creed knocked once on the door.

"Detective Jack Creed, NYPD. I need to speak to you." He opened her door.

It still felt strange saying the call sign, but it was feeling like home.

The office was empty. But the whiteboard had something written on it. Scrawled in red marker were the same words from the storm drain:

Kill the bastards!

The only good boss is a dead boss.

Shotgun says... dead!

He quickly photographed the board with his phone.

He suspected the second suspect wasn't another angry male, but an angry female. Their second suspect was Kellie Fletcher.

CHAPTER 7

Creed didn't give himself time to think. He ran down the stairs to where the management meeting was held.

"Please don't let me be late. Please don't let me be late," he chanted under his breath.

As he ran, he pulled his gun out of the holster hidden under his jacket. He was going to need it. It could be the difference between one casualty and twelve.

As Creed neared the door, he could see HR Manager Fletcher through the glass pane of the boardroom door. She was standing, smiling as if it were just any other regular day.

Her words filtered out into the hallway.

"Team, I know you've been spooked by the events that happened on Wednesday. It's a genuine tragedy. I am truly shocked that no one put the pieces together and followed the trail to Warren sooner. That man was crying out for help and no one heard. You are all a pack of homophobic racists. Gay people are humans too. We have to make sure this doesn't happen again." Kellie reached into the drawer.

Creed kicked in the door and pointed his gun at Kellie Fletcher.

"Don't move an inch. Take your hand out slowly."

Creed watched with eyes unblinking as she did what he told her to do with her fingers shaking.

Her face had turned stark white.

The boardroom was swarming with police before Creed had time to even lower his gun. "Detective Jack Creed." He flashed his badge. "This woman is under arrest."

"What is this about? I have done nothing wrong. I'm taking steps to make sure what happened doesn't happen again," Kellie huffed and grimaced when Creed put the handcuffs on a little too tightly.

"I just bet you are. What do we have here, Ms. Fletcher?" he pulled the drawer open triumphant with a smile on his face when it slowly faded.

Inside were different colored markers.

He pulled it all the way open, but there was no sign she was about to cause these people grievous harm.

No weapon made things complicated in a hurry.

Creed had already stuck his foot in his mouth.

The other officers exchanged looks. Nobody was going to argue with Creed. He was a decorated officer with many stellar years on the force. That was in Australia though.

His private life was one for water cooler gossip. Every hotshot officer usually had a checkered private life. That wasn't news.

Everything had to be done by the book. The lack of a weapon was going to make his case difficult to prove without a confession. The mistake of busting in unannounced with his gun drawn was going to come back and bite him.

He used his phone to call Danielle. The only thing he got was her answering service.

She must've stepped away from the phone. He was going to give her a heads up, but now she was going to have to learn about the arrest when he walked her through the station on the way to the interrogation room.

"I want this place locked down. Take statements from everybody. Get all of their information and send them home. Have forensics go over this place, including her office," he commanded while holding onto Kellie and leading her out into the hallway.

"You've made a grave error, Detective. Why would you think for one second, I had anything to do with what happened here the other day? I didn't even know Warren. We might've seen each other in the hallway," she spoke while he was reciting her rights.

"Do you understand..." He couldn't finish his sentence when she steamrolled over him.

"I understand more than you know. This is going to cause a media outcry. You don't have a shred of evidence to accuse me of any crime, including jaywalking," she stated with this cool and calm demeanor, unlike those that had been caught with the metaphorical smoking barrel.

"Let's not waste the court's time on a frivolous trial. Tell me why you did it? You must've had a very good reason," Creed needled.

Kellie laughed. "Nice try. You have nothing to hold me on. This is going to waste everybody's time and valuable resources." She glared at him over her shoulder. "I believe I have one phone call. Take three guesses about who I'm going to contact. The first two don't count."

"You're going to need all the help you can get. There is the slim possibility you could claim a psychotic break. I don't care what happens to you. Just as long as you are off the street is fine by me," Creed stated with his fingers digging in a little deeper than necessary into her shoulder blade.

Creed would not play her game. It was hard not to when she was being so arrogant and baiting him into a verbal confrontation.

The entire exchange was making his teeth itch.

He had to trip her up under the hot lights, but now she had invoked her right to a lawyer. She hadn't come out and said it, but she inferred it vehemently.

Creed believed in the simplest form of justice. He didn't have a good thing to say about ambulance chasers. They only slowed things down. It would be a circus.

This was the time for jurisprudence. The game was just beginning, but he was certain that once accosted with the circumstantial evidence, she would have no choice but to confess.

So why was he getting this strange feeling in the pit of his stomach?

He noticed the stunned expression on the other police officers' faces when there was no gun found at the scene. He had acted with impulsive judgment, but he felt he had no other choice under the circumstances.

One thing he wasn't expecting was the scene unfolding in front of the building.

A contingent of the press had swarmed in like a bunch of locusts. They were screaming their questions.

Creed had no patience for those looking for a soundbite for the 5 o'clock news. It was strange how fast they could get the story. Somebody must've tipped them off.

"I'm innocent. He's arresting an innocent woman. This is just another example of police brutality. He's hurting me." Kellie motioned with her head to the way Creed was gripping her shoulder.

Creed did nothing to stop the flashbulbs from capturing his supposed over-the-top police action. He couldn't exactly tell her to shut up in front of them without it becoming a feeding frenzy.

He opened the door and slid her into the back seat before closing it. They pressed microphones into his face, but he refused to comment on an ongoing investigation.

"There will be a press conference when we have all the facts. The public can rest easy tonight," he stated in his usual stoic manner, adding nothing.

He had to shove his way through the throng of the press.

He had just got in and turned the ignition when he heard a soft whisper coming from behind him.

"I wonder how they got here so quickly. Maybe somebody predicted what you were going to do. It's amazing how you think you might be smarter than some people. Then you meet somebody that is playing by a whole new set of rules." Kellie whistled while sitting back with an air of confidence surrounding the insipid smile on her face.

That feeling in the pit of his stomach was getting more intense.

CHAPTER 8

They were not exactly applauding when he arrived back at the police station.

He walked the suspect to the bullpen, but this time didn't receive the congratulations for a job well done.

Even his partner Danielle was reluctant to make eye contact. Something had obviously made it look like he had done something wrong in the course of his duties.

He went into the interrogation room and made sure they restrained her to the table. He walked out to let her think about her situation.

Danielle was a little proactive. She grabbed him and found an empty room.

The door closed with the blinds drawn to make sure they would not be interrupted. She walked over to the edge of the desk and sat down with her arms crossed.

"This is bad. No weapon is a serious lapse in judgment. They are going to hang you out to dry for this unless you can get a confession in the next hour. You have a little bit of rope but they hope you're going to hang yourself with it." Danielle crossed her legs without even a hint of a grin that this was some sort of joke.

"She's guilty. I know it," he defended himself, while pacing back and forth in front of the desk.

"You don't have to convince me. I believe in you. We both know it's what we can prove in a court of law. What exactly do you have? I haven't known you long but you have integrity," she said with one hand fiddling with a pen.

She had a hidden nervous habit of clicking it when things didn't go her way. That didn't happen often.

"Look at this. It's what was on the whiteboard in her office. It's the same thing we found in the tunnel," Creed said before he produced the two photographs of the writing on the wall and the whiteboard.

"You busted in while they were busy having a meeting with human resources. You scared the living daylights out of them. Some are screaming about a very hefty lawsuit for psychological damages," Danielle informed him.

He stopped pacing with his lower lip quivering. "I thought she was going to murder everybody in the room. I will not apologize. What I will do is bring you in there with me. Maybe you can talk some sense into her."

"Our superior is distancing himself from this entire mess. A spokesperson from internal affairs is going to be here shortly. You better have your story straight. Let's go get your confession," she said before brushing past him.

"You said you believed me. After everything we have been through in the past few months, I would think that I have earned your respect by now. I don't care about anybody else out there. They can all go to hell and take their self-righteous attitudes with them," Creed blurted out.

"Keep your head in the game. We have the facts on our side. I have a plan. Call me Dani," Dani insisted when she stopped momentarily at her desk to collect a very thick folder. She needed to take things down a notch. Being less formal would help.

She could hear whispers of dissent when they walked through the bullpen. There was no sign of their immediate supervisor.

Creed had one chance to make this work. Nobody had slipped through his fingers, and Ms. Fletcher would not be the first one.

They walked in together to find her alert and smiling.

Creed sat down with Dani, standing behind the suspect. It was intimidation and had worked several times in the past.

"This interview is being recorded. State your full name for the record," Dani urged when she touched her shoulder, only to see her flinch with slight discomfort.

"I'm not saying anything until my lawyer arrives. She should be sure in five minutes," she stated with both Detectives looking at each other puzzled by this comment.

"You've been in here alone the entire time. There is no phone," Creed said, a little flummoxed.

Kellie shrugged her shoulders with the chain connecting her to the table, rattling in response.

There was suddenly a soft knock on the door.

"She's a little early. It might be a good idea not to keep her waiting. The woman is very busy. What can you expect from Miss Williams? Miss Julie Williams. You might've heard of her," Kellie's name dropped without an inkling of panic in her voice.

Dani did the honors of answering the door.

It was only open a crack when Ms. Williams took control of the interview from the moment, she entered the room. She slapped down her briefcase and looked at both the Detectives with a shake of her head.

"I want a few moments to confer before we begin. What are you waiting for? Get out. Whatever is said is covered by client and lawyer confidentiality. I don't have all day," Ms. Williams said with her right index finger touching a very expensive watch encrusted with a string of diamonds around the face.

Creed was about to say something, but he didn't get the chance. Dani was already grabbing his hand and dragging him into the hallway. She had purposely left behind the folder with a couple of pictures prominently displayed.

Ms. Fletcher stared at the dead bodies in the photos, peeking out of the folder without cracking a smile.

Dani didn't like it at all. This was one cold bitch. Nothing fazed her.

CHAPTER 9

Rodrigues went to her desk to find a plain brown envelope left in her inbox. A quick perusal of the contents made her angry enough to want to punch something.

"What is it? I don't like the look on your face," Creed said while looking over her shoulder.

"The IT department can't find anything on those drives. Every piece of evidence, including the diatribe between the two co-conspirators, is gone. They tried everything to retrieve them. It looks like a Trojan virus was released when we read the conversation. We can't even track the conversation." Dani crumpled the paper with the results clearly written in black ink.

"This isn't your run-of-the-mill revenge scheme. Something else is going on here. I don't like it. I don't like it one bit," Creed expressed.

The case was slowly being taken apart, piece by piece. There was still more than enough to charge Warren. He had been caught after the chaos, still holding onto the weapon used.

He showed no remorse.

"Just when we thought everything was tied up in a nice little package. There is no proof Miss Fletcher is his accomplice. I feel so stupid. She played me. She's smart," Creed intoned while staring at the door to the interrogation room.

He desperately wanted to hear what was being said. The law clearly stated a lawyer had every right to confer with her client. This was the red tape Creed hated. It seemed the criminals had more than ample ammunition to make the police officers' life a living hell.

The door opened, signalling it was time to get to the bottom of things.

"My client would like to cooperate. She's willing to discuss what happened. You can call her Ms. Fletcher for the duration of this interview. I'll be here to supervise and advise her when to speak candidly." Miss Williams looked up with her catlike green eyes staring through them.

Creed recited today's date before commencing the interview with the video camera in the corner of the room recording. "State your full name for the record."

"Kellie Emily Fletcher."

"If I feel she is being harassed, this interview is over," Ms. Williams interjected with the sleeves of her white blouse rolled up past the elbows.

"Why did you write those things on your whiteboard?" Creed asked in his attempt to surprise and shock Kellie into becoming flustered.

"I'm afraid I don't know what you're talking about, Detective. I very rarely use my office. You can ask anyone. I haven't been inside in almost a week while I have been traveling on business. I can corroborate everything I say with irrefutable documents," Kellie answered.

Ms. Williams produced said documentation in triplicate.

"This is full disclosure of her whereabouts for the last 72 hours. She just came back from England this morning. These are also affidavits from three of her colleagues. You'll see everything is in order."

Creed was gobsmacked by how efficiently the lawyer was systematically destroying his credibility.

"What do you suppose they're going to find when they evaluate the handwriting on the whiteboard? It's going to be an exact match for you. You think you're smart, but every criminal makes a mistake," Creed said while looking at the documentation provided.

"I can't see how that's possible when I didn't do it. You're barking up the wrong tree. You should be out looking for the real accomplice. How do we know there is one?" Kellie inquired.

"Forgive my partner. He doesn't function without a daily fix of caffeine. We have Warren's computer. His family told us that he has been acting irrationally. They detailed certain episodes where he became withdrawn and sullen. His rants blindsided them," Dani piped in unannounced.

"What does that have to do with me? Clearly, you have the wrong person. I'm not stupid. I know my rights," Ms. Fletcher stated, while leaning forward.

"You should be very careful about accusing an upstanding member of society. She doesn't even have a speeding ticket. I have heard nothing to indicate you have enough to hold my client. If there is nothing else, we will be leaving," Miss Williams said while she was shuffling papers.

It was tempting to hold her for 48 hours. They might be able to sweat a confession out of her.

There was nothing they could offer when everything was erased.

Creed turned away when both client and lawyer strolled out without further comment.

He almost flipped the table, but he remained quietly fuming with indignation. "She knew I was coming. Everything was planned to make me look like a fool. You do see that... don't you?"

"We both know there's not enough to hold her. We have to continue digging to find the truth. You're right about one thing. Criminals do make mistakes. This one is a sociopath. She's loving every minute of this," Dani replied when there was suddenly a shadow in the door.

"I'm Jeffrey Reeves. This is now an internal matter. You are ordered to hand over everything you have on this case. An impartial observer will look at all of your evidence and report to me. I will determine whether action is going to be taken against you. I take no delight in this," he said with one hand combing through what was left of his thinning locks.

He showed his credentials before motioning for two more guys in black suits to come in to retrieve the evidence compiled in the two cases.

CHAPTER 10

It was two days of unpaid suspension. An investigation into his conduct was going to decide his fate.

A jury of his peers. What a joke!

They gave the case to another rookie investigator.

There was some discussion about Warren pleading guilty to the murder charges. It was done under the guise of a psychiatric evaluation. Temporary insanity was going to be his plea.

That part of the process was ongoing and would yield some results in the next 24 hours.

Creed was unshaven with a day's growth of beard. His job was hanging by a thread and he knew it. Drinking would have been the first thing he did, but he refused to give Ms. Fletcher that kind of power over him.

This bout of depression was something his family had to deal with before. They wanted him home for the duration of his suspension, but he refused to put them through another one of his mood swings.

He felt relieved they were still in Australia, tying up some loose ends.

The press had already crucified him in the headlines. The gaggle of reporters on his lawn had dwindled down to a select few from rival stations.

He picked up the coffee cup and looked at the insignia on the bottom of it. How could he claim to be the best dad in the world? He could hardly get out of bed without slapping the snooze several times.

The pity parade was getting annoying.

Phone calls had been left unanswered throughout the night. The machine picked up a medley of messages. Some very close acquaintances claimed to have his back and others castrated him for making the department look bad.

He was called a dinosaur. Maybe they were right. Things were changing. It wasn't the same way to do police work.

It was 3 AM when he finally had enough. The cord was still dangling from the wall where he had pulled it out in an angry outburst. He was just glad nobody was around to see his accidental slip from sanity.

His cell was ringing right next to him on the counter. The caller ID identified an ally. Just how much she could do was something to be considered. He didn't like relying on somebody else to feed him information about the case on the sly.

It went against his moral integrity, but there was no other choice.

Creed pressed the button. "This better be important. I haven't even had my 1st cup of coffee. Tread carefully."

"There's been a development you might want to know about. Another body was found this morning washed up in Hudson. He had been severely tortured. There is a connection to the case. He was Miss Kellie Fletcher's immediate supervisor when she was working in a temporary agency answering phones," Dani informed him while reading from the company webpage.

She flipped to the next page where there was a picture of Ms. Fletcher's sunny disposition at a company barbecue. Everything was found on their website. It was a plethora of information.

Social media was making police work easier.

"She apparently left the company under a black cloud. It's been stamped, classified. I'm in the process of attaining a warrant for the information, but I don't think it's going to be easy. They'll have their high-priced lawyers stomping their feet and yelling about confidential information falling into the wrong hands," Dani continued.

Creed could sense that she was holding something back. The silence was more than deafening on the other end.

"I appreciate you keeping me up to breast on the case, but you might be cutting your own throat. They know we are close. It won't take them very long to put the pieces together if there is some sort of leak. You should distance yourself from me until this blows over," he suggested with a bittersweet taste of caffeine touching the tip of his tongue when he brought the mug to his lips.

"I think we have a serial killer," she whispered conspiratorially into the receiver.

Creed slapped his forehead. "You don't say. I would have never guessed. There is definitely a pattern, but she is very good at cleaning up after herself, as I've recently learned."

"I have to go. Try to get some rest and enjoy these next couple of days off. It's going to be all hands-on deck when you get back. Nobody has even mentioned anything about the disciplinary hearing. No news is good news," she stated.

"It looks like I'm going to have the chance to catch up on my reading," he said with a breath of hot air onto the books covered in dust taking up residence on his shelf.

He coughed into his hand.

"You are going to obsess about this case. The least I can do is offer you free access to information. I'm sending you a secure link. You will have a back door to bypass my password. Don't thank me," she said before hanging up.

An attachment was delivered. He opened it and committed the password to memory. The program instantly deleted the email with no way to retrieve it.

He had no idea she was in contact with someone technologically savvy. It didn't surprise him. She had proven to be resourceful. Cultivating sources was part of the job.

He sat down at the counter with one of his blockbuster novels.

It was about Armageddon and he couldn't even get past the first couple of pages before turning his attention to his laptop.

CHAPTER 11

Dani was at the scene of the crime near the water where she could smell the putrid stench coming off the Hudson River. It was the easiest place to dump a body.

Whoever had done it was a little clumsy in their efforts. The rocks used to weigh down the body weren't sufficient.

She flashed her badge and was immediately afforded the courtesy of taking a look at the crime scene.

The Detective in charge was a recent new hire. He was straight from the Academy and still green around the gills evident by the way he was dry heaving a few yards away from where the body had been found.

He had been given the rubber stamp to become a detective over those older and more experienced than him. His reputation was born in the case of the missing family. He had found them. They were being held for ransom.

Dani placed the palm of her hand on his shoulder. "At least you didn't do it in front of the cameras. A lot of officers have made that mistake in the past."

Detective Anderson wiped his mouth with the back of his hand before responding. "I'm sorry about your partner. I know his reputation. You shouldn't be here."

"Do you want me to leave? I might be able to offer some insight. I have spent time with the prime suspect," she said with a motion of her hand to one of the technicians.

They came over dressed with rubber gloves to keep the crime scene from being contaminated.

"We haven't even done the preliminary assessment. You've been a busy girl. I suppose I wouldn't have expected anything less from somebody with your dedication to the job," he said with a smile, almost flirtatious.

She was older than he was.

It had been a long time since she had experienced the physical comfort of a man of his youthful exuberance. She was not above mixing business with pleasure, but there were going to have to be certain conditions.

Losing the love of her life had hardened her heart. She wasn't looking for husband number two.

"I heard his name spoken over the wire. He had his wallet still intact when they found him. His name is Flip Carson. I ran it through our database with certain criteria being considered. He is just one of a few men linked to Ms. Fletcher. They did run in the same circles a couple of years ago," she explained what she found after putting on the gloves and walking with him to where the body was being photographed.

It was terribly mangled by what appeared to be the sharp end of propeller blades from a speed boat.

The next generation was always about their need for speed. It was dangerous, but the law turned a blind eye to tourism dollars.

Half of the victim's arm was missing.

She kneeled to take a closer look. The stench almost made her lose the blueberry bagel she had for breakfast.

The corpse was bloated but surprising with most of its limbs still attached. That was a little perplexing, considering how long it had probably been in the water.

"You can see the lips are blue. He's been dead for about a week. The cold water preserved the body. It would've remained at the bottom of the Hudson had it not been for the storm last week," coroner Adams mentioned while using a pen to pry open the swollen lips of the victim.

He was missing several teeth and there were bruises all over his body.

"I would say somebody worked him over pretty damn good. I'm no psychologist, but this is one sick individual we are dealing with. I can't be entirely sure how to say this. I think the victim was alive when he was thrown in the water." Adams flinched at the mere implication of what that might mean.

There had been a shuffle in several departments during budget cuts. Adams was once an assistant but was now the head honcho of the coroner's office. His predecessor had been given early retirement with a 'no obligation to talk about' severance package. The young man was new blood.

The Department was shaking things up to avoid antiquated thinking when it came to racism and prejudices.

A new era of police transparency with the public was taking place. Cowboys were either going to have to change the way they thought about the job or end up being left in the dust.

Some people stuck in their ways were summarily dismissed and replaced with bleeding hearts, looking to make the Police Department accountable for their actions.

There was a transitional period underway.

The man behind the whole campaign was the Police Commissioner.

It was definitely politically motivated, but nobody had the balls to question his authority when he was given the freedom to clean up the department from the higher-ups.

It was also an election year.

Adams and Detective Anderson were part of the shakeup.

"I'll know more when I get him back to the lab for extensive testing. It's a little slow since I haven't had time to hire my replacement. They told me to sit tight for a few more days, but that was two weeks ago." Adams threw up his hands and continued recording his findings in a small recorder in the palm of his right hand.

"I'm going to take another run at Ms. Fletcher. Would you care to join me for your first off-site interview? I believe in the sink or swim method of mentoring. I'm offering to contribute to the case with my years of experience on a consultant basis," she said quickly to add that part to make it less formal and more off the record.

Detective Anderson was a blonde heartthrob with a complimentary fan base from his days in the California surfing community. An injury sidelined him from further competition, and he turned his attention to serving the public's interest.

Moving from LA to New York gave him a new experience.

"People are watching me very closely to see how I handle this case. We could compromise. You can't be officially connected to this case. That will send the wrong message," Detective Anderson said while he was scratching his chin.

"What do you have in mind?" Dani asked, already seeing the wheels turning inside his head.

"Nobody can know you are involved. Let me have your cell number. I will have the blue tooth in my ear to listen to you. We can be in constant contact," Detective Anderson proposed a breach of ethics.

"That's very interesting. I can work with something like that," she said, while taking off the gloves with a snap.

"If you don't want my help, all you had to do was say so. Don't come crying to me when you have questions," she hollered for the benefit of those standing around making it seem like she was getting the bum's rush.

"You're washed up. Maybe you should consider early retirement like your partner," he said with fake aggravation, to continue the play on words she had started.

Dani pointed an accusatory finger at him. The one finger was met with a chorus of disapproval.

CHAPTER 12

Dani hightailed it to Creed's temporary residence. It was just a place to lay down his head until his family could join him.

Some cases lasted days and others weeks into months.

She parked her car down the road a couple of blocks away from his place. The house she had chosen was overgrown with weeds and had a for sale sign on the front lawn.

A couple of windows were boarded up. Vandalism was an epidemic in houses left abandoned.

It was almost a long weekend, with Friday's business coming to a close. There would be no viewings. Everybody would be preoccupied with the dog days of summer coming to an end.

She skirted the perimeter, aware that the press had staked out his front yard to the chagrin of his neighbors. He was going to hear it from the tenant board, but that was a problem for another time.

Dani peeked over the fence before scaling over it. She treated the whole exercise as if she was sneaking up on a perpetrator about to commit a crime.

Her senses were on high alert for anything out of the ordinary, including the possibility of a journalist skulking around in the hopes of capturing a candid photo of Creed.

There was a lonely rusted-out barbecue on the back porch. His place was ground level.

She wished her partner could come out of the cold into the future. It was something she was going to have to discuss with him.

"You're going to have to do better than that," Creed whispered to her from behind.

"One of these days," Dani fretted with her fist in the air.

"You're going to have to get up pretty early in the morning to get the drop on me. What do I owe the pleasure of your company?" Creed asked when he took the lead into the house through the kitchen, where the rest of the rooms were in total darkness.

It was a contemporary kitchen with stark white cabinets and stainless-steel appliances.

"We might have something going our way. The Detective assigned to the case is Anderson," she revealed while looking at her phone, waiting for it to ring.

"They really are scraping the bottom of the barrel. You have seniority. I'm sorry that you are being pulled into this mess," he said dejectedly until he was sitting comfortably in his black armchair, which was a recent acquisition.

He had no interest in turning into a run-down cop with no prospects other than walking the beat for a security firm. It made him shiver to envision stopping teenage skateboarders from plying their craft inside a mall.

"He realizes he's in over his head. I managed to get him to agree to work with me. He was the one to come up with the idea of a two-way exchange of information." Her cell vibrated in her hand. "Speak of the devil," she said before opening up the line of communication.

The two detectives listened into Anderson beginning his interrogation.

"Are you sure you don't want your lawyer present? I'm more than happy to wait until she gets here," Detective Anderson said sweetly.

"You're not like the other police officers. It's nice to find one who can actually think for himself. You're more than welcome to ask me any questions. If I feel at any time you are infringing on my rights, then I will contact my lawyer, "Kellie announced, followed by the clinking of 2 cups.

Fletcher was smart. She had learned from the narcissistic President that you can catch twice the number of flies with honey than vinegar.

"Nothing for me. I'm on the job," he said, with the sound of paper shuffling from what was obviously a notebook about to be broken in for the first time.

"Why don't we get started? I've been given a couple of days off. They heard what happened. Detective Creed is certainly photogenic.

Ironically, a new video camera was installed directly on the door to the board room. The police have since confiscated the footage," she stated gleefully, with no way to hide her joy.

"I'm not here to talk about him. He's a cowboy. There has been a recent development. Do you recognize the name Flip Carson?" Anderson paused for dramatic effect.

Creed exchanged a knowing look with Dani. "He didn't learn that from me. I'm guessing he's been hanging around a bad influence."

"What can I say? He's a sponge for knowledge. I sent him a few dos and don'ts. It will help his progress in becoming a well-rounded police detective. He's already getting a bad reputation for having gotten his position through nepotism," she referred to his father, a well-respected member of internal affairs.

Some officers suspected his posting of being politically motivated. He could've been a spy sent in with the express purpose of taking meticulous notes on his fellow officers.

"It does sound familiar, but I can't seem to place a face with the name. Don't tell me you are accusing me of his murder, too?" She fumed at the sound of her nails scratching against something they couldn't possibly see through the receiver.

*****

Anderson was regretting not taking her up on her offer of the caffeine fix he desperately wanted.

It was the one vice in his life.

He also had a penchant for older women.

"I'm not accusing you of anything. You're just a subject of interest. He was your immediate supervisor at your last job posting. He went missing a couple of weeks ago. His family has been terribly worried about him. They are my next stop. I'm not looking forward to it," he said with a deep swallow of concern about how he was going to handle a despondent wife.

"I've been involved in a few of those talks myself. It's not something I envy you. Just lay out the facts. This will at least give them some kind of closure. Some victims' families don't get that luxury," Kellie said, while drinking her tea in a small white porcelain cup.

"How did you get into human resources? If you don't mind me asking. It sounds like such a leap from answering telephones," Anderson posed the question which he heard in his ear courtesy of a little birdie.

Kellie touched his arm. "You're very insightful for someone so young. It would be a pity if you somehow became jaded by the job. To answer your question, I guess I was in the right place at the right time when they were trying to fill the spot."

Kellie wasn't the touchy feelie type but she knew when to use it. She had been in a long-term relationship with a guy who rarely got any marital delights. She would often brag about that to her colleagues, make is laughing stock of her partner. Maybe she was a closet lesbian after all.

"It might've had something to do with your predecessor resigning and moving to Nicaragua with no forwarding address. He doesn't even have any family. It was rather sudden and out of character." he said the words with one eye twitching when he heard Creed.

He should've known Creed would find a way to weasel into the case. Dami was good at her job, but her respect for Creed came with pitfalls.

"I don't know anything about that. My studies were extensively in criminology and human resources. It was fortuitous she stepped down. I was ready for a change and somebody mentioned my name. I guess I can leave a lasting impression," she stammered with a smile behind her cup.

Perhaps many moons ago Anderson thought. The most distinguishing thing about her face was the protruding wart and her cheap red lips. Her butt was now huge and the rolls of fat crinkled her outfit.

"It seems there are bodies everywhere you go. How do you account for that?" He asked, repeating what Dani was now whispering into his ear.

"Bad luck. What else could it be? The simplest answer is always the best one. Hhe got tired of the rat race and decided to find his inner peace in Nicaragua. It does sound good. A tropical setting with ocean breezes and drinks named after celebrities," Miss Fletcher sighed.

"Did you know Mr. Carson? He had some interesting thoughts about you. We found a few disciplinary notations on his computer concerning you. He thought you were undermining his authority," he said, once again taking his lead from Dani without knowing how she was glossing over the truth.

"This is getting into dangerous territory," she said with her legs crossed in an attempt to unbalance the young detective from any further questioning.

Anderson wasn't blind. A large lump had formed in his throat.

CHAPTER 13

Creed clapped his hands. "I don't know about you, but that was highly entertaining. Did you hear her squirm? That was good thinking about mentioning his private notations."

"She never even argued. It was just a hunch. It's something to look into," she answered.

"What now?" Creed asked.

"I'm meeting Anderson to debrief him. We need to know what his thoughts are concerning her reactions. It might be a good idea to hold his hand after he returns from giving the bad news to the wife. He will be understandably distraught," she said.

"I think I'm going to stay out of it. My only connection to this case is going to be through you. See if you can't connect the dots. She must've left a breadcrumb somewhere. Start with Carson's computer at home and at the office," Creed suggested.

"This one is going to be a tough nut to crack. You should know I'm scheduled to meet with Warren. He doesn't even know who was pulling his strings. It's probably best coming from me. You're not exactly his favorite person." Dani checked her phone and then stuck it in her pocket.

"Look who's talking. I seem to recall someone in this room being aggressively rough. It wasn't me. You almost broke his arm," he recounted with a sly grin.

"I don't have to sit here and take this abuse. You won't have me to kick around any longer," she huffed theatrically with her head held high and her chest puffed out.

"You're right about that. There's no telling how much trouble you can get into without me in 48 hours. We are about to find out. Watch out world," he bantered in the same joking manner before escorting her to the back door.

His place didn't feel so crowded as his previous residence. He was actually cooking healthy meals. None of it was coming from a cardboard box. It was something new to try.

"I don't think it's a good idea for me to call you. Don't say anything to the press. Not even a one-finger salute through the blackout curtains. I know you. You just can't help yourself," she said with a soft patronizing pat to his face.

"I want you to keep one thing in mind," he said with the echo of his words, causing her to look at him with one eyebrow raised.

"Don't tell me. Let me guess. You want me to stay frosty and keep my head on a swivel," she paraphrased what she thought he was going to say in a pithy comment.

"More or less. We don't know what she's planning for an encore. I don't think this is over. There are going to be more bodies. Just make sure you're not one of them," he warned in a half-hearted attempt at getting her to watch her back while he was otherwise out of commission.

*****

Dani had already ordered something from the bar. There was no time to go home and change into something more conversational.

She did have several items in her closet dedicated to making a man's jaw drop to the floor.

This was supposed to be a casual get-together. She didn't want to make the mistake of throwing herself at somebody that wasn't available. It was just sex. Something to take the edge off.

It was better to gauge his reactions and see how he would respond.

She was already wired and feeling no pain when he finally arrived fashionably late.

Anderson spotted her from across the room. There was no doubt in his mind she was exceptional in many ways. He had risen from the accusations of nepotism to stand strong against his critics.

"I took the liberty of ordering you sex on the beach," she offered him the beverage, which he eagerly accepted before sitting down across from her in the booth.

It wasn't her usual hot spot.

That was a place near the precinct.

It was always standing room only with officers trying to drown their sorrows in the bottom of a bottle. Commiserating with their colleagues made them feel better about their chosen profession.

They felt accepted into a very exclusive club.

"Why didn't you want to meet at..." He stopped with her finger against his lips.

"I don't want people knowing our business. There's no telling who might be spying for Jeffrey Reeves.," She announced with a hand shielding her mouth.

There was a platter of wings with 10 varieties of sauces. She had chosen to make it a little spicy. That little bite on the tip of her tongue was nothing compared to the burn on her lips.

"You are definitely full of surprises. I would've taken you for somebody that liked the finer things in life," he said while watching her gnaw into a chicken wing with her bare hands.

"What can I tell you? I'm an enigma," she announced with a little bit of sauce clinging to her lip.

CHAPTER 14

Creed paced in front of the computer most of the night.

Creed had his finger moving down the pages. There had to be a thread he could pull. Something everybody else had missed.

His research led him to several accounts throughout her storied history.

Her social media page was a string of smiling photographs in a variety of locales.

Ms. Fletcher loved to travel.

On her profile page, no close associates or family members were mentioned. Nobody had become her friend. She looked lively but there was something cold and detached behind her eyes.

He didn't want to be right.

Another body meant she was just getting started. The woman had an axe to grind and was prepared to run circles around the authorities. Keeping close tabs was impossible when the manpower was severely limited by recent budget cuts.

He found documentation revealing two husbands, one lost in a terrible accident. Those that had investigated found no signs of foul play. The other husband, or more precisely, partner, Vince Daniels, kept a low profile, most likely under the thumb.

Ms. Fletcher had seats on different boards. A paragon of virtue in most people's eyes unless you got to know her. Nobody had an unkind word to say about her.

Their glowing recommendations and praise for all of her hard work were making him sick.

Kellie Fletcher no longer stood on the sidelines. Revenge had become an obsession. Just how far she was willing to go to achieve a measure of satisfaction was anybody's guess. Her narcissism made the President look like an amateur.

It was almost midnight. His eyes were heavy with frustration. The words on the pages blurred as he tried in vain to make sense of her psychological makeup.

A missing piece had him enthralled to solve it. He rubbed the sleep from the corners of his eyes. Something nagging at his consciousness made him put on the kettle for another cup of coffee.

It was going to be a long night. No rest for the wicked.

*****

Walking with him had the desired effect. Dani was no stranger to finding comfort in the arms of those she respected. That was how she found Frank. She had no regrets.

It was novel to think of this young kid as her equal. He was amazingly insightful, but they had reached an impasse.

The neighborhood was filled with urban professionals. Body language talked for them in lieu of any kind of verbal communication.

They stopped in front of his building. A taxi waiting at the curb honked its horn.

"I would offer you a cup of coffee but I don't think that's appropriate. It's too bad they frown on fraternization. I really like you. I think you feel the same way but I would rather not know. Pick me up tomorrow for breakfast at seven. Bring your partner," Anderson stated with a sigh.

His hand touched her face where droplets of rain were slowly sliding down her cheek. He wiped it away with his thumb before turning and leaving her stunned by what was the equivalent of rejection.

Pursuing him gave her something to think about on the way home in the taxi.

There was something appealing about the forbidden. The right thing to do was to keep things platonic on a professional basis, at least until after the case was solved.

She typed on the keyboard. A blow-by-blow description of the evening came with every keystroke. She lowered the phone into her lap and was staring absentmindedly at the rain streaking down the window.

A beep indicated a message was waiting for her.

A lopsided smile had her directing the taxi to an alternate destination on the other side of town.

A good strong drink would hopefully soften her sour mood. She thought about the one that got away. The possibility existed there could be something between them. Thinking about the option of sneaking around made her smile.

Another beep on her cell confirmed Adams had finished the autopsy report. He was anxious to report his findings. It would be the first place she visited in the morning with Creed still cooling his heels.

Two days must've felt like an eternity to him.

The taxi driver of Middle Eastern descent didn't even bother with idle chitchat.

She drummed her fingers on her knees to the beat of Latin music coming through the speakers. She wanted to dance and to let her hair down but it seemed premature to celebrate.

The taxi dropped her off at the front of the courtyard. She walked briskly to the door. A knock announced her presence. A light came on with a familiar face staring at her from between the curtains.

The teeming rain had convinced the reporters staking out his home to come back in the morning. Only one reporter stayed but he had nodded off after a couple of nips from his flask.

CHAPTER 15

What she saw made her consider the possibility her partner had lost his marbles. He no longer took on the appearance of somebody capable of rational thought.

The wall in his living room covered the span of years regarding the comings and goings of one Miss Fletcher.

He was clearly driven by an influx of caffeine until he was practically bouncing off the walls.

"It looks like you have been busy in my absence," she said while looking around incredulously.

A hodgepodge of facts hanging on strips of paper gave her more than she bargained for. Coming over for a drink didn't seem as important as trying to talk him down from the ledge.

A bottle of decaffeinated coffee was found gathering dust in his pantry. She went ahead and added a few scoops before handing him a better alternative.

The water had already boiled.

His eyes were crazy in his head. There was no reason to doubt he had been compiling all of these innocuous facts to find the reward of Miss Fletcher on the receiving end of handcuffs.

"I've been turning over every rock. It's all circumstantial," he said with his fingers shaking when he took a hold of the cup offered to him.

"Come with me. I want to show you something," she urged.

They walked into the bathroom where she reached up and turned his head toward the mirror. She wanted him to see what Kellie Fletcher was doing to him. The sunken cheeks and bloodshot eyes confirmed her worst fear.

The adrenaline from the coffee had to be exhilarating. It was also making him lose focus which was only going to play into Ms. Fletcher's hand.

The drapes were drawn to prevent anybody from seeing his madness on display.

"That's not me. It can't be," he said with his hands on the porcelain white sink until he was leaning closer to the reflection he didn't recognize.

"You need to take a break," she stressed with her right hand on his back.

"There is no time for that. I'm on the verge of a breakthrough. I know it but I can't see it," he said when he returned to the living room flustered and a little out of breath.

There was nothing professional about his attire.

He had on a white shirt open halfway with beads of sweat collecting on his chest hairs. His hair was in disarray, flying and standing up on end. His hygiene was questionable.

The dark sweats pants were tied loosely around his waist.

"Something is here within all of this." He moved his hand around as if he was framing a photograph.

"I have no doubt about that. We can look at this with fresh eyes in the morning. Anderson wants to meet for breakfast to compare notes. We spent the night trying to find different angles to investigate," she mentioned without giving a voice to the sexual chemistry between the two of them at dinner.

A working dinner made them slowly lose their inhibitions until they were openly flirting with one another.

She remembered his words, and they stung.

"Anderson is one of the good ones. I've seen his work ethic. It rivals anybody in the Department. I'm slowing down. It's not something I like to admit. One day, I will hang it up but I will be damned if Ms. Fletcher falls through the cracks," Creed said.

"You need to lie down. Let me do some of the heavy lifting." She escorted him to the room down the hall and turned her back when he started to strip without any heads up.

"We have to put her away before she can do this to somebody else. We are chasing our tails. Her lawyer is worth the expensive retainer. She has a reputation for defending clients with more money than brains. This is different," he said when he suddenly sat down in his boxer shorts completely unaware that she was watching him from across the room.

*****

Across town at the same minute of the hour, Anderson was working with his own process.

He didn't have a wall dedicated to the case. He utilized a program he had devised on the computer. Nothing was connected to the internet.

A long list of characters from her past popped up on an anonymous email.

It had to be from either Dani or Creed.

He arranged everything into categories, systematically finding some sort of organization in the mess provided to him. Everything was correlated to the year and date of what had transpired.

The loop was slowly closing in around Fletcher's neck and she didn't even know it.

He pictured the look on her face several times during his conversation with Dani.

The wings were surprisingly crispy without even the hint of pink meat underneath the skin.

He made some notations in bold indelible red highlights. Everything the suspect said had a hidden meaning. Something struck him.

It was the way she had mentioned some families didn't have the luxury of closure. It wasn't so much the words but how she had spoken them while staring without focus out the window.

Maybe there was something there to investigate.

The late hour had crept up on him. It felt like he was taking one step forward and two steps back.

Creed had done some incredible work on the research. It had to be him.

No way did his partner Dani create this elaborate puzzle with some of the pieces missing. Between the ages of 12 and 16 were missing mysteriously from the collection of facts about Kellie's past.

Nothing more was reported until she was 16 and ran away from home for the first of many times. She always returned with the help of some overzealous police officer.

An incident was mentioned.

He perused the contents of her social media page with scrutiny.

It could've been an obvious error. Some families sent their daughters away to have babies. It didn't fit the span of time. She walked away from her education.

Then there was her brother. They were close' very close.

Her resume impressed him.

To his dismay, he saw the shadow of something coming toward the window. The resounding crash made him jump from his chair where he grabbed his gun and reflexively turned off the safety.

Running to the window revealed a black sedan careening around the corner. It couldn't have been a coincidence. It wasn't likely.

Somebody sent a dangerous message to back off. That was the last thing he was going to do.

He found a cardboard box and did his best to repair the window temporarily. It wouldn't hold up to inclement weather but the rain was petering out.

Tomorrow morning wasn't going to come fast enough for him. His adrenaline was pumping.

One thing came to mind to burn off that excess energy. It involved Dani. Shedding a few layers and jumping right into it gave him a jolt of lightning through his veins. He would love to spar with her in the ring.

Getting sweaty with Dani gave him a chance to slow things down in his mind. Thinking about it suddenly became more than any addict could withstand.

He had an addictive personality.

Those missing pieces from Kellie's childhood could supposedly shed some light on a motive for her actions.

He turned out the lights and gazed one last time over his shoulder at the broken window. He would have to comb the area in the morning to find a material witness.

CHAPTER 16

Creed woke up at precisely 6 AM when the first light of the morning sun lit up his room like the Fourth of July. He struggled to a sitting position when the door opened.

"We have an hour before we have to meet Anderson. He left me a cryptic message last night, but I didn't receive it until I woke up this morning." She produced her phone and showed him the text message line for line.

An attachment contained the systematic organized approach Anderson had taken.

"I think I like this kid more and more every day. He reminds me of me when I had lofty ambitions to change the world. He hasn't become disillusioned but he will over time until he is putting the job second over everything else."

Dani walked to the computer with him following in a staggered formation down the hall.

Her hen pecking with one hand was the true testament to her fighting spirit. The woman's word was her bond, and she took that very seriously.

"When did you get here? The events are a little fuzzy," he said with his sandpaper tongue hanging out.

"Just after midnight. I made you go to bed. Are you feeling any better?" Dani inquired.

"I might've been rambling a bit last night. That much I do remember," he referred to going off on several tangents regarding the compiled evidence tacked to the wall.

"Maybe a little," Dani said while looking at the facts as if she was doing it for the first time.

"I apologize. Lack of sleep is responsible. I swore that I wasn't going to let her get to me. Look at how well that turned out," he said before sitting down next to her.

No sexual chemistry made it easier to bounce ideas off one another. The distraction of getting naked and doing things to each other never entered into the equation.

"Anderson picked up on the fact she's hiding something about her past. A blank page in her history between the ages of 12 and 16 must have some significance. We need to find a way to get somebody to open up to us close to her." Dani lowered the laptop and stretched her nimble hands over her head until her knuckles were cracking and her fingers were interlaced.

"That's going to be easier said than done. There doesn't seem to be any known relatives in the picture," Creed pointed out with his finger to the portion of her family history.

"No surviving relative would be lonely. There would also be certain freedom to move unrestricted without anybody judging you unfairly. Her marriages are more pieces of the puzzle," Dani said while grabbing her coat from where it was lying at an angle over the chair in the kitchen.

"I'm famished. What's for breakfast?"

"Creed, you're always hungry and not necessarily for justice. You must have a hollow stomach. Anderson is waiting for us. He picked the venue. Don't blame me," she said with a turn of her phone.

"I can't afford to eat in a place like that. Appetizers alone will seriously compromise me financially. Two days on unpaid suspension doesn't sound like much. I can't seem to balance my check book but maybe that can wait," He pondered.

"The bill is covered. His family is in high standing with the club. It's the last place anybody would think to look for us having a clandestine meeting behind closed doors," Dani revealed.

"It sounds like our boy comes from family money. It just gets you right here." He punched his fist into his chest. "They grow up so fast. Where did the time go?"

"He doesn't need the job. He does excel in everything he does. It comes from his days of competing on the surfing circuit." She ran her finger over the dust underneath the counter.

*****

There was no point in telling them anything of what happened at his place. A window repair man was scheduled to take a look and make his assessment later in the afternoon.

Nobody had heard a thing.

That gave him plenty of time to sit down with Dani and Creed.

Those Detectives had a reputation for getting their man or woman. It must've been eating him up inside. He would've felt the same way had something similar happened to him.

The warm cognac by the fire was keeping him warm on a chilly morning. The club was primarily built around subtle wood tones. It was very discreet and had a select clientele willing to bend over backward for one another.

It might have become a meeting place for those looking for a safe space to speak candidly. It was the first time the club had admitted a woman but Detective Rodrigues was going to get those tongues wagging around the metaphorical water cooler.

He had just ordered his 2nd cup of coffee when they arrived together. It made him angry to think they had spent the night together.

"We came in the same car. I left you around midnight and haven't got much sleep. He crashed shortly after I arrived. I've been combing through everything you have compiled. You really did go beyond the call of duty. We really appreciate your due diligence," she offered already sensing he was perturbed by how they had arrived together.

Getting off on the wrong foot would send the wrong message and have them fighting each other to be heard.

"I have some inquiries into some group homes in the area. If she has a juvenile record, it's probably sealed by the courts to protect her identity. I've contacted the child welfare office. They are reluctant to speak about Ms. Fletcher," Anderson reported when his eyes were drawn to a western sandwich.

The waiter stood at the ready with his pencil poised over a white pad.

"I'll have this on whole-wheat bread. Bring me a glass of freshly squeezed orange juice without the pulp. My guests will have the same thing," Anderson waved the waiter aside.

"Let's get down to business. Start at the beginning. I want to hear everything including your take on Ms. Fletcher," Creed urged.

The swanky atmosphere made them feel out of place.

It wasn't long before they were comfortable sharing information.

20 minutes wasn't very long. A plan of attack was discussed. Dani would take a trip to Fletcher's hometown where her first husband ultimately met his maker. Shaking that tree might uncover something untoward.

She'd already arranged for an escort from the police officer on those cases in a very small town outside of Boston.

Anderson would continue to dig.

Creed had less than 24 hours before he was back on the job unless something happened before then. It appeared on the surface Reeves was a good and honorable man.

Looks could be deceiving.

Waiting for the hammer to come down had him on pins and needles.

They could take away his career but they would never take away his inscrutable desire to investigate crimes.

CHAPTER 17

Anderson hadn't mentioned the rock. No harm was done. Protocol dictated he make a formal report. The last thing he wanted was a contingent of police officers traipsing through his living room.

He did dust for prints and found none. The culprit must've been wearing gloves when they attempted to intimidate him.

Sparring down at the gym had given him a new sense of confidence with the ladies and on the job.

He wasn't expecting 'him' to tag along. Detective Creed didn't take no for an answer.

"This is my life we are talking about. She's trying to destroy my career and everything I have built. They are already discussing looking at my previous arrest record to see if there are any discrepancies. You might not believe this but I think Reeves has it out for me." Creed was hiding behind a dark pair of sunglasses and a thicker shade of beard courtesy of an application.

"We could just break in and take a look around," Anderson suggested.

"This is about the sanctity of the law. We can't break the rules when it suits us. That would make us no better than the criminals we hunt in the shadows. We do this by the numbers. I called in a favor to a friend of mine," Creed stated with a yawn.

"I'm not going to like this...am I?"

"Everything on the curb is fair game. We are going to do some old-fashioned dumpster diving," he said while donning a pair of white latex gloves.

"Dani should be arriving in Boston shortly around noon," Anderson said.

"Kellie is leaving. It looks like she's going to the gym. That should give us plenty of time to go through her trash looking for anything of interest. Receipts can be the gateway to a confession. Somebody is protecting her," Creed blurted out.

"What makes you say that?" Anderson inquired while watching her drive by without even looking in the direction of the vehicle hidden in the shadow of a tree.

"Think about it. How else could she possibly know I was going to be there? It would explain no gun. It would also explain how the press suddenly showed up out of the blue. It means we have a mole in the Department. We have to be more discreet than ever," Creed stammered with his lips sticking together.

The trash cans were going to be picked up. A quick phone call to sanitation delayed their arrival by almost 3 hours.

The company was more than happy to cooperate with the police. Nobody wanted the bad publicity of an obstruction of justice charge.

The nearest neighbor was down the block and around the corner.

He was senile and over 80 years old on a disability check.

They made sure the coast was clear before advancing on the trash cans. At least there wasn't a dumpster they were going to have to climb into.

Sifting through the remains of the leftover food and banana peels proved to be an arduous task.

*****

Two hours went by fairly quickly. An old friend from the force was playing hooky from his private-sector job.

He had followed Ms. Fletcher to the gym.

A text message was received. They had less than 30 minutes to cover their tracks and make it out of the area before she returned.

"I hate being rushed. Take pictures of everything. I want close-ups of every piece of material. Her timing couldn't be worse. I suppose it depends on your point of view," Creed ordered without any real authority.

"What do you mean?"

"Her arrival will correspond with the delayed sanitation workers coming to collect her garbage to take to the dump. We could follow them there but there's no telling there might be a spy whispering into her ear. I sound paranoid," Creed smacked his face with both hands.

"Not at all. What would ever give you that idea?" Anderson asked in a sarcastic tone of voice.

"You're not too old to put over my knee. I have shoes older than you are." Creed implied corporal punishment was an option.

"I would like to see you try, old man. Let's see how far you can get," Anderson said defensively.

A pile of trash earmarked for the dump was rescued and salvaged. A whole plastic bag of shredded documents would have to be meticulously put together.

It wasn't uncommon for people to shred sensitive material.

The risk of it falling into the wrong hands was better than most people realized. Identity theft was taking the place of vandalism and home invasions. It wasn't a victimless crime.

"What if what happened during that block of empty time is the key to all of this? What was an open and shut case has become complicated in a hurry. We might be looking at this the wrong way," Creed said while seizing the bag of shredded documents from Anderson.

"She's not rattled by anything. We have to be very careful not to step on anybody's toes. I'm sure you realize the penalty for going against a direct order. I'm risking becoming a co-conspirator in the eyes of my superior." Detective Anderson said as he was making a last cursory look through the items she had thrown away.

CHAPTER 18

Dani made the short trip from New York to Boston by taking a puddle jumper.

It was a plane capable of landing on the ground and the water.

Dani cursed her partner's name under her breath. Letting him dictate the terms of her travel arrangements had been a serious lack of judgment.

Gene Milton was retired from air and rescue. He was making bank by becoming a personal tour guide for the area. He also dabbled in bending the law.

"Tell Creed when you see him, this makes us even. You don't want anybody to know where you're going. Sometimes I forget to file a flight plan with the proper officials. They usually turn a blind eye," Gene called out over the wind rushing through the windows.

Dani knew she was way off the reservation. It would be a jurisdictional nightmare.

It was better to claim she was on her day off and could take a trip anywhere she wanted to without having to discuss it with her superiors.

The family of the deceased husbands had agreed to meet with her in private.

The first one would be a half hour after she landed. The second had offered to talk over dinner and she readily accepted the baritone voice of the man proffering the invitation.

"How long have you known each other?" She asked curiously.

"You're going to have to ask him about the details. Suffice to say, he saved my life and I don't think I would be here without him," Gene said with mad respect for Creed.

"You can't just drop a bomb like that and not fill me in on some of the details. The man is a very private person. He doesn't talk about his family. He rarely brings up any friends in the conversation when we are conducting business as usual," she replied, with the landscape of the east coast becoming more than a blip on her radar.

"It's not my story to tell. It's something that happened a long time ago. The statute of limitations has long passed. He wasn't always a choirboy," he laughed into the microphone while preparing for a landing at a small dock where the owner was supposedly on vacation.

"Drop me off here. I'll call you when I'm ready to leave and not one second before," she screamed to be heard with one hand on his shoulder.

She held her stomach where the butterflies threatened to come out of her mouth at any second. She had just finished lecturing Anderson on his inability to hold his lunch.

He would've been the first to call her out on the carpet for being a hypocrite.

*****

"You were right about them. They were exactly where you said they were going to be. I know what to do. You pay me good money to clean these things up before they become unmanageable. Leave it to me," the man in the car behind Creed and Anderson was wearing tight leather driving gloves.

There was a gun hidden under his black leather jacket.

He was weaving in and out of traffic, staying four car lengths behind.

His boss had gotten wind of their attempt to circumvent his authority. Reeves had hired him to become their shadow.

James Spencer was considered top in his field. He moved in secret circles with others whispering their concerns into his ear.

There wasn't a shortage of clients looking to capitalize on his unique skill set.

The car moved forward through traffic. Losing them wasn't an option. Reeves had given him his big break. Getting washed out in the Academy had opened up a different door when that one closed.

James was muscle, but he could also act as a liaison between his employer and whatever entity was pulling his strings. He had no doubt someone higher up on the food chain was making rash demands.

The car they were in stopped next to a post office. The younger one got out and went inside.

The older man had this air of police surrounding him in a stench anybody within a mile would have smelled.

He climbed out of the car with his bad knee acting up. Just a hint of moisture in the air was enough to make the composite alloy in his knee stiff. He had to shake it a few times before crossing the road to the other side.

Using the cover of traffic made him practically invisible.

Nobody really paid much attention to him. He had the face that nobody would remember even if they were standing right next to him. It was good for business to stay hidden.

His job was to get his hands on whatever they had taken from the trash.

No questions were asked.

Killing wasn't in the job description, but he was prepared nonetheless for the eventuality. Doing a cop would come with a premium.

The man was alone in the car. Music was blaring through the open window, masking the handle being pulled on the back door.

He was in.

CHAPTER 19

It was the strangest meeting.

Danielle sat pensively, watching closely to see how she was going to react. The smile told her she was hiding something. Her answers sounded rehearsed.

"She was the best thing to happen to our boy. He could never settle down," Mrs. Olsen stated when she returned from the kitchen with a cup of tea.

"What makes you say that? Why was she the best thing to happen to your boy?" Danielle flipped a few pages in her notebook. "Baxter was on the fast track to becoming a partner in his firm. That never happened," Danielle informed.

"You have to remember something about Baxter. He wasn't very focused on the future. My son was a good man, but he was also a little flighty. Kellie fixed that. She gave him encouragement to reach for the stars," Mrs. Olsen continued.

"What kind of encouragement, if you don't mind me asking?" Danielle questioned.

The house was a shrine to her little boy. Pictures depicting a normal childhood, including accolades from school, were arranged systematically on the wall.

There was one glaring omission. It couldn't be ignored.

"I was a single parent trying to raise a kid with a chip on his shoulder. It wasn't always easy to get through to him. God knows he could be stubborn at times," Mrs. Olsen said while spooning in a couple of cubes of sugar to sweeten the tea.

Danielle raised her hand to stop her from giving her an early onset of diabetes.

"Let's get back to this encouragement you mentioned," Danielle pointed out.

The young woman in front of her had aged prematurely, especially around the eyes. The drapes were drawn heavily. They were disguising a layer of dust over everything. The whole house screamed in desperate need of a housekeeper to come in once a week.

"I don't know what to tell you. She was kind and considerate. My boy didn't stand a chance when he met her for the first-time sailing. They both loved the ocean air. She was more experienced, but his enthusiasm was infectious," Mrs. Olsen stammered with her blue eyes glazing over.

She rummaged around underneath the coffee table before producing a scrapbook of memories. Each page revealed a young man ready to snap at the slightest provocation.

His smile was indicative of somebody that was planning something devilishly evil.

"He had some tough times. Baxter didn't have any real direction. He had considered joining the military. They said that he wasn't psychologically capable of serving his country. What the hell do they know about my boy?" Mrs. Olsen said in a higher register.

The path down memory lane was chock-full of some interesting comments written on the borders of the photographs. It was all there in black and white.

Baxter was a troubled child from early on. He lashed out at students and faculty alike when he attended school, which wasn't very often.

It was clear whoever had written on the margins of the photographs wasn't his mother.

Somebody had taken great pains to uncover the family's deepest, darkest secrets. It was there for anybody to read once they got past the pleasantries at the front door.

"He went to Harvard law school. I was so proud. It made me want to shout it from the rooftops when he passed the bar exam. He wanted to make a difference. He wanted to leave some kind of legacy behind. The one problem he encountered was never being able to stand out from the rest of the crowd. I contribute that to having no father figure growing up," she declared with a pointed finger to a photo of a man that had the face cut out of every single one of them.

"There are no photographs of her. You say she made a tremendous difference in his life and yet there is no photographic evidence of their relationship. Can you explain that?" Danielle asked with curiosity.

"She was so shy. Every time I tried to take a picture; she would stop me. I don't know why. She's very photogenic. The camera absolutely loves her. This is the only one I managed to get, but it was from afar when she was admiring my many varieties of roses in the garden," she said, before placing the pad of her index finger on the only photo of Kellie.

It was as if she was an entirely different person. It was a little fuzzy. Concentrating on the face revealed someone capable of becoming a chameleon. Her smile was dazzling, but there was no life in her eyes despite all indications to the contrary. A bit of a smiling assassin.

Everything she was learning made her think Miss Fletcher was more dangerous than ever, without any concrete proof. Her search for answers had only begun.

Danielle had a feeling she was going to be spending more time in this little town Kellie Fletcher called home.

*****

James was sitting behind Detective Jack Creed. It would have been so easy-to-use piano wire to murder him in cold blood. That was not his job, but the parameters could change quickly if he was discovered.

James had hit the mother lode.

Everything they had confiscated from the trash was bundled up in the back seat. It appeared they hadn't had much chance to go through it, which was a lucky break.

He watched the front seat as he quickly and as quietly as possible slipped every piece of paper smelling of old Chinese food into his jacket. He was holding it with the other hand to make sure it didn't go anywhere.

The young man inside the post office had not returned. There had to be a reason for their visit. It would've been in his best interest to stick around to find out more, but maybe there was a way to do that without being there in person.

A quick and decisive blow to the back of the detective's head was an impulsive move on his part. He was positively elated when he heard the unmistakable deep sigh of inhalation when he passed out over the steering wheel.

He took his wallet and the collection of CDs. It was fortuitous there was a plastic bag lying discarded on the floor. It had the makings of a snatch-and-grab kind of robbery.

James left the same way he came in. He had done what was asked and even more so to keep them from discovering the real reason for the robbery.

He bent over quickly and left a present underneath the driver's side back wheel. There was another similar device inside under the seat, hidden in a small cut in the cloth.

This would give him an audio breakdown of everything that was said inside the car.

A small note with only a few words written in red indelible ink would be found when he became conscious again.

He crossed the street with a limp.

Out of his peripheral vision, he noticed the young man accompanying the detective Creed come out of the post office.

James never stopped. He didn't run to attract attention. A casual stroll was all that was necessary to get back to his vehicle without being discovered. He dumped the contents, including what was found in the trash next to him.

None of it made any sense. It didn't have to when the money was more than made up for the mysterious circumstances surrounding the robbery.

A quick message to his employer was necessary. He was going to have to renegotiate terms. Nobody told him he was going to have to come face to face with a decorated police detective.

It didn't really matter, but the absence of information could be detrimental to his profession.

He sat there for some time, intrigued by the turn of events.

CHAPTER 20

Jack was floating on this cloud with voices calling out to him from a distance. He tried to answer back, but no words manifested out of his mouth. He touched his lips to feel that they were sewn shot as if he was a cadaver.

"He was a good man. The last thing anybody expected was for him to take his own life. I was his partner for years and I never suspected he had mental issues. This case really got to him. I'm going to miss working with him," Danielle sniffled while looking down at the open casket where he lie in peaceful contemplation with his hands crossed over his midsection.

"I didn't know him very well, but I respected the hell out of him. He was one of the main reasons I became a police detective. The man could be hard-nosed and stubborn to a fault, but he always had the instincts to back up his claims. Rest in peace," Anderson said with his arm over Danielle in a protective and loving gesture.

Jack was appalled. He should've had a will drawn up long ago to express his wishes. Being buried among the other rotting corpses wasn't his idea of a peaceful slumber in the afterlife.

Now that he began to think about it, cremation would be his decision once the time came to leave this world behind. He didn't want long goodbyes with tears. He wanted people to celebrate his life with a party in his honor.

His family was standing behind Danielle and Anderson. Dani was there, dabbing her eyes and looking pensive. She never did like funerals.

His wife was dressed in white. It seemed unusual considering the circumstances of everybody getting together. Black was usually the normal color for grieving a loved one.

He thought for a moment they would say a few words, but they were understandably distraught. His wife was being consoled by close friends and family members.

The one thing he regretted most of all was how little time he had spent with his family lately. It was as if they had become strangers. They only reunited during special occasions and holidays.

It wasn't enough.

"The job meant everything to him. He fought the good fight to the end. It's too bad he took the coward's way out. I didn't see the signs until it was too late. He lost his way and was never able to find his way back," Danielle choked on the words.

Her face was covered with a black veil. There was some kind of stain on her dark blouse spreading out as she uttered those final words. It was a eulogy.

She dropped to her knees with her hands next to the hole dug into the ground. Blood was dripping out of her mouth. Behind her stood a woman with a cool expression of restrained excitement, holding a knife.

Kellie Fletcher was twisting it for good measure. The pain must've been excruciating, but would only last a few more seconds before it was all over.

Ms. Fletcher continued to stab her over and over again.

Nobody was intervening. They didn't seem to notice what was going on, even though it was right in front of them. The blood splatter was flying everywhere, becoming raindrops landing on those attending his funeral.

The woman was positively mad. She was laughing uncontrollably while continuing to leave her bloodied fingerprints at the scene of the crime.

"This is what you do to everybody around you. Why don't you see the hell you put people through?" Anderson yelled, with little bits of spittle flying from his mouth down into the hole of the face of its recipient.

Danielle was thrown into the hole on top of him. Her dead body with its vacant eyes was staring right at him. It was almost as if she was asking why he didn't stop Ms. Fletcher when he had the chance.

"Nobody is safe when they are around you. Do something good for once in your life and just let go. You bring nothing but death and misery to all that stands with you. I'm not going to go down the same road,"

Anderson expressed with his hands deep into the pockets of his black pants.

Anderson was leaning over him slapping his face when he finally opened his eyes to the reality.

"Don't try to move. You might have a concussion. It looks like you took a very serious blow to the back of the head," Anderson commented while holding onto his head to alleviate the blood flow with a little bit of pressure.

"What happened?" Jack asked, a little dazed and confused.

"We can talk about that later. An ambulance is on the way. Try not to talk," Anderson warned with a look of grave concern when he saw the blood dripping from his fingers.

*****

Danielle sat there, completely engrossed in every word coming out of her mouth. If she didn't know any better, she could've sworn she saw the invisible strings being pulled.

The fleeting image of Miss Fletcher smiling behind Mrs. Olsen's back while pulling her strings made her understand an important fact.

Kellie had predicted somebody was going to dig deeper into her past. Mrs. Olsen was telling lies. It was a form of misdirection.

What was a good reason for Mrs. Olsen to lie to her? Money and bribery were two good motives. It could've been either one.

"I hope I was able to help. Kellie made my boy better for knowing her. It was a tragic accident. She was found several miles offshore clinging to a piece of driftwood. The Coast Guard remarked it was amazing that she even survived the night in those frigid waters," Mrs. Olsen said with a hand, wiping fresh tears from her eyes.

"That is my next stop. Maybe they'll be able to shed some light on the accident. I appreciate your time, but I think I have to get going. Lots to do and not enough hours in the day to get them done," Danielle got up and took one last look around.

Mrs. Olsen was still grieving. Living in the past was the only way to keep her boy alive in her heart. The psychological trauma of losing her husband and son was killing her a little more each day. She was the walking dead with a smile painted on her face.

"Let me show you the way. This place is a maze if you don't know where you're going," Mrs. Olsen said while tiptoeing around bundles of old newspapers tied in twine.

It looked like she had bought every copy pertaining to her boy's disappearance. The story had international implications.

They had covered the story until something better came along to report on.

It was a hoarder's nightmare come to life. It didn't appear Mrs. Olsen threw anything away, including an old retainer from when her boy was barely in his teens.

Mrs. Olsen was going to drive herself crazy. It was possible she was already screaming for help and nobody was able to hear her.

Every mention of Kellie made her left hand shake. There was a noticeable scar between the index finger and her thumb. This was something Danielle was going to address, but figured a trip to the hospital might find the answers she was looking for.

They stood in front of each other at the front door with the smell of old paper permeating the air.

"Again, I'm sorry for bothering you so early in the morning. You've given me a lot to think about. Perhaps I might stop by before I leave to have a few final words. It's been very interesting talking to you," Danielle said, bewildered.

She noticed out of the corner of her eye three table settings. She was playing house in her mind when nobody was around to see her.

It made Danielle feel sorry for her.

Danielle stopped at the curb and glanced back to see Mrs. Olsen watching her from the living room window through the curtain. The pastoral colors had these tiny little daisies stencilled into the fabric.

It wasn't lost on her how she had quickly grabbed the phone. She didn't need anybody to write it on the wall. Mrs. Olsen was in league with Ms. Fletcher.

Mrs. Olsen must've suspected there was foul play. She didn't even want to think about what Ms. Fletcher would do to silence her. It could be the threat was more physical than emotional.

The hospital records would give her some insight.

Danielle walked briskly across the lawn when the curtains fluttered but remained open a crack. The window was ajar and she could just pick up the last tail end of a conversation.

"You don't have to remind me. I did exactly what you told me to do. Don't call me again. I never want to hear from you. Do I make myself clear?" She inquired while standing at the wall separating the dining room from the kitchen.

Danielle strained to hear the whispered words before she slammed down the receiver hard enough to echo through the house.

CHAPTER 21

Anderson was worried, but not necessarily about Creed. He was understandably concerned for the man he held in high esteem.

There was more to it.

The blow must've come from behind. Somebody had gotten inside the car. It only showed how Creed had lost a step. His instincts were dulled. He wasn't bleeding internally.

That was the first thing they checked into the hospital.

Anderson had already picked up on the fact every scrap of paper they had taken from the trash was gone. Creed was also missing his wallet and a collection of CDs.

Anderson was impeccable when it came to his attention to detail. Nothing remained out of his purview. It had the earmarks of a robbery, but there was also something personal at stake.

He took out the note in the waiting room and looked at it one more time.

"You took everything from me and now I'm taking everything from you. Don't think for one moment this is over. I'm your biggest fan... Not." It wasn't signed.

Anderson wanted to believe it was a relatively unknown enemy coming out of the woodwork to exact some sort of revenge.

It was all a smokescreen to hide the fact Ms. Fletcher had people doing her dirty work behind the scenes.

He couldn't go and accuse her of any wrongdoing. There wasn't anything to lead the investigation back to her doorstep. He'd already requisitioned a blow-by-blow description of all of her telephone calls, but that was going to take time.

He got to his feet, dropping the magazine with the face of Roseanne Barr on the cover.

I'm Dr. Stanley. Your partner is in recovery. We are keeping him for 24-hours for a routine evaluation. He will be released in the morning unless there are complications. There was a hairline fracture of his skull," Dr. Stanley regurgitated the word written illegibly on the chart in some kind of ungodly shorthand.

"What is his prognosis? Give it to me straight. I can take it," he uttered.

"He's going to need to take it easy for a few days. No moving around and no exerting himself in any way. I'm going to be giving him a mild sedative so he can sleep. I don't predict any complications, but you never know about this kind of injury.

He will be monitored closely and I will be informed of any problems," Dr. Stanley explained while casually looking at his watch and realizing he was a half hour late for an important date.

"That is a relief. Do you think that I can see him for one moment? I promise that I won't tire him out," Anderson encouraged with a gentle hand of persuasion on his shoulder.

"Keep it brief. Don't upset him," he ordered before walking away and mumbling something under his breath.

Anderson followed him to a room down the hall. He entered without knocking to discover Jack already on his feet, frantically looking through the closet for his clothes.

"I don't want to hear it. I'm leaving. Don't try to stop me," Jack stated with a hand to his head.

Anderson walked up to him and made sure that he wasn't going to faint.

"I wouldn't dream of telling you what to do. Stay here. I'll get a wheelchair for the old man," Anderson remarked sarcastically.

There was absolutely no color in the room. Everything was pure white except for the green Ralph Lauren shirt Jack was wearing.

Creed was taking it off and didn't show an ounce of shame in his birthday suit. The door was closing when he finally found his clothing. It was bundled up in a white bag at the top of the locker.

He was about to escape the captivity of the poking and prodding of doctors and nurses. Be damned their diagnosis. He had little doubt Miss Fletcher was the cause of his misfortune.

The robbery was a ruse to get their hands on whatever they had taken from the trash.

The one mistake they made was not taking his phone. He had taken the precaution of photographing every piece of paper. They might've had the originals, but his copies could easily be the smoking gun he was looking for.

*****

Danielle had already pirated a copy of the medical records. A badge and a little flirtation went a long way to acquire the cooperation of an orderly. He easily obtained every single detail pertaining to Mrs. Olsen.

She had promised not to take the folder out of the hospital. Sitting down and reading through the report was alarming.

Mrs. Olsen had been seriously injured. They had to surgically reattach her thumb. She had claimed to be cutting vegetables and slipped. There was a notation from her doctor. It was at the bottom of the page.

"It wasn't a clean cut. The injury does not match up to the patient's recollection of events. I turned this matter over to Detective Michael Moore. She will require a follow-up a few weeks after surgery. I'm confident she will attain almost 70% functionality. That is a conservative

number..." He went on for a few more paragraphs, but it was all in medical jargon.

Each piece of evidence was leading back to Ms. Fletcher.

She made a photocopy of the medical report. Nobody said anything about making copies. They probably would frown on such an action, but nobody was around to stop her.

She folded the paper and stuffed it into her purse hanging over her shoulder. The clasp was undone. She had a plethora of different things contained within.

Every woman was prepared.

Danielle didn't have a leg to stand on. It was all circumstantial. Damning material, but still circumstantial without corroborating evidence.

There was no reason to bother the orderly. She left the file folder on the table where he could easily find it when he came back to continue flirting with her.

He was a strapping young man.

A message was waiting for her on her phone. Her hand immediately went up to her mouth in shock.

Jack had been injured severely enough to require a 24 hour stay in the hospital.

She almost laughed when she thought about him sitting there uncomfortably while everybody fussed over him. He would feel like the walls were closing in on him. Nobody was going to make him stay anywhere unless he was in no shape to walk out of the hospital on his own power.

There was a moment she thought about cutting her trip short. It was exactly what Ms. Fletcher wanted her to do. The first thing Jack would remind her of was her duty. Leaving was out of the question.

She didn't notice the young man in a lab coat following her.

CHAPTER 22

Jack was accosted by Reeves when he came out of the hospital. He wasn't in the wheelchair any longer than it took him to cross the threshold.

"Why am I the first to hear about this attack? You're supposed to be on suspension and not running around town. Do you mind telling me what compelled you to stick your nose where it didn't belong?" Reeves stood there calmly with his arms across his chest, looking at both Jack and Anderson.

Jack felt like he was under a microscope, but he was no longer content sitting on his hands doing nothing. It was time to shake the tree and see what fell out.

"Somebody made it personal. They left me this note. It's probably somebody from my past. I've made my fair share of enemies during my career, albeit in Australia" he said before handing over the letter.

Reeves read every single word verbatim while moving his lips with nothing coming out.

"I'll have the lab go over this. You should have called me. This is a police matter. What was taken?"

"Nothing of importance. A few CDs and my wallet. I should've heard him get in the car, but I was a little distracted. I think you can understand after everything I've been through. I'm not exactly myself these days," Jack fumed with his nostrils flaring.

"That's not my fault. I'm just doing my job," he said with the vein at his temple throbbing.

"You keep telling yourself that," Creed muttered.

"I don't appreciate the tone of your voice. Go home. I'm extending your unpaid leave of absence for one week. Don't even say anything. I don't want to hear it," Reeves replied before turning on his heels.

He got into a white Crown Vic before driving away in a plume of black smoke puffing out of the muffler.

"How much do you know about him?" Creed asked Anderson.

"Not much," he replied.

"I haven't been able to get a read on him. There's got to be a reason why he's gunning for me. I just cost myself five more days suspended without pay. It was worth it to see the look on his face." Jack walked gingerly to the car.

"Don't bleed on the upholstery. I just had it cleaned," Anderson joked while flipping the bird at Reeves in his rear-view mirror under the guise of scratching his chin.

"We need more than just a hunch. Reeves intends to put me out to pasture. He doesn't like my cowboy style of police work. It doesn't matter my arrest and conviction record speaks for themselves. He wants my head on a platter, and I want to know why. What does this have to do with Kellie Fletcher and her reign of terror?" Jack rattled on as he made himself comfortable in the seat before strapping the seat belt over him.

Anderson turned to him with both hands on the steering wheel. "All good questions. We might've just made some headway. What happened with Miss Fletcher is feeling like just the tip of the iceberg. We have to hit the ground running."

"What do you suggest? I'm all ears," Jack said with both fingers to his ears.

"We have to come at this from several angles. We will get more done by splitting our focus. You concentrate on Reeves. I'll continue in my capacity as lead investigator to talk to some of her colleagues. They can't all have glowing recommendations," Anderson proposed.

Jack nodded absentmindedly while perusing the photos he had taken of the papers found in the trash. There was one receipt for 10 bags of Lyme. She had ordered them online.

"I'm going to walk. There's something I have to do. I don't need a babysitter," Jack huffed before getting out and walking away from the hospital, still looking at his phone.

He had to admit, Anderson was a good fit. He might've been a little green, but he was obviously holding onto a man crush.

Jack was nobody's hero. He could never be somebody's mentor.

Jack still had his badge, but no authority to use it. It wasn't like anybody else knew about his suspension, especially in the private sector.

That was something he could use.

*****

Danielle was on a mission.

It could've been an accident, but she seriously had her misgivings. Kellie Fletcher was very good at putting on airs.

She had a few moments to spare and wanted to check in on Jack. Creed could be his own worst enemy.

A dog with a bone was a good way to describe him.

Sitting at the café looking at the other patrons made her feel like a fly on the wall. It was interesting to people watch. Everybody had a story to tell. The expression on their faces could be a mask to hide whatever pain they were trying to keep from being uncovered.

A young woman in a tasteful black and white ensemble was casually flipping through some kind of report. She stopped once in a while to punch in something on the laptop next to her.

A man nervously checking his watch was obviously waiting for an afternoon rendezvous. The woman approaching was also feeling those butterflies while struggling with fidelity.

Fiddling with the wedding ring was a sure sign she was having second thoughts. One look at her prospective suitor changed her mind. The nerves were exchanged for excitement at doing something taboo.

A couple was speaking French holding hands and looking longingly into each other's eyes. They were newlyweds on their honeymoon. Their choice of venue was understandable with the soothing sounds of the ocean.

Boston was a melting pot of nationalities.

Danielle dialled the number by pressing one button.

"Didn't anybody ever tell you to have eyes in the back of your head?" Danielle asked before Jack could even answer after the third ring.

"You're funny. I'm fine. You don't have to worry about me," Jack deflected.

Danielle was trying to come up with the right words. "Just be more careful. We are poking a Hornet's nest. Fletcher is at the epicentre but she obviously has long arms. I just got through talking to her first husband's mother. Every word was sickeningly sweet."

"What does that tell you?" Jack asked.

Danielle knew he was using it as a teaching moment. "It told me somebody has already been to visit her. She had a scar between her thumb and index finger. I got a hold of her medical records. Don't ask me how. You really don't want to know."

"Perish the thought. What did you find?" Jack asked.

"Not anything we can use in court. She was injured, but it was more severe than the scar would indicate. They had to surgically reattach her thumb. She's going to lose 30% mobility, but that never came up in our conversation. You have to wonder why," Danielle said with a firm recollection of Mrs. Olsen touching the scar every so often without even knowing she was doing it.

"We have a few leads we are checking out. Anderson has gotten under her skin. We intend to capitalize on the relationship. I'm on my way to check out something else," Jack said.

"You're being a little more aloof than you usually are," Danielle said with her hand wrapped around the cup until she brought it to her lips.

The caffeine was a good wake-up call to keep her on alert. There was no telling if somebody from Kellie's camp was watching her.

"I'm just being extra cautious. I'm going to send you some information. Read through it and then discard it." Jack hung up.

She sat there and waited until his instructions came in loud and clear. He was being paranoid but had every right to believe somebody was out to get him.

It was good to see him acting in his own best interest, no longer wallowing in self-pity.

110

CHAPTER 23

Creed found the shop nestled between a grocery market and a real estate office. The nursery was family-owned with a placard on the front door claiming 25 years of service to the community.

Creed stepped into the air-conditioned environment with a chill running down his spine.

A dizzy spell made him stop short at the counter. He raised a hand and used the other one to pop a pill given to him when he injured himself on the job a few years earlier.

It was expired medicine. The effects hadn't worn off.

If anything, they were stronger than ever and took almost a full minute to kick in.

The receptionist was understandably concerned.

"Do you want to sit down? Can I offer you a glass of water?" The receptionist inquired with a hand touching his grizzled fingers.

Creed looked up with an impassioned smile. "That would be nice. I just got out of the hospital. It's nothing serious. Just have to keep taking my medication."

A quick check confirmed there were no cameras over the counter.

The receptionist went in back to fetch a glass of water. It turned out to be a plausible excuse to get her out of the way.

There was no need to flash a badge when he easily acquired the information by skirting the law. It made him sick to do it but he didn't want Reeves to find out about his visit to the nursery.

That would get back to Kellie.

Creed had learned a lot about computers, surprising for an old dog. He searched the database and found a record of the transaction. It was made a few days ago. He pressed a button to print out a copy and he quickly snatched it from the copier.

He had just enough time to ball it up in his fist before she came back with the water. That hand was behind his back. He took the glass with the other hand and felt the cool liquid sliding across his tongue.

"I guess I might have left the hospital a little too early. Isn't it just like a man to act stubborn and invincible? I appreciate your compassion," he said with his hand lowering until he spotted something out of the ordinary on the wall.

His eyes grew a little bit larger. "I was just admiring your wall of fame. Does every one of your employees have knowledge when it comes to planting and gardening?" He asked out of curiosity.

"Most of our employees are temporary students. There was one that came off the street. She was surprisingly knowledgeable. There wasn't much we could teach her. She still comes in from time to time to chat," the receptionist said before taking down the year of 2001.

Jack was staring at the mocking image of Miss Fletcher but that wasn't her name. The one she had used in her employment was Kellie Daniels. Perhaps there was an air of hope that Vince may one day pop the question. But after ten years he was in no rush. Maybe the wart on her face had deterred him?

"You wouldn't know it from looking at her. She doesn't even seem interested in having her picture taken," Creed mentioned.

"I think I remarked she should've been in magazines. The woman is simply stunning. There wasn't a man alive immune to her charms ahem including my husband," the receptionist revealed with a catch in her throat.

The photo showed a slimmer woman and no wart; something which was onset later.

"You don't sound bitter about it," Creed addressed.

"The one thing you can't do is stay mad at her for long. She was right. If he was really faithful, then he wouldn't have been tempted to be with her. She did me a favor by showing me his true face before we renewed our wedding vows. I think I dodged a bullet," The receptionist stared at the man next to Fletcher with the fury of the damned in her eyes.

"Are you sure there are no hard feelings? It would be perfectly understandable. I'm no stranger to the sting of heartache," Creed said reflecting on many lost opportunities in the past before he met his wife.

It was an old actor's trick when trying to bring out emotions. Danielle had taught him that. It only proved you could teach an old dog new tricks.

There were many layers to Kellie Fletcher. Jack had barely scratched the surface.

"I hate him. She can rot in hell for all I care. I mean, he can rot in hell," she said in what was considered a Freudian slip of the tongue.

Creed was about to leave when she added something to her story.

"It's too bad about the fire," the receptionist said.

"What fire?" Jack asked already knowing it was going to be just another piece of the puzzle.

What he heard next didn't necessarily surprise them. It did put things into perspective.

The woman was turning into a black widow with eight legs stretching from the past to the future.

*****

Anderson was uncomfortably sitting in front of a red light when he was called. The caller identification on his cell told him Reeves wanted a private word with him.

He was going to ignore it but he wanted to hear what Reeves had to say for himself.

There was some bad blood. Jack knew there was some kind of underlying reason for his animosity.

"When I call you, I expect you to answer immediately. Never make me wait. You do value your job, don't you Detective Anderson? Do I make myself clear?" Reeves said with an icy reception.

"I'm in traffic. What can I do for you, Sir?" Anderson asked with his head on a swivel.

"What were you doing with, detective Creed? Be careful how you answer. The last thing you want is to get on my radar. I want you to tell me the truth as if your job depends on it," he threatened in a backhanded way.

"I was just looking in on him for a friend. She was worried," Anderson referred to Danielle Rodrigues with a smile on his face.

"She's just as bad as he is maybe more so. They don't understand the chain of evidence. We don't have room in the Department for cowboys. Bad publicity is only going to cause all of us more harm than good. Do yourself a favor and distance yourself from the two of them," Reeves suggested.

"Are you ordering me to stay away from them in the course of my duties?" Anderson asked.

"I'm not telling you how to do your job. I'm just saying it's in your best interest not to associate yourself with people that will drag you down into the mud with them. You have a promising career. Don't blow it," Reeves spoke defiantly.

"I wouldn't dream of it. Thank you for your counsel. It will take it under advisement," he said coldly.

"I'm glad to hear it. Get back to work. Whatever you find, I want to hear about it first. Don't let them make you part of the problem when you can be part of the solution. We have nothing but good things to say about you. That can change in a hurry," Reeves stated before cutting off the communication with only the dial tone left behind.

He had barely moved from one block to the other during rush hour traffic in New York. He was famished and could definitely use a bite to eat. He heard good things about the Halal Guys.

The food truck could be found on their Facebook Page. There was also something to say for a quiet night in with a home cooked meal. He chose the latter.

His choice of dinner companions might've been questionable. Making the phone call was as easy as pressing the digits one after the other.

"Hello, Detective Anderson. It's nice to hear your voice. What can I do for you?" Kellie asked.

"Do you have any plans for dinner? I still have a few things to ask you but I see no reason why I have to drag you down to the station," Jack proposed.

"I do have some pressing business but I suppose everybody has to eat. Where would you like to meet? Nothing fast food. I'm trying to watch my waistline," Ms. Fletcher stated in a timid tone of voice.

"Would it be unprofessional to invite you to my home? You won't be disappointed," he invoked his license to home-field advantage.

"I think that can be arranged. What time were you thinking?" She pressed.

"How about 7 PM? That would give me plenty of time to freshen up before you arrive. Bring a bottle of wine," he encouraged before the line went dead.

He sat there for a few moments drumming his fingers on the covered steering wheel. He didn't know what compelled him to reach out to her other than a very serious curiosity to learn more about her.

Maybe he was playing into her hand but there was only one way to find out.

CHAPTER 24

Nobody was ever going to accuse her of being subtle when it came to investigating a crime. She felt a little out of sorts sitting across from this man of wealth and fame.

"I apologize for making you wait. It was unavoidable. Business comes first over everything else. Not all the markets close at 5 PM," Chase Adams mentioned while applying the cold blade to the lobster tail soaking in garlic butter.

"I guess that makes sense. You could have been setting the tone for this meeting by making me wait. It only puts me on the defensive," Danielle mentioned without even bothering to taste the culinary delight lying on her plate.

The meeting was arranged ahead of time. The confirmation came with the attachment of information leading her to a fancy restaurant next to the water.

She was beginning to like her time in Boston, however brief it was going to be.

"I wish you could've changed into something a little more comfortable. That pantsuit doesn't do anything for you. It's a little bland and simply uninspiring," Chase spoke with his head shaking from side to side.

"This isn't a date. I'm here on a fact-finding mission. What can you tell me about Kellie Fletcher that I don't already know?" She asked before reaching for the glass of red wine.

Chase stopped cutting into the lobster tail halfway down the center. "I was hoping we could discuss something else. She's not my favorite person for obvious reasons. That gold-digging tramp has been the bane of my family from the moment she came into it."

"How so," she asked while using one hand to cut the lobster tail until the succulent meat was revealed.

The predominant ingredient of garlic had penetrated the shell already soaking in the juices.

"Don't get me started. My brother was an idiot. I tried gently to warn him but he didn't want to listen to me. She killed him," Chase accused while holding onto the knife until his knuckles turned white.

Danielle sat straight up. "Care to elaborate?"

"She took a knife to his chest and carved out his heart," he said with his hand moving the knife over his heart without touching the expensive Italian fabric of his dark shirt.

"Why didn't you report this to the police?" Danielle interrogated.

"You've got the wrong idea. She didn't commit a crime per se. My brother was head over heels. He gave her everything, and she wanted more.

The last straw was when he gave her his seat on the Board of Directors without first consulting us," He seethed before stabbing the table with the knife until it was driven into the wood at least an inch.

"Why would he do something like that?" Danielle continued to ask the pertinent questions on the tip of her tongue.

"Why does any man do anything for a woman he hardly knows? I can only imagine the sex was phenomenal. He couldn't wipe the grin off of his face. He would have done anything for her. They were only together three months before he married her in a private ceremony. None of us were invited to the nuptials," Chase expressed himself with every muscle flexing in frustration.

"Calm down. You don't want to break a blood vessel," she implored.

"It just burns me up inside to see him used for her own selfish needs. The ink was barely dry when they decided to take a drive in the country. She claimed it was the wet road that made him lose control. I beg to differ," he said with one hand pushing the plate away from him, no longer interested in dining with his pretty companion.

He had lost his appetite for food.

"You suspect that she was involved somehow? Did you find anything to warrant the suspicion? It could've been something small. Anything you say is not going to leave these four walls," Danielle said a little flustered with a flush to her cheeks.

"Nothing that I can put my finger on. It seemed like she was playing a game when she came to tell us the awful news. My mother had a heart attack. She is not expected to live past the end of the week," Chase lamented with his eyes welling up.

He unbuttoned the sleeves of his shirt before rolling them up to his elbows.

"I'm so sorry. Family is the most important thing in the world," she said forlornly while touching his hand to demonstrate her ability to show some kind of compassion.

"It doesn't make a difference. The family is ruined. She holds 51% stake in the company. That is what is considered a majority stockholder. We are basically at her mercy. I've even tinkered with the fantasy of killing her with my bare hands," he fretted with both hands on the table.

"I'm sure you're not the first man to express the same thing. Just remember crossing the line is something you can never take back." Danielle squeezed his hand.

"I would never give her the satisfaction of wrapping my hands around her throat. What goes around comes around. She will get hers one of these days. I just hope that I'm around to see it," Chase said with one hand slapping the table hard enough to rattle the cutlery.

"It doesn't sound like you have anything more than conjecture. That's not enough to prosecute her. It does shed some more light on her lack of character. You might be called to testify against her," she said before taking her first bite of the garlic-soaked lobster.

"Gladly." He sat back suddenly clutching his collar.

"Take a drink of water," she said with one hand pushing the carafe of water over to him.

He gasped and pitched forward with his head smacking the table. The plate went flying as he fell from the chair and began to convulse in a spastic fit.

"Is there a doctor in the house?" Danielle screamed the question.

A man with a distinguished air of experience pushed his way through the collective murmurs of the crowd. His full mane of white hair made him look experienced.

"I'm retired, but I have practiced medicine for the last 20 years. Give me some room. Back up and give me some room," he ordered before kneeling next to the patient.

"Did he have a heart attack?" Danielle asked.

The man ripped open his shirt and began to perform life-saving measures. He pounded on his chest and breathed air into his mouth several times. The chest rose and fell but didn't continue to breathe normally.

It was as if somebody had turned off the light switch. He was there one second and gone the next.

Exhausted and heaving, the doctor sat back on his heels. "There's nothing more I can do for him. He's gone. Time of death 6:45 PM..." He made a notation which he scribbled on a napkin to give to the paramedics when they arrived.

Danielle was understandably distraught.

He was a vibrant man and somehow was cut down in the prime of his life.

It was just another body associated with the name Kellie Fletcher. Just how many people were going to have to die before they brought the woman to justice was anybody's guess.

CHAPTER 25

It was uncommon for Creed to grieve unless it was in private away from the prying eyes of others.

He didn't even know the man, but he still felt a deep kinship. Their ages were very similar.

The report from Danielle devastated him. They were so close and yet so far away from nabbing her.

Jack made up his mind to continue in his pursuit of justice.

Kellie Fletcher thought that she was above the law. That somehow, she was untouchable from those in power and authority. The woman was slippery.

He sat and compiled his notes. This time, he didn't care about his career. Something had to be done before somebody else died as a result of coming in close contact with a killer with no conscience.

He was alone with his thoughts.

There was only one thing on his mind. Bringing Kellie Fletcher into the station in handcuffs with no wiggle room for negotiation.

It was going to drive him to the brink of insanity but he was willing to take that chance.

"You've been a very busy girl as of late. You have airtight alibis but I have no doubt your fingerprint metaphorically speaking can be found at every crime scene. Danielle is in trouble. She knows more than she should and there is going to come a time you are going to want to silence her. Good luck with that. She has nine lives and will always land on her feet," he spoke to the air and to the photo of Ms. Fletcher staring at him from across the room.

The wall was quickly filling up with innocuous details about her life. There was still the unspoken question when it came to those years between 12 and 16.

Just where did she go during that time?

He had an appointment with the child welfare office in the morning. It was time to tread carefully when there were obviously eyes and ears working for Ms. Fletcher.

She thought it was a damn game and wanted him to play by her rules. He had made the first mistake, and she was happy to have him chasing his tail.

The one thing she couldn't possibly predict was Warren naming her as his accomplice. That would've been too easy. She recognized Warren's vulnerability and used it to fuel the fire until he was ready to act.

"I see you. Everybody else is fooled. My partner and I are on the same page. Anderson still needs a little convincing but I

125

think he's no longer in the dark floundering around trying to find his way. The three of us have joined forces. God help you because I won't," Jack said vehemently to the same picture mocking him on the wall.

He had different colored strings connecting the dots from one colored pushpin to another. It might've been old-school, but this was considered old-fashioned police work at its best.

There was no telling when another body was going to drop. No further leads led them anywhere concerning her old superior.

The investigation was becoming a moot point.

The investigators tasked to go after the evidence were rookies. They didn't have the experience. Other seasoned detectives had grumbled but never ventured any further than casting shade in a bar after indulging a little too much.

"Somebody on the inside is working for you. Reeves is one of them. Everything that has happened leads to only one conclusion. The corruption is at the highest level of the department. A lot of people are going to fall from their lofty perch when I'm through with this investigation," he said with his finger pressing against the smug arrogant smile on her face.

The microwave dinged.

There was a pop and fizzle followed by an electrical charge through the wires.

Jack had his hand almost on the handle when he was blown out of his metaphorical boots. He felt the electrical discharge through his fingers.

His mind was a jumble of images as he lay there on the floor laughing like an idiot.

"I'm getting a little too close for comfort. It means I'm on the right track," he said with one fist raised with his fingers sending out pins and needles.

He wasn't even going to bother with an investigation. She wasn't going to leave evidence behind. It was good to know things were coming to a head.

Creed was going to need a few moments to get feeling back in his lower extremities.

It could've been far worse. Lady luck was on his side for a change.

*****

The shock was wearing off after being grilled by the local cops. She didn't mention any kind of conspiracy. It wasn't her investigation and not her place to meddle unless they specifically asked for her help.

"We have your contact information. Your superiors have nothing but good things to say. If we have any further questions, please make yourself available to answer them. It looks like natural causes,"

Detective Amber Benton stated.

There was no point in arguing.

Danielle walked away from the restaurant feeling hopeless. Chase was essentially a Playboy on the prowl for suitable companionship for the evening.

The path of the conversation had taken a drastic turn when it came to the subject of Kellie Fletcher.

The woman was going to have to make a serious mistake they could pounce on. That didn't seem likely when she considered all the angles before concocting one of her schemes.

She was ready to go home, but she felt this nagging compulsion to go back and talk to Mrs. Olsen. Now she knew she was putting on a front. It was time to treat her as a hostile combatant instead of a cooperative witness.

That would be tomorrow. Tonight, was a time for self-reflection.

Something told her it revolved around Jack Creed. Their paths must've crossed somewhere during his illustrious career. He hadn't been able to provide any insight in this regard but maybe it was a matter of jogging his memory.

One more discussion with Mrs. Olsen and then she would go home.

That was her plan until a few drinks changed her mind.

CHAPTER 26

Anderson had gone all out on the pretence of romancing the pants off of her. He had the roast simmering in the oven. It was accompanied by baby potatoes and small carrots he had picked from his garden.

Nobody knew his penchant for getting his hands dirty. They could never suspect he had a green thumb.

He had just finished marinating the roast in its own juices. The spices added to his culinary masterpiece made it a mouth-watering example of a four-star general in the kitchen.

He had dressed for the occasion. There was a dark suit in the back of his closet gathering dust. His hair was completely slicked back with not a lock out of place. He still couldn't understand why he was bending over backward to impress her.

It came naturally.

It was probably what other men felt when they were on the receiving end of her flirtatious advances.

Somebody was knocking on the door. She was fashionably early which was something he hadn't considered. His psychology degree was being wasted.

He thought for sure she wasn't going to show up until the very last minute. This was out of character and somewhat confusing when it came to the basic mechanics of human behavior.

"You're a little early for dinner but maybe we can break open a bottle of wine while we wait," he finished his spiel when he was faced with a moral dilemma in the shape of a woman, he had almost kissed. "Oh, it's you," he said deflated and somewhat amused at the same time.

"Were you expecting somebody else?" Danielle asked with a bottle of wine hidden behind her back.

"I'm sorry but you caught me at a bad time. Maybe you can come back tomorrow morning," he said nervously fidgeting with his tie.

"Something smells good. You didn't have to do this for me." Danielle looked at him and could see that he was fumbling for the words with his mouth agape. "I'm kidding. I won't keep you very long. I just wanted to stop by on my way back from the airport," Danielle said when she stepped into the kitchen and pulled open the stainless steel stove for a closer look.

"You've been incommunicado for the last 12 hours. I was beginning to think you fell off the face of the earth. It was tempting to send out the military to find you," he jested.

"You don't get off that lucky. I had an interesting day off. You already know the pertinent details. I just received word from the authorities in Boston. His death is being ruled natural causes but I think we both know she had her hand in it," Danielle stressed.

"I wish we had more to go on than pure speculation. It's not a good idea to go around accusing people of murder when they are 1000 miles away. Not every death is connected to Kellie," he mentioned when he caught sight of Ms. Fletcher standing in the doorway.

"It's Kellie now, is it? When did that change?" Danielle asked.

"My personal life is none of your business."

"I couldn't have said it better myself. Will you be staying for dinner, Danielle," Kellie said in an effort to disrespect her by using her first name.

"I think not. This is where I say good night. Don't do anything I wouldn't do. You might want to consider sleeping with one eye open," Danielle warned with a sideways glance toward Kellie.

"I doubt there will be much sleeping done. Have a good night, Detective," Kellie said with an inflection of hatred seeping through every word.

Anderson tried to pick his tongue up from off the floor. It was more than a little exciting to see them verbally sparring while he was watching temporarily stunned into paralysis.

Danielle stormed out and slammed the door behind her with as much enthusiasm as she could muster. She was seeing red and wanted to wring Kellie's neck until she squealed. It was starting to dawn on her how she felt for Anderson.

What she thought was an infatuation for a much younger man was turning out to be something even deeper than she realized.

It was the only way to explain why she had given him the cold shoulder when Kellie showed up unannounced.

She wanted to believe Anderson was playing her to get information. It was the way he looked at her. Something more was going on than a casual observation.

The woman was notorious for getting men to spend time doing whatever it took to impress her.

She needed a drink and the last thing she was going to do was help her partner to fall off the wagon.

*****

Creed was fast asleep on the sofa. He had worked himself into a tizzy until he couldn't see straight.

There was something there but he just couldn't see it. Fresh eyes in the morning might provide a better insight.

He was awoken by the disturbing sound of somebody banging against his front door. He wasn't expecting to see Danielle hanging her head in defeat.

"You've been drinking." He looked her up and down. "Don't tell me this has something to do with Anderson. He's not worth the time or effort. He's still old enough to know better and young enough not to care," he said before stepping aside to watch her stumble into the room inebriated and stinking of vodka.

"You don't know the half of it. I came home looking for a little comfort. I thought mistakenly I would find it in his arms. Do you know what I found instead?" She asked with a finger in the air.

"I could take a stab in the dark. Another woman?" He asked already knowing the answer.

"Bingo. You nailed it. There's one thing you don't know. Can you guess what woman he is spending his time with?"

"Pray tell," he encouraged while putting on the kettle.

The microwave was unplugged and there was a black char mark on the receptacle. The wire was frayed. Somebody had cut it. He didn't need a crystal ball to know who had come looking to silence him with intimidation.

"I can't even say her name without wanting to throw up in my mouth a little," She slurred her words until she had a hand over her mouth with her eyes bulging out of her skull.

"The bathroom is down the hall to the right," Jack directed with one finger.

She rushed past him and almost didn't make it in time.

She was over the toilet getting rid of too many shots of tequila. It did make her feel no pain but she could never forget the look on Kellie's face when she stumbled upon their love nest.

Jack came in and leaned against the counter with a cup of coffee in his hand. "I think you need this more than I do. Are you able to speak?" He asked while offering the cup of coffee which she gratefully accepted.

"What is he thinking? The man must've lost his mind. She was wearing this red dress off the shoulder with a little too much skin showing. She didn't just show up out of the blue. Anderson was cooking for her something that made my mouth water with anticipation. That would've been far better than what I consumed after leaving his place."

"I've never seen you like this. You barely know him, Danielle."

"I've harbored feelings for quite some time. I just never wanted to talk about it. She has her hooks in him. Kellie 'god damn' Fletcher." She looked up from where she was kneeling over the toilet.

"What about her? Wait, a minute. You're not saying what I think you're saying," Creed said with his mouth going dry.

"That's who I found at his door. The conniving little bitch is going to rue the day," she said when she suddenly passed out next to the toilet holding on to the cup of coffee that didn't spill a drop.

Jack knew Anderson was going to have some explaining to do in the cold light of reality.

There had to be a logical explanation. He didn't want to think about the alternative.

CHAPTER 27

Creed had spent the night watching over his partner. It was a thankless job, but he felt protecting her was a priority over everything else.

The one thing that remained unclear was how far down the rabbit hole their ally had gone.

Danielle was nursing a hangover with a homemade remedy in front of her. Her nose curled at the mere mention of alcohol.

They were impatiently waiting to meet with Anderson in an undisclosed location.

It was a seedy bar in the middle of nowhere. The morning after was desolate, with only a few motorcycles remaining in the dirt parking lot.

"Do you mind keeping it down?" Danielle asked with her thumb and forefinger stretched out about an inch.

"I didn't say anything," Jack responded in a whisper.

"You're breathing too loud. The annoying whistle you make is starting to get on my last nerve." Danielle held the glass with this green concoction with little bits of things she didn't recognize floating on the surface.

The bartender was an informant with the Hell's Angels. He kept his eyes and ears open for anything he could use to capitalize on.

Harper had always been an opportunist with his body a landscape of tattoos. He had lost his hair at a young age. He was one of the pioneers to tattoo his skull to replace those lost locks. The muscles on his forearms bulged under his denim shirt.

The bar was a front for other activities behind the scene. He was privy to back alley deals over a game of pool.

"That's a new one. My wife says I snore. Nobody has ever accused me of breathing too loud. We should get something to eat from the kitchen. They make a mean breakfast dish. I hope you like jalapenos," Jack said before signalling Harper.

"I can't even think about food. I'm still trying to stomach this," she said, with her eyes rolling.

Harper was ready to listen and learn from the master. It wasn't just a contractual obligation. Nobody would take them for friends. It was better they didn't know Jack on the other side of the metaphorical tracks.

He screamed something derogatory on his way into the kitchen.

Harper considered himself a culinary genius. He did like to dabble and had a few well-chosen guinea pigs, including Jack, ready to partake.

"What is taking him so long?" Danielle inquired.

"He's probably trying to find his pants." Jack felt the punch of a woman scorned. "Too soon," Jack snickered under his breath.

"I don't know why this bothers me so much. We don't exactly socialize in the same circles. He's more comfortable in a club where they cater to those with money to burn. I enjoy a cold beer around a bonfire with some friends talking about the job," Danielle said with her head lying on the table.

"Maybe it's a case of wanting something you can't have. It's the oldest story in the book." Jack inhaled the aroma of the fresh jalapenos being chopped in the kitchen.

"I can't remember the last time I've been drunk," Danielle lamented with a groan while speaking out of the left side of her mouth.

She did remember, but the thought of the gun loaded on the table drifted away.

"I blame Kellie Fletcher. Let's look at the case with an unbiased eye. We know she was bullied, but nobody is willing to come forward. Don't you find it ironic?" Creed posed the question.

"I'm in no shape for 20 questions," she groaned again with her head pounding.

"I'm just saying she was the one being bullied and now the roles are reversed. She's using money and influence to get what she wants. I think if we continue to dig, we are going to find skeletons in closets nobody wants us rooting around in. Namely Reeves, just to name one." Creed shook his head in frustration.

Danielle lifted her chin from the table to look at him through the rose-colored sunglasses. "I don't know what you did, but he doesn't like you. The man has been on a warpath with all of his resources directed at you."

"I do have that effect on some people," he recalled many suspects in court screaming how they were going to get him when they got out.

"Rubbing people the wrong way isn't always a good idea. Have you ever heard a little honey is a lot more effective than vinegar? I think that is how it goes, but I really can't think straight," Danielle said before pushing away from the table when the spicy breakfast dish arrived.

The predominant ingredient was aged jalapeno peppers.

"Harper, I don't suppose you have heard anything about a woman by the name of Kellie Fletcher?" Jack blurted out in a conspiratorial whisper.

"I don't think her name has been mentioned. I'll discreetly make some inquiries. How much is this information worth to you?" Harper inquired.

"Let's see what you come up with before we talk about compensation," Jack said before dismissing him with a wave of his hand.

*****

Anderson woke up to the sound of birds singing on his windowsill.

He stretched his arms above the sheets. He couldn't remember how he had gotten into bed.

It had been a long night of trying to use alcohol to coerce a confession. None of it could be used against her. She would claim that she was under duress.

Any information would at least give them a place to start to build a case against her.

That tactic quickly went out of the window.

His tongue felt like sandpaper and two times its normal size. An empty glass of wine sat lonely and dripping with condensation onto his black lacquered night table.

There was no coaster.

His ears perked to the sound of the shower. It couldn't be.

Both hands gripped the sheets and lifted them to reveal how he was somehow naked. He didn't remember taking off his clothing. Somebody had to do it for him.

"You better get in here before I use up all the hot water. We can continue what we started last night and into the morning. I have to say you were an unexpected surprise," Kellie called out from the bathroom.

Anderson didn't know what to say. A double take confirmed he was almost 30 minutes late.

They were just going to have to postpone the meeting until he was better prepared for their accusations.

Trying to piece together the evening wasn't possible. Those memories had been fractured into tiny little images.

He seemed to recall kissing her, but there was no context for a physical relationship to develop between them.

His head was swimming.

It was a mistake to invite her to dinner on the pretence of pumping her for information. Ethically, it was wrong to have any contact with her without her lawyer present.

She didn't seem concerned when she walked through the door.

"I hope I didn't wear you out. I didn't take you for a wild animal. I think I'm going to have to invest in some new clothes. It's a good thing I brought with me something to change into," she hinted that the dress was no longer a viable option.

Anderson peered over the edge of the bed to see what was left of the dress. He seemed to have a vague recollection of having his hand around her waist.

The sound of the fabric ripping made him understand what happens when somebody leaves him to his own devices.

"I have a few minutes to spare. Can I interest you in a little morning delight? The temperature is rising, and it has nothing to do with the weather outside." Kellie jiggled in a towel around her waist at the door with one leg poised against the entrance.

Anderson gulped but quickly got a hold of himself figuratively and not literally.

"Would you look at the time? I just remembered I need to be somewhere. We are just going to have to pick this up later," he said while using the sheet to wrap around his naked body.

"You don't have to be bashful with me. It's not like I haven't seen it already. We are two consenting adults. Sex is a natural endorphin high. Are you sure that I can't convince you to stick around?" She pondered with a finger tracing her glistening cleavage.

Fletcher was totally opposite of the frigid persona she displayed to her work colleagues and to her partner Vince. Christmas and birthdays were not guarantee of any action from her.

But with strangers, Kellie was very different. Perhaps she liked to escape through role playing with men and women.

"I'm afraid I'm going to have to take a rain check. Get dressed," he said with a little more edge to his voice.

"This is priceless. You don't remember what we did last night. That might have something to do with polishing off the bottle of wine. I suppose all good things come to an end. Let me just freshen up my makeup," she laughed with her voice suddenly muted when the door closed behind her.

Anderson was frantic and running around like a chicken with its head cut off.

He stopped in his tracks when he saw a vessel of information staring right at him.

Her cell was left unattended on the nightstand next to the empty glass of wine.

It was his one chance to sneak a peek. That would be spying. Could he really cross the line?

This was up for debate as he stood there and looked at the phone with no visible password to punch in. He could easily access her list of contacts and call history.

It was going to be risky with her only a few feet away.

A decision had been made within the next couple of minutes.

CHAPTER 28

Creed wasn't exactly happy, but he had to admit the cryptic message from Anderson gave him a little bit of hope.

There were no witnesses present when they arrived at the location.

It was an isolated area inhabited by nobody. A warehouse shut down was now vacant, with the previous owners washing their hands.

The for rent sign on the front door was askew.

"Are you sure this is where he wanted us to meet him?" Danielle asked from where she was lagging behind by a few steps.

Jack looked around but saw nobody lurking. It wasn't even fit for the homeless. They had more respect for themselves than to be caught dead in a rat-infested warehouse.

That alone should have told him it was a bad decision to let Anderson dictate where they were going to meet after missing their first-morning briefing.

He wiped some dust and grime from the front door. Inside was a hodgepodge of machinery abandoned after the textile plant went bankrupt.

It was a dark day for almost 30 employees. Nobody knew anything was amiss until they showed up in the morning to see a padlock on the door. Their jobs were being sent to India.

Nobody was there to explain.

The note written by the management was still visible. It stated emphatically their jobs were no longer needed. The plant had been closed. There was no compensation or any mention of some kind of settlement.

"It doesn't look like anybody's home. We are a little early. Let's take a look around. The one thing I hate is being blindsided," Jack stressed.

He could've sworn there was something off.

"Sundays are for rest and sleep in. What are we doing here?"

"Danielle, I think it's called trespassing on private property," Jack said before taking off his jacket and hanging it over his arm.

"What am I going to say to him? I made a fool of myself in front of a prime suspect. She must've had a good laugh behind my back," she fretted.

"Join the club. You're not even in my league when it comes to being manipulated by that witch. We need to watch each other's backs more than ever. What I'm doing here is nothing official. I'm just a civilian with a badge I can't use," he said while peering into the shop to see stagnant water lying on the concrete floor.

Something scurried, but he didn't get a good look, even though the hairs on the back of his neck stood up.

"This is ridiculous. I can't stand this waiting any longer. Call him," she requested.

*****

What Anderson had found was damning, but wasn't enough to charge her for a crime. There had to be a second phone.

Her last call was to Reeves. It confirmed they knew each other.

She tried unsuccessfully to unbutton his shirt when she came out of the bathroom.

Dodging and weaving around her was the only way to prevent him from doing something he was going to regret. The details were fuzzy. Some of it was slowing coming back.

He needed something that wasn't going to stand out like a sore thumb. It was possible the woman he had spent the night with was keeping tabs on him.

A car sitting in between two others was a little suspicious when he escorted her to the door. The one thing they couldn't afford was having their whereabouts known to anybody that wasn't in their close circle of confidence.

He hadn't heard from Danielle or Jack. He thought they would be livid. All of his attempts to reach them went directly to voice mail. He had left several messages in one hour.

His neighbor was out of town. Anderson had a set of keys to look in on his place while he was away. They did each other favors but weren't considered friends.

Anderson was a police detective with a great standing in the community for going above and beyond the call of duty. It all started when he was patrolling the streets in uniform. He gave people a smile and wave, but also the benefit of the doubt.

He was the one that had implemented a neighborhood watch program.

Anderson could still smell her on him. The whole place would have to be aired out to get rid of the pheromones trapped inside.

He went out the back and crouched next to the hedges until he was able to access a series of backyards.

The car was watching the front door for any movement.

He got to the garage with little difficulty. A bead of sweat was running down his spine when he punched in the code for the security system.

It beeped once before going dormant.

Inside was a man cave dedicated to frivolous toys for boys. A Pac-Man arcade was stationed tight in the corner. A few road signs decorated the walls with a fridge straight out of the 1970s. It had been restored meticulously.

The fresh teal paint job was accented with a stainless-steel handle.

A poker table and billiards were right in the centre of the garage. Two leather armchairs in front of a 75-inch big-screen television were where they spent many afternoons screaming at the home team to rally back from a deficit.

The motorcycle was his friend's pride and joy. There was a porcelain white skull with smoke coming out of its eyes and mouth stencilled on the front. The metallic blue was a nice touch.

He pressed the button with the door lifting. The helmet was strapped on with the visor, hiding his true identity from onlookers.

What he experienced was a sense of vertigo when a pair of headlights blinded him.

He was sitting astride the magnificent beast.

He couldn't see the driver of the car. The vehicle was a relic from the early 80s. The engine revved over and over again until the wheels began spinning clockwise.

It was coming straight at him and didn't look like it was going to slow down.

CHAPTER 29

It was the second time they were depending on Anderson to come through.

Something told him they shouldn't hold their breath.

"Are we judging him unfairly? We should hear his side of things," Danielle suggested.

Creed grabbed her and shook her. "Do you hear yourself?"

"Don't you think I know he can't be trusted? Sleeping with the enemy wasn't exactly the best decision he has ever made. We don't know anything for certain. It could be his invitation was strictly professional. Yeah, I hear it now," Danielle bent down to look in the window.

"A man his age is susceptible. It would be interesting to get a look at her little black book. It's probably a list of some very familiar names." His phone began buzzing in his pocket. One look made him stare at it quizzically. "It's Harper. That didn't take him long at all. We just left his establishment an hour ago." He looked at Danielle to see her pointing at the screen display.

"Are you going to answer it? Don't leave me in suspense. You never know. It could be the big break we have been looking for. Answer it," Danielle encouraged.

Creed touched the button and was about to speak, but he didn't get the chance. "The number you have reached is no longer in service. Please dial again. I'm just pulling your leg."

"Who is this?" Jack asked while taking a few steps back, still holding onto his phone in the palm of his hand.

"I'm afraid Harper can't come to the phone. He's tied up at the moment," a digitized voice responded.

"What have you done to him?"

"Some things are better left unsaid. Remember that. I can assure you Harper is never going to forget it for as long as he lives. I suspect that's not going to be very much longer," the digitized voice informed them.

"This isn't over. Do you hear me?" Creed fumed.

"Haven't you learned your lesson? This has been fun and I do hope we can catch up very soon. Harper is no longer your informant. He won't be saying anything to anybody ever again. Ta-ta for now, Detective Creed," the digitized voice signed off with both Jack and Danielle staring at the phone.

"We both know who that was. I'm starting to get mad. This is no longer just a regular case to be solved. I'm positively incensed," Danielle announced with her fist shaking and fingernails cutting into the palm of her hand.

"How is she always one step ahead of us? I have a meeting tomorrow when the doors open at the welfare of children's offices. We better not get stonewalled. Where the hell is he? I'm not going to wait here all day," Jack said with one glance at his watch.

"I don't like this," Danielle replied while biting her bottom lip.

"Standing us up once is more than enough. I have a bad feeling. We better get over to his place. Get in and hold on to something," Creed said over his shoulder while dangling the keys around one finger.

The explosion forced them both against the car. They were flattened against the hood.

The warehouse had imploded with some help. It wasn't lost on them how they had been just standing at the door peeking in the window.

*****

It was fun to be the smartest person in the room. That didn't stop those that felt small from lashing out against her.

It had been happening most of her life, but it was only recently she began to fight back by using the tools at her discretion. No longer was she hiding in plain sight, waiting to be accepted by society.

The man in front of her was screaming, but she didn't hear his pleas for mercy. The electricity attached to his privates was an electrifying experience to witness.

His bloody tongue was still hanging from the pliers she used to rip it out of his mouth. It was a symbolic gesture. Loose lips and all that jazz.

Harper was jerking and thrusting against the chains.

The battery was fully charged. There was no need to question him when he had nothing to contribute. What he had was information that couldn't fall into the wrong hands.

Kellie smiled while administering her own form of inhuman torture. Hearing his painful anguished screams was music to her ears.

He was dead minutes after she stopped gloating on the phone. She just had to figure out the best way to reveal her handiwork for public consumption.

She lifted his head to see those vacant eyes.

Another thorn in her side was dealt with. It was becoming easier with each new victim in her cross hairs.

Kellie prided herself on being a different breed of animal. It was repugnant for her to kill the same way twice.

There was no creativity in being predictable.

Warren was scheduled to go to trial on Monday. She was going to be there for the preliminary hearing. She wanted everybody to see her in the courtroom, front and centre, for the opening arguments.

This was a man that was capable of bending the law for his own selfish needs. She was devising a plot to get him out of jail. He was no good to her behind bars.

Cultivating another ally was going to take time she didn't have. Her endgame was going to have her name on everybody's lips.

One glance confirmed everything was going according to plan.

Who did Anderson think he was? It was time for him to learn a valuable lesson about having sticky fingers. Did he really think he had gotten away with anything?

She wasn't an idiot. There was no incriminating evidence on her phone. It was the principal of him taking a peek.

Creed was going to have to learn the hard way having allies meant that she had somebody to target. It was too bad. She really did like Anderson, and they could've had fun, at least in the interim.

CHAPTER 30

Anderson was frozen like a deer in the headlights.

One hand was still holding onto the key in the ignition. The other one was instinctively going for his gun.

He jumped from the bike seconds before the car sent it careering into the back wall of the garage. It landed on top of the Pac-Man machine. The bells and whistles went off.

Anderson rolled until he came to a stop in between the two leather chairs. He aimed and fired with the safety off. The bullets took chunks out of the glass windshield.

The driver was trying to put it in reverse.

Anderson stood up with his arm extended. His hand wasn't shaking as he walked with purpose and confidence. His face was expressionless as he continued to fire indiscriminately into the windshield.

The bullets should have perforated the man behind the wheel. It appeared it wasn't normal glass. This was reinforced to take the blunt end of lead projectiles.

The car was stuck with one wheel wedged next to an old weight machine. The wheels were spinning with black smoke peeling off the rubber of the tires. It made his nose curl.

"Come out with her hands up. Do it nice and slowly," Anderson ordered while in the process of reloading the clip.

The window on the passenger side rolled down until he saw the beginning of the end.

The cannon was indicative of something Dirty Harry would use in one of his movies

He couldn't see the face of the perpetrator when he was staring down the barrel of the gun. It was something custom-made.

The chamber moved as the trigger was pulled.

There was no chance to get out of the way. The bullet careened in a dangerous trajectory. He felt the impact in his chest before he was blown off of his feet. The pain radiated through his ribs as he was lifted clear off the floor.

His body was propelled over the back of the chair with one hand slapping at the big-screen television suspended from the ceiling.

Glass shattered as he came down heavily on his left shoulder, twisting it at an awkward angle. His hand was cut deep enough to require stitches.

The chairs provided some coverage when the perpetrator continued to fire, undeterred. The holes punching into the upholstery of the leather made the stuffing turn into a snowstorm of violence.

The man behind the wheel decided discretion was the better part of valor. His anger was amplified when the car finally broke free from its confinement.

The front end lifted into the air and came down with sparks dancing below the undercarriage. The rear end turned sharply until the green beast was fishtailing onto the road.

Anderson saw the scar on his face before everything went black.

*****

Danielle gasped out loud when she saw the ambulance idling in the driveway. A stretch of black tar from a set of wheels made it to the road.

"She wanted to kill two birds with one stone," Jack said.

Two paramedics, one older with snow white hair and a young woman with a blond ponytail, were working on Anderson.

Jack grabbed her shoulder. "Expect the best, but be prepared for the worst."

She very carefully removed his hand from her shoulder, one finger at a time. "He's one of us. We can't just sit here and do nothing."

"Listen to me. We can't be anywhere near the scene. Nobody can know we were here. It would be just the ammunition

Reeves would use against me. I'm already hanging by a thread. He's just looking for a reason. Sit tight," Creed encouraged with plenty of gentle persuasion in the tone of his voice.

"What is going on? I can't see a thing," Danielle said while craning her neck over the dashboard.

"We can't get any closer. Let's see what we can do about getting a better look," Creed mentioned when he stuck his hand into the glove compartment.

He produced high-powered binoculars, which were immediately taken from him. There was no point in protesting when he knew any argument was going to fall on deaf ears.

She peered through the lenses and soon focused on the scene playing out in front of her.

They were crowded around his body in the garage. It wasn't even his place.

There had to be a reasonable explanation.

Danielle couldn't stop staring and could barely recognize her partner's voice trying to calm her down before she did something stupid.

The other hand was holding onto the door handle, refusing to let go.

"She is going to make a mistake. Mark my words, we will be there when she does. She is becoming too confident. Thinking that she can't be caught is what is going to get her a one-way ticket to a jail cell with her name on it," Jack enthused.

"From your lips to God's ears. I guess nobody really knows what they are capable of until they are facing something they couldn't even imagine in their worst nightmare. He dies and all bets are off. She won't even see me coming," she threatened with thoughts of violence.

"I didn't hear that. You have a duty to make sure she sees her day in court. We both have reasons to detest her. She's having fun at our expense, but there's always a method to her madness. We are getting close," Jack answered.

Her heart was hammering in her chest. The breath was caught in her throat. She didn't blink in fear that she was going to miss something important.

"You want to talk about right and wrong? Gene might have something to say on that subject," she mentioned, without even meaning to dig at the scab from his past.

"What did he tell you? We made a pact," Jack interjected.

"Your secret is safe with him. I'm just saying don't throw stones at glasshouses. You preach about the law like its gospel. Something happened."

"Don't go asking questions you don't want the answers to. What I did wasn't against the law. I didn't kill anybody, if that is what you're worried about."

"Everybody is capable of cold-blooded murder under certain circumstances. I'm already contemplating several ways to get rid of the body. It's just a fantasy, but it sure does make me feel good," Danielle smiled.

"That just creeps me out. Stop that. That's the difference between us and the criminals. We might think about doing something illegal, but we would never actually go through with it," Jack said.

"I bet you would give anything to have one more crack at her. Somewhere behind closed doors where you don't have to worry about doing the right thing," she said with a sneer of derision.

"You're right about that, but you didn't hear it from me," Jack said while shifting in his seat.

"She has a lot to answer for. This game is getting more dangerous by the day. Every moment she's free is another body waiting to show up unannounced," Danielle said with her eyes burning with rage.

"Don't remind me. I'm already dreading the day we get called to the scene where Harper's body is going to be located. I'm going to miss the idiot. I'm just glad my family is safe," Jack sighed.

"Are you sure about that? I think you better make damn good and sure about that before you make that claim. You should use one of our safe houses. Better yet, find something out of the way nobody knows about, including me," she stated when she finally got a look at Anderson.

He was sitting up with bandages around his ribs. They must've had him on some very powerful painkillers. He was looking straight at her, but really didn't see her.

"You might be right. Nobody is safe, including my family, with that maniac still running around free. I'll make a few phone calls. There's no telling what she is capable of," Jack said while sending an encrypted text message to his family in Australia.

"Thank God. He's alive. He was wearing a vest," she revealed when she saw it lying next to him on the floor.

She couldn't bear the idea of losing anyone else.

"You have your answer. We can't stay here any longer," Jack said before backing up and turning around to go in the other direction.

Danielle sat there pensively, thinking about all the ways she was going to hurt Kellie.

She was afraid of what she would do when they came face-to-face.

She knew Jack was right. Creed was anything but subtle. They just had to keep digging until they unearthed the metaphorical smoking gun.

One last look in the rear-view mirror confirmed he was alive and kicking.

He was already becoming belligerent and pushing the paramedics away from him. They would insist on taking him to the hospital to evaluate his condition under medical observation.

The one thing she knew about him was his fear of hospitals.

"I want you to do me a favor," Danielle whispered.

"You don't have to say it. I do have a connection. I'll make sure he's taken off the case," Jack referred to Anderson, almost getting killed.

CHAPTER 31

Jack had his daily influx of caffeine ready in a Styrofoam cup. Toby Estate coffee, an Australian brand, had made its way to New York. Thank God Creed thought. The Yanks make shit coffee. Percolated liquid piss to me more descriptive.

There was no way he was going to miss the preliminary trial. It was becoming a media frenzy. The story kept people glued to their devices.

Forensics had combed through the warehouse, but everything had been burned to a crisp. It was done by a pro. Most likely a seasoned arsonist.

He saw the defendant conferring with his lawyer. Warren was dressed to impress. He had already pleaded guilty by reason of temporary insanity. It was exactly what he thought he was going to do.

"Whatever you do, stay calm. She just came in and she is not alone," Danielle whispered.

Ms. Fletcher came in with a young man hanging on her every word. He looked book smart, with a pocket protector and a calculator in his hand. It had to be a metaphorical marriage of convenience. He had something she wanted.

The courtroom filled up quickly until the doors were locked. Nobody was allowed in or out until the judge convened.

Jack didn't know the judge, but had heard rumors stating that he was a stickler for the law. He very rarely showed any kind of compassion. That was good news.

"I was wondering when she was going to slink out from whatever rock she was hiding under. It should surprise me to see her here but it doesn't. She doesn't get out of bed unless it benefits her in some way. This is going to be interesting." he stopped when the judge banged his gavel for silence.

"We are here today to determine the fitness for trial. Testimony will be heard from a variety of sources including psychiatric professionals. Let's start with the opening remarks," Judge Arnold Davenport motioned for the prosecution to state their case as eloquently as possible.

Prosecutor John Stevens stood with his blond hair coiffed. He was clean-shaven and sporting the intellectual look with dark glasses perched on the edge of his nose. He didn't look old enough to address the court.

John Stevens was the youngest lawyer to become District Attorney at 25. He loved his job with a conviction record supporting his superior's belief in him.

"There is no jury. We are simply here to determine whether or not the defendant is fit for trial. The prosecution has damning evidence. That's not in dispute. We believe Warren is as sane as any of you in this courtroom. It's up to the defence to prove otherwise. Your Honor, if it pleases the court, we will issue into evidence affidavits from the arresting officers on the scene. Sworn testimony from his own family including one very convincing letter from his daughter," John presented and produced the said documentation.

The defence attorney turned out to be another wolf in sheep's clothing. His name was Miles Shapiro. He had a long-standing arrangement with several high-profile clients. His retainer was quite significant something the defendant shouldn't be able to afford.

"This guy is good. He has a reputation for getting his clients off with mental disabilities. He will parade a number of psychiatrists renowned in their field. They have been paid extremely well for their testimony and expertise," Danielle stated.

Jack didn't answer quite content in listening to the testimony while watching Kellie Fletcher out of the corner of his eye. This had her fingerprints all over it.

"Your Honor, this case is not going to be settled with a guilty verdict. My client has been under a doctor's care for almost 6 months. He has had blackouts where he wakes up having no idea how he got there. When everything is said and done, my client will get the help he so desperately has been crying out for." Miles had a slight English accent.

He was wearing something understated with a vest that he was able to stick his hand into during his auditory exclamation.

"Is it my impression the defendant is not going to take the stand?"

"That is my client's prerogative." Shapiro placed his hand on his client's shoulder.

"That is highly unusual but we will continue with that in mind. Call your first witness to the stand," the judge urged with his hand lying on the bench.

Jack noticed the absence of a wedding ring. There was a white patch of skin where there should have been one. It meant the divorce was recent, and the wound was still fresh in his mind.

Jack listened to the psychiatric evaluation with very little interest. His job was done. He had brought the culprit to justice. It was now in the hands of a clown courtroom where they would determine how best to proceed.

He was more curious about Ms. Fletcher and how she was sitting in his corner whispering words of encouragement as the trial progressed.

"I would give anything to hear what she's saying to him," he sighed deeply while polishing off the last of his coffee which had turned lukewarm.

*****

Anderson was standing in front of Reeves with his hands behind his back. He was at attention completely taken aback by being called into the office the moment he entered at exactly 8 AM on a Monday morning.

The weekend had been spent in the emergency room before being released late Sunday afternoon with a strong prescription for painkillers. He hadn't even popped the seal.

"I don't know what the meaning of this is but I don't like it. I just got a call from the Chief of police. He informed me of your intention to be taken off of the case. That's a little surprising to me. We both know you are on the fast track in your career. This little setback could derail it by several months maybe even years," Reeves stated from behind the captain's desk where he had temporarily taken up residence.

"Permission to speak freely," Anderson proposed.

"This isn't the military. Say what is on your mind, Detective," Reeves said while sitting back with two of the legs suspended in mid-air.

"I don't know where this request came from but it wasn't from me. I'm more determined than ever to bring this case to a close. We're still compiling evidence. Rest assured no stone will be left unturned," Anderson answered with a scratch of his neck perturbed by somebody trying to meddle in his affairs.

The internal affairs man on the scene leaned back a little further until the chair hit the wall. "I'm glad to hear that. There's a lot of heat coming from upstairs on this one. You have until the end of the day to close the case. I hope that won't be a problem."

Anderson wanted to say something but wasn't looking to be some kind of Cowboy like Jack Creed. Admittedly, Jack was good at the job but sometimes, he glossed over certain details to make sure an arrest stuck.

"I'm going to deny the request at the risk of rubbing the chief of police the wrong way. He didn't tell me where the request came from but I can make an educated guess. You were almost killed," he referred to the bandage on his hand.

"A couple of cracked ribs and a cut that I could've gotten shaven isn't going to take me out of the game," Anderson said with a grimace when he felt the bandages around his waist tugging too fiercely.

"This case isn't going to make your career. Nobody can blame you for coming up short. Tomorrow is a new day. Put this case to bed and I might find you something worthy of your talents," Reeves stressed while clicking a pen incessantly with his initials emblazoned on the side.

There was no air-conditioning. The technician was scheduled to arrive in less than an hour to overhaul the entire infrastructure. Everybody was pretending with cool thoughts but the afternoon temperature had risen dramatically until it was almost stifling.

New York was in the middle of a very strange heat wave. Temperatures were estimated to rise above 100° and that wasn't including humidity. The nights were going to be restless for the next couple of days.

Anderson was already irritable completely side swiped by how brazen his colleagues could be. He had no doubt Jack and Danielle had pulled some strings. Their efforts had been thwarted.

He knew he was on thin ice. Danielle probably told Jack about his unofficial meeting with Ms. Fletcher. He was still trying to piece the night together. He didn't remember drinking much of the wine yet the bottle had been polished off when he woke up with this strange taste in his mouth.

He had never battled alcoholism. His main vice was a pretty face with long legs attached to it. Danielle was different. She was recently widowed and raising a kid on her own.

The woman was strong and reserved but there was passion waiting to be released.

CHAPTER 32

It had been long and agonizing with the final few moments becoming interminable. The judge had requested a 10-minute recess to go over everything.

Jack decided on impulse to rattle her chain with the direct approach.

"You're not going to get away with this. You might not see a jail cell tomorrow but there's enough circumstantial evidence to bury your accomplice in the meantime," he whispered.

Kellie turned to face him with a smile. "Detective, I haven't seen you since you arrested me for no good reason. Should we discuss the lawsuit? Kellie asked.

"You're not going to get a red cent. I'll make sure of that," Jack seethed with his words becoming clipped and icy.

"That's not what my lawyer tells me. You should be careful with your blood pressure. It's not good to get upset," she revealed how she knew about a medical condition.

"I'm warning you," he said with a finger stuck in her face.

"You're nothing but an inept ineffectual police officer past his prime. Don't you understand? I'm smarter and I'm always going to be one step ahead of you. I have to admit sicking your dog on me was interesting. His technique is far more preferable than your strong-arm tactics," she giggled with a hand over her mouth and her eyes lighting up like the Fourth of July.

"He's young and impetuous. Just the type to fall easily for your, shall we say, questionable morals? I'm not easily swayed. My job is to put criminals like you behind bars where you belong. I won't rest until that happens," Jack stammered between clenched teeth.

"Do you know most accidents occur in the home? It's an interesting statistic don't you think? I hear some microwaves can easily short-circuit," she referred to the appliance that almost electrocuted him.

"You're not the first one to think they are untouchable. Where are they now?"

Kellie frowned and shrugged her shoulders. "I'm sure you're going to tell me."

"They are cooling their heels in prison. Everybody makes mistakes. You're not going to be any different. Too many bodies are going to be your downfall. You might be better at cleaning up after yourself but I'm betting, you were careless when you first started your downward spiral into insanity," he said with a hand on her elbow to insinuate himself into her private space.

"This is bordering on harassment. I think we should go back to our seats and come out swinging another time. This conversation isn't over. Everybody knows one small thing can turn their lives upside down until they have nothing. Wait and see." She backed away from him while holding his gaze until she turned and sat back down.

Jack didn't get very far with the Inquisition. She did mention the microwave, but it was only in a hypothetical way.

The comment about accidents happening in the home couldn't have been clearer.

*****

Danielle had slipped out unannounced. The coroner had been waiting to go over his findings. She was still a little stunned and walking around dazed. The killer had purposely and maliciously tortured the man to the inch of his life.

Nobody had heard from Jack's friend. Maybe his body wasn't going to show up. It only meant Ms. Fletcher had gone way too far.

There could've been evidence left behind to point directly at her which wasn't going to bode well for her continued freedom.

The coroner had given his report cold and clinically without getting personally invested.

She listened to every word and was reminded of when her husband was slain in the line of duty. They had dug out the bullet and found it registered to a gun stolen by a rival gang against the Hell's Angels.

The morgue was a sore spot. She tried to avoid it during the scope of every investigation but this one needed a special and personal touch. Just stepping into the air-conditioned environment brought back a flood of bad memories including identifying the body on a slab in a drawer.

She remembered the ashen face with all the blood drained out of the body. Her husband deserved some respect for all of his years of service. To be poked and prodded to determine the cause of death was an insult to his memory.

She stood in the hallway unable to breathe. Her legs threatened to fall out from underneath her but she refused to give in to the panic trying to grip her by the throat.

It wasn't a good idea to show weakness, especially as a female. It would be just the ammunition the other officers would need to ridicule her mercilessly.

Being strong didn't mean having no emotions.

It meant keeping them hidden from the real world. She could always cry herself to sleep against her pillow at night where nobody could see her falling apart.

She wiped her hands on the knees of her dark pants while bent over at an angle trying to stop herself from hyperventilating.

A plain brown bag indicative of what a homeless man would use to hide his liquid bounty was suddenly in front of her face. She looked up to find Anderson leaning back against the wall.

"I thought I would find you here. Don't worry. Nobody is going to hear about this from me. It can't be easy coming here every time you are summoned. It's only been a few months. We don't have to talk about it. I'm here if you want a shoulder to lean on," he said while fiddling with the change in his pocket.

She snatched the bag from his hands and began breathing into it.

It wasn't long before she had weathered the storm. Grief could come over her at the most inopportune times. It was getting better but she could still feel the icy chill of his passing every time she closed her eyes at night.

She looked up still holding onto the bag. "You don't look like someone that has lost his best friend. I'm sorry. I lost my head when I saw the paramedics. Don't blame Jack."

"I just came back from a friendly conversation with Child welfare. Jack missed his appointment. I figured he would be preoccupied with what was happening in the courtroom. You were probably on your way over there. Don't waste a trip," he said hiding a brown office folder with Kellie Fletcher's name on it.

"You always did have a way with the ladies. Too soon," she said with an attempt at a snide smile.

"We'll talk about that later. Not that my love life is any of your business. Take a look at this. It was a juvenile record sealed by the court. I'm not supposed to have it and you're not supposed to be able to see it," he said with the file folder open to an incident involving Kellie Mitchell.

Danielle combed back a lock of dark hair hanging over her eyes. She began reading through the transcript. It was very disturbing and certainly did point to a pattern of erratic behavior.

Her eyes widened when she saw what she had done.

"This only proves she has a penchant for violence. We already knew that by finding out the hard way. She almost killed you. It wasn't her holding the gun, but she was the bullet in the chamber. She also tried to kill Jack and myself at a warehouse with a text message supposedly from you." Danielle moved down the page to the outburst in court.

She had threatened everybody including the judge. Death threats were serious business.

They didn't pay attention and maybe they should have. The arresting officer was killed three years later in a drive-by shooting. The prosecutor was dead of a heart attack.

"She's been a busy girl." Danielle scowled.

CHAPTER 33

The silence in the courtroom was deafening. The judge had returned with his verdict. The press had a ringside seat with several recognizable journalists taking up the first row. The recorders were set and ready for his proclamation.

"I've been a judge for almost 20 years. People have come and gone. Some of them, I don't remember and others will be forever imprinted on my mind. This case falls into the latter category. It bothers me these things happen all the time. You hear it in the news more often than not," the judge started with a shuffle of papers.

Jack watched Warren for any kind of reaction. He hadn't taken the stand on his own behalf. It had to be a tactic. The prosecution would have eaten him alive on cross-examination.

He wasn't exactly rational. He didn't even look like he was there in the courtroom, simply staring off into space without even saying a word.

"I have no doubt a serious crime has been committed. This evidence can't be denied. What is in front of this Court isn't the guilt or innocence. He already issued a statement of guilty by reason of insanity.

I've seen nothing to detract from that statement. Everything convinces me this man is in desperate need of some time with a qualified professional. How long that is remains to be seen and will be determined by those in charge of his care," he droned on for a few more seconds before declaring Warren unfit for trial by a jury of his peers.

Jack was not amused when he saw Ms. Fletcher talking to one of the professionals sent to evaluate his psychiatric condition. It was a set-up. He couldn't prove it but he could feel his gut telling him it wasn't over.

Warren was escorted from the courtroom in handcuffs to an awaiting white van outside. He was strapped in for his own safety with the psychiatrist sitting next to him speaking in a gentle tone.

"Don't you love it when the law gets it right? Mental illness isn't a joke. It's not like you had anything to prove he was completely sane. It's funny how transcripts can disappear into smoke on the cloud. The right program is all that it takes. So, I've heard," Ms. Fletcher needled Jack with parting words outside on the courtroom steps.

She whistled and clicked her heels down to an awaiting taxi without bothering to hear what Jack was going to say. She could see he was stunned into silence. There had to be a part of him that knew this was going to be the verdict and that somehow she was going to orchestrate his escape from captivity.

Warren would continue his mission with her whispering encouraging words into his ear. Money was the gateway to his freedom. Blackmail was better.

Dr. Anniston was riddled with fear.

His testimony was falsified. She had him over a barrel with incriminating evidence to ruin his career and to burst his little happy bubble.

Jack had no knowledge of how far she was willing to go but he suspected this was going to be the outcome. He just wanted to be there to look her in the eyes and make her understand his mission in life was going to be to take her down.

He slapped his forehead when he remembered his meeting with child welfare. He had plum forgotten about it. That wasn't going to make him any friends. Not that he had gotten into police work to make friends.

His phone vibrated. He reached for it having no idea of what he was going to see but certainly not prepared for the one-two punch.

*****

Anderson sat in the car drawing inspiration from the vape pen. It wasn't illegal. It certainly wasn't pharmaceutical-grade marijuana. It was a substitute for nicotine.

He never wanted to look at another cigarette again after witnessing what had happened to his grandfather.

The hole in his throat when he visited the hospital was the wake-up call he needed. His subsequent passing two months later broke him of the habit. It was not something he wanted to think about and declared himself no longer an addict.

"They say those are even more harmful than cigarettes," Danielle mentioned while continuing to peruse the document obtained from the welfare agency without going through the proper red tape.

"Don't lecture me. I'm down to one puff a day. What does that information tell you about Ms. Fletcher? Bear in mind I have a personal relationship with her that I can't seem to remember for the life of me." Anderson shook his head while watching a meter maid perform her duties with an irate customer shaking his fist.

He was amazed by how easily she was able to dodge any sort of violence by staying calm throughout the altercation. She would make a fine officer. That kind of calm under pressure wasn't easily taught in the academy.

"Have you considered you were drugged? I certainly wouldn't put it past her to put something in your drink when you weren't looking," Danielle proposed a theory.

He summarily dismissed it until he began thinking about it.

"It's something to consider. It's easy to disprove. I have the glass. I can make subtle inquiries with the lab. The first thing I need to do is bag the evidence. We should stop by my place. It's on the way to the station," Anderson suggested when he began honking the horn and really laying into it.

It wasn't considered road rage in New York City. Drivers could get under his skin. Construction workers toiling away without even bothering to pick up a tool made for some interesting rush hour driving.

It was almost noon with everybody piling out of their skyscrapers to find something to eat suitable for one hour of consumption. Some brought their lunches in bags and sat in the park getting in tune with mother nature.

Others packed the local restaurants. Some lucky few had reservations in air-conditioned high-class establishments catering to the elite with more money than brains.

"It's going to take forever to get to the station. Your place is nearby," he said while clearing his throat with his hand up to his mouth.

"How would you possibly know that?" Danielle said with a light-hearted jab to his shoulder.

"Don't tell me I'm the only one to research those he works with. Everybody has skeletons in their closet. Some are easy to find and others take some digging. Want to guess what I found out about Fletcher?" He hinted about having inside information.

"If this has anything to do with his misspent youth, I don't want to hear it. I'm not even sure it's a good idea for me to be looking at this," she said with a tap to the folder already having read every single paragraph three times.

"She is a piece of work. Stabbing the teacher five times must be some sort of record. Somebody with a lot of clout made most of the charges disappear," he related what was in the file by condensing it down to a few concise sentences.

"She spent three months in a juvenile corrections Centre before she disappeared. There is no record of her anywhere officially or unofficially. She came back after reinventing herself. This is the picture taken when she was arrested for the stabbing," she said before showing him the mugshots.

"She had a lot of work done. The teeth are not the same. Her eyes have been nipped and tucked. Her breasts were augmented twice the normal size. That takes a lot of money. Who was funding her transformation?" Anderson inquired.

"I don't believe it," Danielle said before pointing a finger

CHAPTER 34

Jack had pulled over when he received a call. It was from Danielle. He didn't get to it in time but instead listened to the voicemail with avid interest.

Mondays were the worst.

There was no other day where you felt more downtrodden and stepped on by the little guy. It was a long time before being able to unwind on the weekend.

"I'm here with Anderson. You should get down here. I'm sending you the address. I don't want to ruin the surprise. Trust me, you are going to want to see this for yourself instead of hearing it second hand," Danielle informed him.

He had to admit that his curiosity was piqued. It had to be important enough to get him to drop everything. It was nice to know they were on the same page.

Nobody else would have gone to the trouble of taking his place at the welfare office for children. He was reminded it wasn't her when he looked at the digital copy of the juvenile transcripts.

It didn't make him happy to learn Anderson was the one that was thinking clearly. He couldn't be trusted. The fact he had a sexual relationship with the defendant wasn't something anybody wanted to come to light in the press.

He raised his hands in the air to figure out how he was going to address this issue with Anderson. His love life wasn't his business. That changed when it affected an ongoing investigation into a seemingly cold-blooded serial killer.

"I hope this isn't a colossal waste of my time. I could be sitting and stewing in a bar with a bottle of cold beer. What am I saying? They don't serve anything remotely close to a real Australian ale." He thought about the cold beer in his fridge bought from a boutique market.

They specialized in bringing in imported liquor including his favorite brew. It was more expensive but worth every single penny. Those bottles would have to be used sparingly.

That wasn't going to be easy during a heat wave. Everybody was one argument away from killing one another.

His car stalled at a red light. He turned the key several times with the engine trying but unable to ignite the pistons under the hood. It was one of those days his mother warned him about growing up.

He could still hear her in the kitchen dispensing her wisdom. *"Every day is a blessing. There's always going to be that one day where nothing goes right. That's when you should have stayed in bed under the covers. Just make sure you are wearing clean underwear for when the paramedics arrive*," she chuckled while stirring frantically to make a cake worthy of his birthday party.

New York was a ticking time bomb.

There had already been several cars in fender benders. Several calls for domestic problems came with the heat wave making things extra tense in an apartment the size of a shoe box.

He wanted to be anywhere other than the streets of New York City during lunch. He had left the comfort of his apartment to watch the travesty of justice in the courtroom.

A veteran down on his luck began spraying his window. It was just one of the many idiosyncrasies the city had to offer. He was just trying to make a buck, but he was smudging the window even more than it was with his dirty water and sponge.

He rolled down his window to address the man with his tongue hanging out of his mouth. "I don't need my window cleaned. What I need is my car to start before a tow truck drives by and sees dollar signs in his eyes."

"I was a mechanic in the Army. Pop the hood. I'll take a look," he said suddenly alert and no longer looking like a zombie going through the motions.

Jack thought about it for a second before popping the hood. He didn't have anything to lose and everything to gain.

The man was tinkering for less than a minute before he craned his head around the hood. "Turn the key and give it some gas," he suggested with his fingers sticking out of threadbare leather gloves.

He wasn't expecting anything but was mildly amused when it turned over on the first shot. He fished out a $20 bill and gave it to him with his card.

"I might have a job for you. It won't pay much but more than enough to get you off the street. You could use the money to buy a ticket to anywhere other than here," he said thinking three steps ahead.

He almost laughed out loud when the man pulled out a cell phone and gave it to him to put in his digits. It just proved one important fact. Digital was the only way to go.

He drove away with a newfound respect for those that served in the military with distinction.

He came to a sudden stop when he saw a police officer conducting a sobriety test on none other than Miss Fletcher.

It was just too good to be true.

*****

Anderson and Danielle were inside a small Mexican restaurant with native music playing through the speakers. They had a ringside seat for Miss Fletcher's sobriety test.

She was definitely above the legal limit.

She swayed back and forth and could barely touch her nose while giggling uncontrollably. The officer was a flatfoot not remotely knowledgeable about the case.

"Can you believe it? This might be the leverage we need to get her to talk to us on the record. She apparently has two strikes against her for drinking and driving under the influence. That's a bit of an oxymoron," Anderson stated while he was looking at a digital printout of her misdemeanor crimes.

"Three strikes and they throw the book at you. She does have a very expensive lawyer. That's going to play an important factor in all of this. She is drunk. You know what that means," Danielle hinted with a knowing wink.

"They will have to impound the car. We might be able to get a good look inside. It's also possible we could use her inebriated condition against her. Getting her alone in a room isn't going to be easy. Reeves is still sniffing around," Anderson informed her.

"What about Jack? He's missing all the excitement. The man is positively going to flip when he finds out about this," Danielle stated while chewing on a taco with very spicy seasoning.

She dropped it on the plate and began to fan her mouth. She grabbed the glass of water chilled with ice cubes and drank half of it before coming up for air.

"I warned you but you wouldn't listen to me."

"Look what the cat dragged in." She pointed to a car across the street.

Anderson could see Jack smugly leaning back against his car with his arms crossed. He might as well have a bag of popcorn to enjoy the festivities.

185

"He shouldn't get too close. Most of these officers know his face. He was only transferred a few months ago. It's amazing what kind of impression he leaves behind. It doesn't help that he brought down a dirty cop on his first week," Anderson referred to the scandal.

"We should get him out of here before somebody notices. We can discreetly go down to the station and get in while she is being fingerprinted. She's in no shape to invoke her right to a lawyer until she sobers up in the drunk tank." She paid the bill with a generous gratuity of over 50% on top.

They used the crosswalk after it blinked it was safe to get to the other side.

Danielle whispered into Jack's ear. He turned and smiled.

It was the first good news he had heard in days.

CHAPTER 35

The tricky part was getting into the police station without being seen.

Jack knew most of the officers didn't give him the time of day. They respected him and the reputation of being hard-nosed but they still felt he was unnecessary.

That would work in his favor.

Anderson and Danielle were going to create a diversion. They never mentioned what it was going to be, and he never asked.

His credentials consisted of more than a badge. He also had a key card to access the department after hours. It would be recorded on some fancy device loaded to some sort of data stream.

Jack didn't know much about technology and really had no interest in learning. He still had a VCR blinking 12 o'clock. He woke up with an old-fashioned alarm rattling on the nightstand. It had to be rewound every time, but it was a sense of normalcy he couldn't live without.

It was getting late with the dregs of society pulling themselves out of whatever hole they were hiding in. A man down on his luck wearing his displeasure on his face came down the alley. He was missing one tooth. He stared at him for a moment before advancing to the garbage bin.

Jack was told to wait for the signal. Not knowing what it was going to be made it difficult to prepare. He did like Danielle more than he wanted to admit. She was a consummate professional with a long-standing career with the Department.

It was after dinner when a skeleton crew remained to oversee what was going to be a long night shift. New York never slept and there was always some kind of crime being committed with the express purpose of getting away with it.

He jumped when he heard a crash and then the subsequent blaring of an alarm. Raised voices called out to him from the dark of night. It wasn't the caped Crusader. No light in the sky announced the presence of a nocturnal visitor.

"What do you mean you didn't see me? I swear young kids are going to drive me crazy," Danielle fumed with an indignant attitude.

"Maybe you should get glasses. My mom has a prescription. I'll be happy to get her to call you with a recommendation. You backed in without even signalling," Anderson professed.

"I'm tired and it's been a long day. Don't test me, little man," Danielle answered.

"You are a maniac behind the wheel. You change lanes recklessly without any thought to your actions. This is just another infraction. Somebody should take the keys away from you," he proposed with a snicker.

"You are dangerously close to getting on my last nerve. Let's not push it any further. I'm not opposed to punching you in your face in front of everybody. Looks like we got ourselves an audience," she announced practically telling Jack to go inside.

Jack couldn't see them. He could almost imagine how they were standing up to one another. Neither one was going to back down. The other officers would stand back and wait to see if things escalated beyond the verbal sparring.

Jack pressed the key to the antiquated device in the back of the building. It remained red. He had to try it a second time and then a third before it finally recognized his newly appointed access card.

The green light made his heart start beating again.

The door clicked and opened a crack.

He placed his hand in between and pulled it open with one final glance at the man rummaging around in the trash. He never paid attention or even looked up from what he was doing. He was already quite enthralled by his find.

Jack stepped into the hallway with the door closing behind him. The sound was reminiscent of jail cell bars. He almost imagined what the suspects felt when they were finally trapped in a corner with no way out.

It made him smile to think of Ms. Fletcher feeling like a wild animal in desperate need of chewing her own arm off. The liquor would help to numb the senses.

Photographs adorning the wall made him sigh deeply for those that had lost their lives fighting for justice and the American way. 911 was a dark day indeed. It had claimed too many lives.

The faces were a photo album of old and young alike. Crime never made the distinction between someone starting their career and those that were close to retiring on a pension that wasn't worth much after a long distinguished career.

The bullpen was deserted. Those that stayed behind were close to the window to watch a juvenile playground argument between colleagues.

"I don't know where you got your license. Maybe it was one of those crackerjack boxes you mentioned. It's the only explanation," Anderson mocked with his voice carrying through the window to the snickered applause of those officers standing close enough to hear it.

He gingerly walked to the counter and quickly lifted the keys to the back room cells.

They had waited long enough for her to be processed. She would be sleeping the effects of the alcohol off before screaming for her lawyer in the morning.

Jack backed up with the key firmly grasped in between his fingers. One of them could easily turn and question the reason for his presence. It appeared they were more interested in the fight than in anything he was doing.

*****

They had them eating out of the palm of their hands. The fight was making her blood pump. It was reminiscent of fighting with her late husband. The excitement of really laying into each other made for some explosive moments under the sheets.

"Why don't you get in your clown car and leave?" She referred to his electric mini car.

"Pardon me for wanting to limit my carbon footprint. I'm still choking on your exhaust." He mimicked coughing into his hand.

"You're going to be coughing up teeth if you don't quit flapping your gums," She said with a press of her hand against his chiselled chest.

The move made those watching gasp in mild amusement.

"That's an interesting turn of phrase, grandma," he teased while pressing his chest against her hand even harder than it already was.

Anderson was not immune to the fire he saw in her eyes. It could've resulted in a moment of unrestrained pleasure. He had to be careful to keep things from overheating. He didn't want people staring and pointing. That was something he would never be able to live down.

"You need somebody to take you out behind the woodshed to teach you about manners. I might be older than you and should know better but you are really making it difficult to turn the other cheek," she said with those fingers against his chest squeezing until her nails were biting into his skin through his shirt.

"Here we go again. We know all about the way you got up at the crack of dawn to walk 6 miles to school," he exaggerated with a flurry of hand motions.

"This is the last thing I wanted to be doing tonight," she uttered.

"Let me guess. You have a big night ahead of you. A bag of popcorn and a cheesy romantic movie until you fall asleep in front of the TV," he teased.

"That's far better than picking up your next conquest at the supermarket testing the firmness of the zucchini. You are a grown man. Start acting like it," she argued by using his past dalliances against him.

They were just getting started and had the attention of a hypnotized audience of police officers. It was fun to lay into him and use his reputation to screw him figuratively.

CHAPTER 36

Jack moved to the back slowly to find nobody watching the inebriated prisoners. They had been subjected to a strip search. Some were dejected and hanging their heads in despair, wondering how they were going to make that one phone call to their significant others.

The women were surprisingly chipper, wearing scandalous outfits ranging from black leather miniskirts and crimson red halter tops to hot pants and a top that looked more like a bra.

A few whistles had them coming closer to the bars, with a storm of different perfumes assaulting him. He waved them off as they tried to reach him through the bars with their manicured nails.

"Come a little closer. You could benefit from my teachings. The only thing it will cost you is a free pass out of here. Shop around. You can't get a better deal than that," Charlene stated with her pouting flaming pink lips, beckoning him to come closer.

Her caramel skin was smooth to the touch, and she had read reviews from clients in the New York ZIP Code. She was high-priced, with a reputation for being discreet. It was the first time she had been hauled in during a routine raid at one of her favorite clubs.

Jack gave her the once over appreciatively and then blew her a kiss, which she grabbed from mid-air and placed against her over-inflated chest.

"Come back. You haven't lived until you have spent one hour with me. I will ruin you for other women. They will never compare and you'll come crawling back to me begging for more," she expressed with conviction, knowing full well her talents had become a sought-after commodity by many individuals, including those in the Department.

Jack had no doubt her skills would leave him penniless and divorced.

He finally stood in judgment over Miss Fletcher. A couple of hours had barely sobered her up. She wasn't alone. A lump on the cot near the wall caught his attention. The person snoring was completely out of it.

Ms. Fletcher was lying back on the bench with her hand covering her face.

"I'm sure it's not what it looks like. Why don't you tell me what happened?" He asked while leaning into the bars with both hands holding onto them.

She looked up with her eyes bloodshot, unable to comprehend the tall drink of water addressing her. He wasn't much more than a blur, but there was something familiar about the insipid smile plastered on his face.

"I had a few drinks. Maybe more than a few. You should open these doors and we can celebrate together back at my place. I'm sure I have a bottle somewhere," she said while trying to stand before sitting back down with the room spinning in a clockwise motion.

"You're famous around here. The others think you are going to slip up. I don't think so. You're too smart and well-connected for that to happen. It's too bad your lawyer isn't here to spring you," Jack said in an attempt to lead her into making a confession that wasn't going to stand up in court.

"I've never had a problem making people jump when I told them to," Kellie said, with her tongue sliding across the roof of her mouth.

"What you need right now is the hair of the dog. Don't tell anybody. I keep this little secret at the bottom of my desk for rainy nights. Take it. You need it more than I do," he said with an old-fashioned silver flask produced from inside his black windbreaker.

She smiled sweetly with her fingers stretching toward the bars without being able to reach them. "You're going to have to come closer. I don't bite. I might nibble a little bit. Ask any of my husbands. That's right, you can't," she laughed.

"I'm not sure I want to do that." Jack kneeled and slid the flask through the bars until it was perfectly positioned against her feet.

"You are a gentleman and a scholar," she said with the flask up to her lips before she took a good slug.

Jack knew with a little more prodding she might reveal something incriminating. A set of footsteps approaching delayed the inevitable. He had to move within the shadows a few feet away from the bars.

He could only hope Miss Fletcher had the good sense to hide the flask.

*****

"You have some nerve speaking to me like that. Be careful what you say next. It might be the difference between a bruise or a night in the emergency room," Danielle said with her teeth showing.

"I'm so scared. Can't you see I'm shaking?" Anderson replied with his hand completely steady.

"I would advise getting that hand out of my face before you lose it," Danielle said.

"That's enough. There is nothing to see here. Get back to your desks," Sergeant Ansell said with his hands on his hips.

There was a chorus of disapproval, which was met with a glaring report of authority in response. They grumbled and started to move up the stairs.

They had to give Jack more time to grill the suspect. The sergeant had intervened at the most inopportune time. His words held some weight with the other officers.

"This is none of your business, old man," Danielle insulted his tenure in one breath.

"I don't usually agree with her, but this time, I have to. Take your self-righteous attitude and over-inflated ego back behind your desk where it belongs," Anderson piled on.

"The both of you are old enough to know better. This bickering is only going to cause a public outcry. We've already had reports about this incident. It's surprising a journalist hasn't jumped at the opportunity to record your outbursts for posterity on the evening news." Sergeant Ansell stated.

He placed a hand on both of their shoulders where there was a bundle of nerves. He escorted them up the stairs and back into the bullpen. They were no longer on the street, creating a mockery of the department.

"I'm not done by a long shot. This kid is barely old enough to register a firearm. I have shoes older than him. What gives him the right to think he's better than me?" Danielle continued, undeterred by the interruption.

"I should have known you would run to daddy for help," he mimed with his voice a character from a cartoon.

They stared at each other for quite some time before she lost her composure. She turned her back, and it looked like she was going to leave, but then she turned and lunged at him.

CHAPTER 37

The officer standing at the bars drinking a cup of lukewarm coffee heard the commotion. He almost spotted the flask in her hand before he almost spilled the coffee on his pristine blue uniform.

"They had to bring their argument into the bullpen. It was going to be a quiet night away from my bickering family. They are acting like children. If they are going to act like children, then I'm going to treat them like children," he said before taking off his belt in a universal sign of corporal punishment.

He accidentally dumped the coffee into his shoes. He cursed in Italian and went into an unrestrained litany of words that would've made a grown sailor blush.

Anthony came from a proud Italian heritage.

Jack was envious when he talked about extended family dinners on Sunday evenings. He could barely get his family to sit down long enough to enjoy a meal. Everybody had things to do and not enough time in the day to do them.

He stepped out of the darkness and back into the dim light. "That was a close one. I think we should finish what we started. You obviously have something to say. I'm not going to tell anybody," Jack insisted.

Kellie drank the rest of the flask before setting it back down beside her. She wiped her mouth with the back of her hand. "That hit the spot. You have good taste in liquor. I would estimate that was 9% proof. Tell me that I'm close."

Jack extended his thumb and forefinger an inch away from one another. "Exactly 12%, but who's counting? It will tear the tar paper off a house," he jested.

"My first husband tried his hand at making moonshine in the bathtub. He was a curious sort. Money was no issue for him and his family. I was always considered the black sheep when I married into a family of vipers," she regaled while stretching her eyelids with her hands.

"That's as good a reason as any to kill him," Jack pressed for more details, but didn't want to be too obvious.

"I'll never tell. My lips are sealed," she said with a finger pressed to her mouth.

"Nobody is here. You don't have to be so damn secretive all the time. It has to be pretty damn lonely being the smartest person in the room," Jack sympathized, but it was merely an act.

"I suppose it wouldn't hurt. It's not like anybody can prove anything. Let's say hypothetically he couldn't stop snoring. That hypothetically, I devised a plot to make it look like an accident. He was practically asking for it," Ms. Fletcher revealed, without showing all of her cards.

It was juicy but nothing more than conjecture. Getting her to talk made him smile. She had always been one step ahead. Her inhibitions had lowered significantly.

She wanted somebody to know how absolutely delicious her plan could be. He only had to wait for her to fill in the blanks. Silence was golden. That awkward moment had her itching to spill the beans.

Jack had waited for a very long time to have something to hang over her head. Listening had become a lost art. His patience was about to be rewarded.

*****

Danielle had him by the throat, splayed out on a desk with papers flying everywhere. A chant had begun. A mob mentality was looking for blood. They all had silent bets on which one was going to get the better of the other.

"Is this the best you can do?" Anderson squeaked.

"It's about time somebody shut you up. Don't you think everybody is wondering why you insist on living a lie? Your family has more money than the gross national product of some foreign countries. Why are you slumming it with us when you could be living in the lap of luxury?" Danielle asked while at the same time addressing the elephant in the room.

The same question was on everybody's lips, but nobody was brave enough to ask him to his face. They left tiny gifts in his locker, but it was all locker room antics with a real underlying animosity for everything he stood for.

Anderson applied pressure to her wrists and finally released her fingers from around his throat. It wasn't very ladylike for her to go off the handle like that. The act had turned into something more than they bargained for.

They had brought up some painful topics of conversation during the heated argument.

He shoved her back before adjusting his tie, which was askew. "Sue me for enjoying the finer things in life. I passed all the requirements with flying colors. Is that what you are sore about? I seem to recall breaking one of your records when it came to the accuracy of shooting."

"You can't be good at everything. Surfing, shooting, police work... it's all so easy for you. Why should any of us believe for one moment you're taking any of this seriously?" She asked again the same question in a different way, still with an audience begging for an answer.

"My father always thought that I was going to follow in his footsteps. He respected how I wanted to do things on my own. He showed his support, but I knew he was always disappointed. A man has to make his own way." he swallowed with his left eye twitching.

"That's true for most people. I can't speak for anybody else, but if I had that kind of money, I don't think that I would be risking my life on the streets. I'm sure that I could find something less likely to murder me on the job," she replied tersely while looking at her fellow officers to see them nodding in agreement.

"I've always been interested in police work. Surfing was a passion until I no longer could do it. That's when I decided to live my dream. I'm just like the rest of you. I still put my pants on one leg at a time," he said with his dark humor eliciting some smirks.

"I guess I can understand. We haven't really given you a chance to explain. We still have to talk about my car. The bumper is dragging on the ground. You can afford to compensate me. Money is nothing more than paper currency to you," she said in a calming voice when she spotted Jack sneaking out the same way he came in.

The time had come to wrap up this little production. They no longer had to keep the other officers from discovering Jack questioning a suspect without her lawyer present. Nothing was going to hold up in court, but they needed a clue.

The unorthodox method would hopefully reap the rewards.

"You make a valid point. I have a guy. I'll give him a call and schedule an appointment to look at your car. Let's call it a draw. We were both wrong." Anderson smiled and fished out a card for a local body shop his family used.

Those watching walked away unsatisfied. There was no bloodshed. It was like watching a boxer dance around in the ring without making contact with his opponent. They had all of this pent-up aggression that went nowhere.

"I hope I didn't go too far," Danielle whispered.

"Nonsense. I'm a big boy. It's going to take a lot more than insults to get under my skin. You have to remember on the circuit, there was a fair amount of psychological warfare going on. We could get pretty catty with each other to get the upper hand in the hopes the other guy would make a mistake," he explained how he was able to remain calm under pressure.

CHAPTER 38

Jack sat in his car, drumming his fingers on his way back to his apartment. Driving on the wrong side of the road was becoming more familiar. He couldn't believe his good luck. He had to admit the very notion of tripping her up seemed like a pipe dream.

He recalled the rest of the conversation verbatim. Being stuck in traffic made him go over every detail. It was somewhat disconcerting to hear her admit to any kind of wrongdoing when she had remained impassioned about her innocence, even though she was mocking him.

"What did you do?" Jack asked in that moment in front of the cell where she was temporarily trapped like an animal.

"Wouldn't you like to know? Those stupid police officers thought that I was going to fall apart under the hot lights. It was fun making them chase their own tails. You would be surprised what crocodile tears will do to a strong and strapping young man," she sobbed, with real tears streaming down her face.

"You're pretty damn smug. I will give you that. What did they miss? It was ruled an accident. Nobody suspected foul play. I'm sure some had their suspicions, but nothing could be proven. There was no evidence to suggest you had anything to do with his untimely demise," Jack continued to push the issue.

She was ego eccentric and capable of some amazing feats, but she was also human, in desperate need of validation from her peers. Under the influence made her susceptible to his questions.

"I wasn't even on the boat when the accident happened. They couldn't tie me to anything incriminating, no matter how hard they tried." She tossed the flask through the bars without even touching them.

Jack caught it and stuffed it into the back of his jeans, away from prying eyes.

"They were just doing their job," Jack defended the officers without even knowing all the details.

"Keep telling yourself that. They wanted me to be guilty. It would've made them happy to see me fall from my lofty pedestal from where I was looking down on them. They didn't even let me talk to a lawyer for 24 hours. It was inhumane and against my Miranda rights. Some of them lost their jobs. It couldn't happen to nicer guys," she said.

"I can't condone what they did during the investigation. It must've made them mad. You're not exactly the easiest person to talk to," Jack pointed out.

She sighed and stretched her arms over her head. "I've never been good with authority. Not everybody is guilty by association. Sometimes being in the wrong place at the wrong time can destroy lives. I'm not innocent. We can both agree on that."

"You're not going to get any argument from me. I know what you did. Nobody can prove it. Detective Creed is a good man. He didn't deserve your smear campaign against him. It was pretty crafty to make him look flawed," he spat it out with the venom of the words sickening him.

"Detective Creed is a rare breed of animal. I knew if I played my cards right, he would walk right into my trap. The man is predictable. It's actually a little sad when you think about it. His entire career hinges on an investigation that has already been decided. It's the waiting that's going to kill him softly," Kellie mentioned when she suddenly slapped her hand over her mouth.

"What did he ever do to you? He hasn't even been in New York that long. It feels personal, but I can't see how that can be when you hardly know each other. What am I missing?" Jack questioned.

He looked down the hallway to make sure the officer in charge wasn't going to destroy all the legwork he had done to get her to open up to him.

"I'll never tell. He might not know me, but I know him better than he knows himself. Everything fell into place when I arranged for his transfer to the states. Nothing was by chance," she admitted with her eyes closed and her head lying against the brick wall behind her.

"What does that mean? Come on. Don't pass out on me now," he said with his fingers turning white around the metal bars, anxious to hear the rest of the story.

No further discussion meant that he had run the gambit. A few more pieces had fallen into place during the exchange. He had run afoul of her at some point in his career.

The connection would be found in Australia.

The honking horns made him look into his mirror after being drawn back into the present. He had some friends in Australia that could do him a solid. He was getting used to the American slang, but he was still flummoxed by some of the things the officers said behind his back.

He never thought for a moment Australia was where he was going to find the smoking gun against Ms. Fletcher. It all seemed as if the answers were in her past and not his.

The mistake of underestimating her was his cross to bear and one that he would carry alone. If this truly had Australia to blame for all of this, then he couldn't ask Danielle and Anderson to go any further.

*****

Danielle sat pensively behind her desk, looking at the phone display. Every attempt to reach him had been met with the drone of his voicemail. Something had to have happened for him to go completely off the grid without any forwarding address.

"The party you are trying to reach is out of the area."

She wanted to throw the phone across the room. Her anger could sometimes get the best of her. It came with her Latin bloodline. She had always been a little hot-tempered. It was one of the things her late husband loved about her.

Their first meeting was with him in the emergency room after taking some liberties in a bar. She felt bad about cracking his tooth. The knee to the crotch would have sufficed, but once again, she had her Latin temper to blame for her outburst.

Her husband had shown compassion with no charges laid for assault. That kind of thing could destroy her life. He agreed to let bygones be bygones on one condition. She had to have dinner with him some place nice with linen napkins and tablecloths.

She smiled at the memory of sitting down uncomfortably in a posh environment. The night started silently with her sitting there amicably without a word.

He never said anything about being a conversationalist.

He had said something to make her smile and before she knew it, they were getting along famously. He had spoken of his job with a passion that was lacking in hers.

He was the one to help her navigate getting into the Academy. He drilled her with questions day and night into the wee hours of the morning. Nothing sexual happened between them for several months while she prepared to break the glass ceiling for other young women looking at her as a role model.

It was only when she graduated from the academy that things turned physical. The celebration took on a life of its own, with several bottles of champagne flowing.

They stumbled into her apartment, where they suddenly became overcome with a passionate release of endorphins. The man had somehow restrained himself for several months while she contemplated a career change to make her parents cringe.

The length of time between their first physical interaction and the birth of their child was inconsequential. She thought he would balk at the idea of having a child. That wasn't the response she got when she sat him down and delivered the news as calmly as possible.

His silence spoke volumes in her opinion. He surprised her by suddenly smiling and lifting her into his arms.

She wanted lightning to strike twice after he was laid to rest 6 feet under. Anderson could be an interesting diversion, but it wasn't going to be a long-term solution.

Distraction was the mother of all inventions. She needed some kind of outlet to burn off that access energy. Her child could be vexing. Acting out was normal after losing a parent, but it didn't make it any easier.

It didn't help that her partner had suddenly gone radio silent. She wasn't going to let that stand without a good explanation.

Tracking him down would prove to be quite difficult when he didn't want to be found.

CHAPTER 39

Jack decided not to answer his phone. Disconnecting it and leaving the apartment seemed like the prudent thing to do. He had a lot to think about with his years of service in Australia playing out in his mind over and over again.

The man at the counter was perfectly content taking his money. His long frizzy while hair was a throwback to his days singing on stage for his supper.

The storage unit housed boxes from the move. Some of the furniture from the house in Australia was being kept under lock and key until they agreed on a place to live.

That decision wasn't going to be made by him unilaterally without first consulting his wife.

He never thought for a moment he would live in abject squalor inside the storage unit.

Nobody knew he had it, and he wanted to keep it that way. Some of those boxes had copies of cases from his stellar career.

He sat in the middle of the storage unit, surrounded by an array of files. The hodgepodge of evidence never amounted to too much. Cases left unsolved were in the thousands. He was lucky to have only a select few dogging his every waking hour.

An unanswered phone call from Reeves could be the final nail in his career coffin.

There were five messages from Danielle, with each one increasingly getting angrier. Talking to her would only convince him to come out of the cold.

Unsolved cases were always going to be something any police officer would never be able to forget about. Friends had travelled down similar paths with varying degrees of success.

The mistake had been his from the moment he tangled with Miss Fletcher. She had purposely orchestrated everything to make him look bad. Cultivating the right resources, including having something hanging over Reeves, made him compliant with her wishes.

He had spent most of the morning going over the files before separating them into categories. The ones with a pink label were barely much more than a misdemeanor swept under the rug by red tape bureaucracy.

The ones with a blue tag were more serious. Breaking and entering and arson was supposedly a victimless crime unless the unexpected happened.

Those with white tags were murderers hiding in plain sight.

He didn't limit himself to unsolved cases.

It might easily be something connected to someone he put away. There was no shortage of those claiming to be innocent of the charges levied against them.

It would've been nice to have another set of eyes peering over his shoulder. It was shameful to think his past was coming back to destroy his career.

He had no doubt Danielle would continue to pursue every angle without his help. His disappearance would only put a fire under her. It was possible even Anderson would feel the slight when he couldn't bring himself to answer his phone calls.

That would make them dig even deeper.

He had to admit it was nice to know somebody had his back when the rest of New York was looking for his blood. His head remained on the chopping block, waiting for the final proclamation from the investigation against him.

The day had gotten past him until it was almost supper time. He would need to refuel some place out of the way where nobody was going to recognize them. He had spied a quaint diner dedicated to those traveling out of state.

It would be nothing fancy. Comfort food would definitely hit the spot. He thought about an old-fashioned meatloaf with all the trimmings His stomach rumbled in anticipation of the first bite.

*****

Two weeks wasn't a lot of time, but it felt like an eternity. She had exhausted every measure to find him. His voicemail was full, indicating he had no interest in talking to anybody after his meeting with Ms. Fletcher.

He had to know giving up was not in her vocabulary.

A development had happened during his absence.

Warren had been released after getting a clean bill of health from psychiatric services. They had stamped him sane with no further judicial action against him. He had killed with impunity and had received the equivalent of a slap on the wrist.

He hadn't been responsible for his actions and was now reunited with his family. Bullying and mental health are very topical.

A book deal had been offered by a big-name publishing company. He had scheduled several interviews with his five minutes of fame stretching out longer than most people.

The man was never going to be a choir boy. She had made preparations for somebody to be watching him around the clock. Paying somebody to do that was out of Anderson's pocket, which he was happy to provide when he learned of his release from the psychiatric institution.

"It's not your fault. He had good representation. That is sometimes the difference between justice and injustice. We did everything by the book. It's too bad his disturbing blog was deleted. The jury of his peers gave him the benefit of the doubt without knowing every single detail," Anderson spoke while leaning on her desk.

"Where the hell is he?" she asked with her nostrils flaring and her upper lip quivering.

"I have some people working to find out. They are very good at their jobs. We have to remain under the radar," Anderson related.

She threw up her hands in frustration. "Not everything can be solved with money. Ironically, your idea to source this out was surprisingly astute. He can't hide forever. Somebody is going to recognize him from the news broadcasts."

"You're referring to how his disciplinary hearing was leaked to the press. They are painting him as the bad guy. They want reforms and they have to start with him being drummed off the force. They just can't find him to make him the scapegoat," he said.

Danielle shuffled some papers before she lost her composure.

She screamed and threw those papers into the air before storming out of the building. Nobody dared follow her except for Anderson, hot on her heels.

"I need some air to think. Maybe what I need is a change of scenery. What about your place?" She suggested with that anger about to be used in a more constructive way than punching the heavy bag.

"That sounds great, but it's not the answer. We need to continue to dig on his behalf. I had to close the case, but it

215

doesn't mean we can't work together after hours. Leaves of absence happen all the time. I've recently been reminded that I don't need the money," he joked in a half-hearted attempt at making her smile.

"We come back to what we've been fighting about all this time. My mother is looking after the little one for the night. We don't have to deny ourselves," she hinted with very little subtlety about what she wanted.

"What are you trying to say?" Anderson stared at her with questioning eyes.

"What does a girl have to do to get laid around here? Does that make it any clearer? Perhaps I need to hit you over the head with a club and drag you back to my cave," she said sexually frustrated.

"I still don't think it's a good idea. We need to remain steadfast in our belief in his innocence. The distraction of sleeping with you would be pleasant. It would also play heavily into Miss Fletcher's hand." He moved an arm's length away from her.

"Don't remind me. Her lawyer is screaming for blood. They have video footage of Jack talking to her without proper representation. They don't know for certain it's him. They haven't been able to verify his identity." She got in her car and motioned for him to join her without proffering an audible invitation.

He leaned on the window. "Get some sleep. We'll tackle this again in the morning. I know I'm going to regret this, but I can't take advantage of you. It just wouldn't be right," he sighed deeply while tapping the hood of her car with his hand.

"You would remember a night with me. I hope that keeps you up at night thinking about the opportunity you let slip through your fingers." She started the engine and revved the motor.

"Did you really have to say that? I'm going home to take a cold shower. You might want to consider doing the same thing. Take some time. You have a daughter to think of," he stated while strolling back to his limited-edition electric car in Kermit green.

Danielle knew that Anderson liked to stand out from the crowd. He dressed with the mindset of a fashion model walking down the runway. His car made for some interesting jokes behind his back but he let it wash off of him.

Danielle wished she could do the same thing.

CHAPTER 40

Kellie Fletcher couldn't believe how stupid she was about to drink herself into a stupor. The three-strike rule didn't apply to her after her lawyer made some compelling points.

Julie Williams was worth every penny of a very sizable retainer to keep her on speed dial.

She could hardly remember the conversation, with only pieces coming back to her in disjointed fragments of conversation. The headache the morning after hit her like a sledgehammer.

It was enough to make her angry. That anger manifested into blaming Reeves. Shit ran downhill. He, in turn, made those around him miserable by pointing out discrepancies in protocol to make him feel better.

The pool was a crystal blue persuasion.

She dangled her bare toes in the water. The oversized mirror sunglasses gave her plausible deniability. The young boy cleaning the pool made her hunger to teach him the finer points of the female anatomy.

He could learn a lot by listening to her wise words of encouragement. It was too bad she didn't have the time to dedicate to making the boy into a man.

"This means you are going to have to spend some quality time with your family. Take them out to a public dinner. Make them see you are a changed man," she said, with her toes skimming the water.

"Don't get me wrong, I'm grateful for everything you have done for me and my family. Those guys deserved everything they got and more. I told the doctors exactly what you said to the letter. It was a slow progression, but the results spoke for themselves," Warren stated with the sun bronzing his almost naked body on the white chaise lounge next to his co-conspirator.

"We are not finished. Do you still have the list?" She asked with him responding by tapping his temple with the tip of his finger.

"I made sure there were no copies, but I don't need a reminder. Those names are permanently tattooed on my mind. They think they got away with it. I would love to be a fly on the wall when they learn of my release." He smiled while enjoying his newfound freedom in a luxury he had become quite accustomed to.

"I did that for you. It was necessary. Having you behind bars made things a little more difficult for me. We need to be extra careful. Go about your life as if nothing happened. Make everybody believe you were sick and needed somebody to throw you a lifeline," she said while staring at the Adonis with very little experience under his considerable belt.

"What are we going to do to make them pay? I don't want to get caught again. We can't just walk up to them and shoot them. We need to be smart about this," Warren suggested while sipping from a very strong pina colada.

The condensation was dripping down the sides of the glass with the sun blazing from above.

"We finally agree on something. I blame myself for your incarceration. I've already started by going after them where they are going to hurt the most. They have already suffered some setbacks in their investment portfolio." Miss Fletcher sat up to get a better look at the chiselled Greek God skimming the pool.

"It sounds like you have a plan to deal with them. Does that include Detective Creed? Maybe you might want to add Danielle Rodriguez and Detective Anderson to the list," Warren fidgeted until he was reading a crime novel already bookmarked to where he left off.

"I'm way ahead of you. They have been a thorn in my side for too long. It's about time they learn what happens when they stick their noses where they don't belong. The law can be a fickle mistress," she said with her sunglasses lowering until they were on the bridge of her nose.

*****

The pounding on the door woke her from a dead sleep. She thought it was a dream until she heard muted voices. She swung her legs onto the floor before reaching for the black robe on the back of the door.

"Keep your pants on. I'm coming," she said with a glance at the empty spot next to her.

It didn't feel good to be rejected even if it was the right thing to do. She had convinced her mother to babysit. It meant she had the night free from the constant barrage of alternative music coming from the bedroom down the hall.

"Open up. This is the police. We have a warrant to search the premises," the voice commanded while she was still trying to shake the cobwebs.

"What is the meaning of this?" She asked when she flung open the door to see Jack holding a paper bag.

"Get dressed. I brought you something for breakfast. You're going to need all the strength you can get." He barged in and took a seat with his hand shaking on the bag.

"You pound on my door at 6 AM and walk in like you own the place. This partnership is going to drive me to drink. I'm very angry with you," she stammered while reaching for the coffee pot until being rewarded with the sound of the percolation of caffeine.

"We don't have time for this. Put something on a little more comfortable." He opened the bag and placed two blueberry muffins on the counter before peeling one out of its shell.

She walked briskly to her bedroom and relieved herself of the robe until it landed at her feet.

Seeing him after almost 2 weeks made her want to give him a piece of her mind.

She slipped into a pair of black slacks and a yellow sweater to accent the positives. She ran her hands through her hair before touching up her makeup.

Her natural beauty shone through without any additives.

"You have some nerve showing up like this unannounced after leaving me to wonder if you were dead in a gutter somewhere. I've been looking all over for you," she called out with her head in the closet before pulling out a sensible pair of shoes.

"I know and I don't appreciate having to have eyes in the back of my head. This beard is itchy. I'm surprised you recognized me," he answered in a muffle with a fair chunk of the blueberry muffin in his mouth.

She stopped to admire her reflection.

Danielle clipped her badge to her waist on her way down the hallway. She stopped when she noticed something different about her daughter's bedroom.

She could have sworn the door was closed when she came home last night.

She lifted her gun and felt how heavy it was while clasped in both hands. The safety was off when she lightly kicked the door open. Nothing seemed to be out of place but then she noticed the window slightly ajar with the white curtains shifting in the breeze coming through.

"We have a lot to talk about and not a lot of time. I got a heads up and came here to get you. Reeves is on his way here. I think we can both agree it's never a good thing when he shows up at the crack of dawn. You shouldn't be here when he arrives," Jack said.

She heard him but wasn't paying much attention. The bed had moved with one corner hanging. She held her breath and lifted the mattress with both hands. What she found puzzled and confused her.

She could hear Jack creeping closer down the hall until he was turning the corner into a bedroom with brocades of pink everywhere.

Danielle leaned over the bed and then turned with a bag of cocaine lying in her hand.

CHAPTER 41

Jack had heard enough to know through a reliable source to act quickly without first thinking things through. He suspected Reeves was going to turn his attention toward Danielle.

He could only stand and stare at the bag of pure cocaine.

"Somebody planted this in my daughter's bedroom. I probably would have missed it but they made the mistake of not putting back everything they had disturbed. My attention to detail is uncanny. My daughter can attest to that. She can't get away with anything. It helps to have a network of parents to keep an eye on her when I can't," she droned one with the bag lying heavily in her hand.

"Flush it. Do it now. There's not much time," he commanded when he suddenly noticed three plain sedans driving up to the curb.

Danielle ran past him to the bathroom.

She opened the lid and used the pin from her badge to open the bag. She dumped the contents and flushed repeatedly until the bag followed suit.

The pounding on the door was a little louder than was necessary. "This is Reeves. Open the door. Don't make me knock it down."

Jack had watched her but now needed to find some place to hide in a hurry. They would search but most likely would concentrate on the bedroom where the anonymous tip had pointed them in the right direction.

"There is no reason for that. I've been up for hours. I'll be there in one second. This better be damn important to wake me up in the middle of the night," she said while brushing past him and pointing to the kitchen.

Jack opened up the cabinet underneath the sink before making room for himself beside all the cleaners. It smelled like ammonia.

He heard her footsteps and then the door opening to address Reeves most likely standing there with a contingent of police officers ready to serve a warrant to search the premises.

"I don't like this any more than you do. This is a warrant to search the property. Stand back and let us do our job. You can stay but only if you don't interfere. Say anything I don't like and you will be escorted to one of the cars outside. How would that look to child welfare?" Reeves stated.

"What is this about? I think I deserve an answer," Danielle stammered with her hand on her badge.

Jack could see everything through a crack in the cupboard hinges.

"Nobody is above the law. You can always call a union rep. I would suggest you get in touch with them immediately. Don't say a word. I did you the courtesy of coming with unmarked vehicles. That's more than anybody would have gotten under similar circumstances," Reeves announced.

"Be still my heart. You're my hero. Why don't you come in and make yourself comfortable? It's not like this is an invasion of my privacy," she mocked with her hands over her chest while staring daggers.

"Keep her here and out of my way. The rest of you follow me. Turn this place upside down starting with the bedrooms. I'll take the little girl's room," he smiled behind her back.

Jack understood what was happening. This was the next plot twist in a story that started with bullying and had ended with three lives becoming nothing more than a footnote in history.

It evolved to several more bodies including his friend within the Hell's Angels.

He was dead yet no body had been found.

He saw the uniform of a police officer standing right in front of the cupboards. The smell of caffeine was rather strong.

*****

She watched Reeves pretend to do his job. He didn't look under the mattress. He was purposely avoiding the one place he probably knew the drugs would be found.

226

She was standing in the right position to see him fumbling around in her daughter's dresser. She also saw the officers in her bedroom dumping the contents of her pleasure chest onto the bed.

The embarrassment of having her belongings on display gave her Latino temper a run for its money. It wasn't anything that wouldn't be found in anybody's tickle chest. An assortment of interesting implements had been found.

It did make for an interesting conversation starter.

A cat of nine tails plus furry handcuffs didn't make her blush. She enjoyed the pleasures of the flesh. Her husband had introduced her to some of the more interesting aspects.

She hadn't invited anybody to look under her bed. Those toys were sacred. She would only share them with somebody worthy of her affections.

"I'm sure your wives have a few secrets of their own. You might want to talk to them before you throw rocks at glasshouses. It's perfectly natural. I'm not going to stand here and try to justify anything to the two of you," Danielle said while fostering thoughts of revenge.

"Drop everything you are doing in there and help me with this," Reeves ordered with the two officers unable to look into Danielle's eyes.

"Lift when I tell you to and not before. On the count of three. One... Two... Three." They lifted the mattress to find nothing underneath.

There wasn't even any residue when he ran his hand under the bed with a white glove.

He took out a knife and began stabbing into the mattress repeatedly without mercy. He destroyed the bed with stuffing floating around the room.

"The department is going to get a bill for that. I think you should leave before you make any more of a fool of yourself. I don't blame them. They are just following orders. It's you I take exception with," she said with a finger poking his chest to illustrate how he was going to rue the day.

"That's it. You are assaulting an officer. I can have you arrested and charged," Reeves blustered.

"That's not assault. This is assault," she slapped him hard across the face with her fingernails making direct contact with his cheek.

She grabbed his hair and slammed his face into the wall. "If you are going to arrest me for assaulting an officer, then we may as well make it look good."

She held him there with the sticky texture of whatever was in his hair rubbing against her fingers.

The other three officers were temporarily stunned but now they were holding her back with her arms behind her and handcuffed.

Reeves was shaking his head and dabbing his bloodied lip with a napkin. "Your career is over. Anything you say can be used against you in a court of law. Hell with it. You know your rights. I don't have to waste my breath." He pointed to the door with the officer holding her.

"You're not much of a man without that badge. I bet your wife cringes when you try to touch her at night. She probably thinks it is better to get it over with. Five minutes doesn't take much out of her day. That's if you can even get it up," she seethed with a bombardment of insults.

"Put her in the car. I don't want to hear another word. We will settle this down at the station. You made a serious mistake striking a superior officer," Reeves called out from the front door.

"The only mistake I made was not kicking you in the balls when I had the chance. That's right, you don't have any. They are currently in Miss Fletcher's purse." She stared at him while being forcibly put in the car with one officer holding onto her head.

Reeves followed to the window where he stood with his hands on his hips. "It's been a long time coming. This isn't going to end well for you. There might be a way to make all of this go away."

"Let me guess. You can't find him so you want me to do your job for you. I'm not going to do that. He's not the problem. I'm looking at the problem. I have no idea how you got your position. Maybe it was on your knees," she rattled on with the other officers trying not to laugh at their superior.

Reeves was flustered and could barely utter another word. "I don't know what you're talking about. I'm a happily married man with children."

"I think somebody is protesting a little too much. Did I hit a little too close to home?" She replied through the window.

"Just tell me where he is. Don't go down with him. He's not worth your loyalty. He's not going to come out of this with his career intact. He will be lucky if he doesn't spend some time behind bars with those he has put away," Reeves responded with his words clipped.

"Do you hear yourself? The only one that should take a cold look in the mirror is you. One of these days karma is going to catch up with you. I just hope I'm around to see it. Nobody would shed a tear if you were suddenly tossed out on your ear," Danielle spewed her rhetoric while looking straight ahead and not bothering to look at him.

"I don't think you're squeaky clean. Sit tight. This warrant gives me the right to execute it in whatever way I deem necessary. This is going to be fun. Definitely not for you." Reeves stormed back into the house with his dark suit jacket flapping in the breeze.

Antagonizing him wasn't a good idea, but it certainly made her feel better. Just mentioning his sexual preferences had gotten the desired results.

Maybe it was time to dig deeper into his closet of secrets. Bringing to light his past indiscretions would bring a smile to her face.

She imagined his wife would have some interesting stories to tell off the record.

She could only hope they wouldn't find Jack. He wouldn't be so stupid to stay where he was while they were dragging her from the house. Under the sink wasn't exactly a permanent solution.

He would be smart enough to leave by the back door where nobody was stationed.

"Look what we have here. I knew you were hiding something. This doesn't look good for you, Detective Rodriguez. I use the term loosely. Harboring a fugitive would be bad enough but this is going to get the book thrown at you.

He walked out of the house with his hands behind his back. She glared with avid interest expecting to see Jack being hauled in.

That would've been preferable over the alternative.

He lifted the bag of cocaine over his head triumphantly. It appeared there was more than one bag planted.

CHAPTER 42

Jack had never had a more complex case. It was the first time in a long time he had to dig down deep to find the strength to fight another day.

He was already hidden away from the rest of the world inside the only place they would never look for him. The storage unit wasn't even under his name.

He sat there scratching his beard trying to make sense of it all. It all stemmed from the past. The time he had spent in Australia with his partner Jo Boston-Wright had been some of his memorable moments.

He was going to have to get in touch with her without anybody knowing. The last thing he wanted was for her to get pulled into something beyond her control.

He had vacated Danielle's house while the police were busy trying to calm her down. That wasn't easy considering her Latin temper could be her own worst enemy. He had a feeling she was putting on an act to give him time to leave before being discovered.

He saw her strike Reeves. It couldn't have happened to a nicer guy.

Learning of her arrest and subsequent incarceration was weighing heavily on his mind. He wanted to do something but had no idea what strings to pull. He was a relatively new recruit transferred from Australia with no real friends to speak of other than his partner.

That was his problem. He thought people would disappoint him and he had always been proven right. There were only a select few including Danielle to make him believe in the possibility people could be relatively sane most of the time.

He remembered fondly the spirited debates between his wife and himself. Those angry outbursts had given him a rush. It made making up much more pleasurable but still, the underlying reasons for their animosity toward one another were there.

A text message from Anderson came in with a vibration that was making his phone dance to a tune of its own.

It appeared Danielle had been put on leave without pay while the investigation was ongoing.

She had done the right thing and had requested union representation. They would definitely tell her to keep her mouth shut. She wasn't the type to quietly go off into the sunset never to be heard from again.

The woman was going to make some noise. Reeves was going to have a hard time getting a confession out of her when she had done nothing wrong. It wasn't the first time some disgruntled suspect had tried to get revenge by making another officer look bad by planting evidence.

He had all the information in front of him including boxes from his old life in Australia. Everything was correlated to the best of his ability. The whole thing was a big puzzle with no way to know where the pieces fit to make the picture whole again.

He was working around the clock for the last 48-hours. The caffeine was store-bought and made in an old-fashioned coffee pot. The electricity was connected to a generator to keep him warm at night.

He knew Miss Fletcher and Warren had other plans. Getting them out of the way meant they could go forward without any undue stress. They had a list, and they had checked off a few names but they were far from finished.

Nobody could blame her for what happened to her two husbands. It wasn't like they had tried very hard to pin the crime on her. She was very good at digging up skeletons and using what she found against influential people to get them to do exactly what she wanted.

He woke up every day thinking there was going to be a big break. It was that positivity that kept him going despite the little voice in his head telling him he had met his match.

There was no way he could believe that.

He just had to keep plugging away hoping for about one tiny thread he could pull to unravel it all.

*****

She was tired and extremely upset to be of any use to anybody. The last couple of days had been spent being treated like a criminal. They had nothing other than the bag of cocaine with no fingerprints to prove she had even touched it.

It was an interesting snow job and quite effective to leave her on the outside looking in. The only saving grace was Anderson was still in the fight. He could inform her of what was going on but he would risk losing his job if anybody found out.

She had on a dark hooded sweater covering her face to make it impossible for anybody to identify her. The inclement weather helped to give her some time alone with her thoughts on the trail next to her home.

She stopped to pretend to tie her shoe on a bench located halfway down the trail. It skirted a lake to make jogging more pleasurable for the residents. She enjoyed the sound of her shoes slapping against the wet ground. It made her feel safe despite various reports of women being mugged in similar circumstances.

"You are one of the good ones. This whole thing stinks. What have you learned?" She asked in a whisper.

"There's not much to report. Reeves is pushing to have you fired. He is getting a lot of flak from the higher-ups. They want something concrete to throw at you," Anderson said from behind some foliage with the water dripping from the leaves onto his shoulder.

"He's not the only one with powerful friends on the force. He should've done his research before coming after me. I have an extended family tree with many cousins. We always get together on Sunday for big family meals with all the members including the kids," she recalled chasing after them while laughing at the top of her lungs having the time of her life.

"I would've figured with somebody with your Latin roots there would be those willing to go to bat for you. I've already made some inquiries about what happened with Ms. Fletcher during those missing years. The altercation was just a start of a downward spiral of criminal activities," Anderson informed her while glancing up and down the path to make sure they were not going to be interrupted.

"I told you what happened at the child welfare office. The woman to speak to is behind the scenes. Did you find out anything about her? I'm sure you dug up something I can use," he said with his collar pulled up.

She had chosen wisely for their once-a-day meeting.

The weather helped to limit the possibility of a trespasser showing up unannounced. Not many would venture out with those black ominous clouds and rain coming down in sheets.

"That's very good. You're going to have to do better than that. Use your considerable charm and take the lady out to a nice dinner. I have it on good authority she's been lonely since losing her husband two years ago. It's despicable but I want you to use that against her," she referred to the woman at the child welfare agency.

"I'm way ahead of you. We have dinner plans tomorrow night at a fancy Italian restaurant. She didn't take much convincing to take our harmless flirtation to the next level. I know she's hiding something that's not in the permanent records." Anderson cleared his throat when he spotted an errant jogger wearing a flamboyant pink and white tracksuit.

He passed while humming something from whatever music was playing in his ear. He never looked at them twice or glanced over his shoulder to indicate his curiosity had been piqued.

They remained quiet until he rounded the corner and was soon out of sight.

"We both know what Ms. Fletcher will do if she learns about your impromptu meeting with her. What is her name?" Danielle inquired while checking her pulse rate with her watch in an attempt to complete the picture of someone jogging to relieve stress.

"Her name is Christine Thompson. She hasn't been there long, but she keeps the records impeccably intact. She is the first to change things over to a digital format. It's not like those records can't be accessed. You have to have a specific code." Anderson explained the process.

"If you can get the code tomorrow night, I will do a little digging of my own after-hours. If you catch my drift?" She said with a droplet of water collecting on the tip of her nose.

"I didn't hear that, and you didn't say it. Just be careful. People are obviously watching you. They are waiting for you to slip up to give them a reason to haul you in for something more than a bag of cocaine that could clearly be planted in your house without your knowledge. They want the proverbial smoking gun." Anderson checked his watch to make sure they didn't go over the prerequisite five-minute allotment.

"Any word from Jack? I haven't heard from him?" She lied to keep up the pretence.

"He's like a ghost. Reeves is on a warpath. He has every available officer looking for him. There's no telling what resources he is going to use. I doubt that he's going to go through proper channels. He can't fire him if he can't find him," Anderson snickered.

"Don't worry about him. He'll find us when he's ready. Trust me on that one," she said with two fingers on her neck before she began running in place.

Anderson had made a hasty exit using a footpath until he was back at his vehicle which was a rented sky-blue Subaru. There was no sign of anybody around.

He didn't notice the man on the hill training a pair of binoculars on him.

CHAPTER 43

The night was young and the two seemingly close lovebirds had decided to take an evening stroll along the river. The moon was full with a few clouds to obscure the full blanket of stars above.

They had their fingers entwined and kept touching each other when it was necessary to do so. They enjoyed playing the part. The meeting was not by chance. It was planned from the moment they were reunited after his unfortunate stint in a mental institution.

"This is fun," Warren said.

"Don't get carried away. This isn't going to be easy. He has a full complement of guards. You could say he's paranoid after what happened to the others. We're not here to do anything more than to get a lay of the land," Kellie stated with a picnic basket between them.

To any observer, they would appear to be about to have a midnight picnic near the river. They arranged everything a mile away from their target. A champagne bottle on ice accompanied a few finger sandwiches and fried chicken dripping in grease.

"He didn't do anything to me but he knew what was going on. Those reports go directly to human resources. You saw my first-hand account. Then you sent it to your superiors. They buried it, hoping to avoid the bad publicity of a harassment charge within the company," Warren said with a bite of cucumber and mayonnaise hanging on his lip.

She very carefully removed it with the pad of her thumb.

They were lying under the stars feeding each other with loving expressions of endearment. It had to look good so they could spend the time necessary to clock how the guards would change shifts every couple of hours.

The house was situated next to the water. It was an investment strategy but also gave the owner the best vantage point if anybody came knocking on his door late at night.

She reached under the basket to retrieve a pair of binoculars. It was camouflaged and easily hung between her breasts just barely peeking up over the ridge of her sweater. She wasn't blind to his casual glances, but she didn't mind the attention.

It kept him wrapped around her little finger.

"Dr. James Carver is the worst of them all. He claims to be your friend and willing to listen but he always has an agenda. The big boys pay him extremely well to look the other way. I'm not even sure the doctor in his name is an official title or something that he gave himself to make him sound more important than he is," Warren protested with a handful of sand collected between his fingers when he made a fist.

"Easy does it, big fella. We both know he's only part of the problem. You just made mention of the big boys. They will have to be dealt with. We just have to keep our heads down low. Reeves has been a friend. He's not happy about it but there's not much he can do when I have my foot on his throat," she said with a perfect view of a wall of windows most likely fortified against any sort of upfront attack.

"You never told me what you have on him," Warren pressed for answers while licking his fingers of the greasy residue from the chicken.

"There's a good reason for that. I'm the only one with that knowledge and it's going to stay that way. He's already losing it. The only way to keep him in line is by protecting his secrets. Ironically, I could easily send those images to the web where it would become viral within minutes," she said with a smile while thinking about the consequences of his dirty laundry becoming public knowledge.

"What about Detective Creed? I hate that guy. He never had to deal with bullying. What gives him the right to judge me? It's not like anybody else was lifting a finger to help me. I'm sorry that I didn't see you as an ally. You did the right thing by staying in the dark," Warren stated on his back with his elbow planted on the ground while enjoying a momentary reprieve with a glass of champagne.

She looked at him and felt pity. "You didn't deserve any of it. Those guys claimed to be your friend only to get you to open up to them. They wanted leverage. When they couldn't get it, they resorted to underhanded tactics and name-calling."

"Revenge is best served cold. The look on their faces is something I'm never going to forget," he said with a grin while reliving the day he finally took matters into his own hands with her help.

Kellie knew he was only a patsy but a useful tool in her arsenal. They made a great team. She had assured his loyalty by getting him out of the institution. His hatred for those looking down from above was something she could use to her advantage.

*****

Danielle was reminiscing about her past. Her daughter was playing loud music in her bedroom. She wasn't very happy to find her mother trying to sweep up the mess the officers made in their search of the property.

She had made sure her daughter was kept away from the ugliness of her detainment. It was more of an annoyance with no public record. They were very careful to avoid the unnecessary drama of making an example out of her without a signed confession.

She hated the music coming from down the hallway.

Getting a new mattress after Reeves had stabbed the other one repeatedly was a bit of a hassle. She had to use her union representation to call and make the order while she was still being questioned.

Detective Robert Engler wasn't exactly her biggest fan. It didn't surprise her to learn that Reeves had assigned him to grill her. He was constantly sweating and moving his fingers through what was left of his black mane of hair.

The man wasn't exactly accustomed to working out with the other detectives. He was happy to skate through until his pension in the next few months. She remembered how he glared at her and tried every tactic in the book to make her break but she refused to give him the satisfaction.

"What are you doing?" Her daughter asked.

It gave her a start, and she temporarily lost her breath with her hand to her chest. "It's not nice to sneak up on me. I was just feeling nostalgic. Your father always told me recording those milestones was important. It's all here labelled by the year. It must've taken him hours to compile all of these pictures into the album." She said with a flip of a page.

"That can't possibly be me," Jessica pointed out with her finger touching this innocent face of a young girl barely out of diapers.

"You came into the world kicking and screaming. Your father took one look at you and said you were trouble from the moment you were born. He also said he would protect you and keep you safe from harm for as long as he lived," Danielle said with her eyes welling up.

She felt tiny fingers wrapped around her from behind. "I know I have been making your life a living hell. It wasn't your fault. I'm just angry all the time. I will try to be better."

Danielle reached up and touched her arm as a sign of solidarity. "I figured the best thing I could do was give you some space. You have every right to the way you feel. Don't let anybody tell you differently."

"I did hate you for a long time. I'm worried about you all the time. I don't want the same thing to happen to you that happened to daddy. I can't sleep most nights when you're not down the hallway. I'm afraid of getting the knock on the door," She sniffled while hugging her mother tightly.

"You're old enough to know bad things happen to good people. The one thing I can promise you is that I'm careful. I have everything to live for. I want to be there to see you have your first kiss. Become heartbroken. Walk down the aisle wearing a beautiful white dress. Don't become a police officer. Be true to yourself and follow your passion," she referred to her artwork.

She was always drawing. It was a talent passed down to her by her father. Danielle couldn't even draw a stick figure. Her pride had no bounds.

There was a rare moment of civility between them.

"I know it's probably bad but do you want to have some ice cream?" She said while sitting on the floor with her daughter showing her how much she meant to her.

"Rocky Road?" She said with a clap of her hands.

"Is there any other kind?" She asked with a smile before following her daughter into the kitchen where she was already digging into the freezer.

She stood there looking at her and then sent her eyes skyward. She knew her husband was watching. It made her feel close to him while they sat and enjoyed the chocolate chip pieces in the ice cream.

There was still a lot of work to do but at least she could stop her brain from working overtime for a few moments to enjoy the simple things in life.

CHAPTER 44

Jack couldn't seem to get in touch with his old partner. She had gone off the grid after making a powerful enemy of her own. They had put her into what was the equivalent of witness protection.

Nobody was willing to lift the gag order to her whereabouts when only a couple of people knew where she was hiding out until after the trial.

It wasn't what he wanted to hear but there was very little he could do about it. The best he could hope for was to ask a few colleagues to make a few discreet inquiries on his behalf.

A few boxes were discarded until he was left with 25 files to go over with a fine-tooth comb. It wasn't going to be easy to make heads or tails out of many of the arrests made without some sort of context.

"You've been hiding a long time in plain sight. It's about time somebody makes you answer for the crimes you have committed. Everybody makes mistakes. It's human nature," he said with his finger going over pertinent information.

There was still the discrepancy regarding what happened during those missing years. She had virtually disappeared without a trace until suddenly showing up with a chip on her shoulder.

"You're not going to get away with it. The last thing you should've done was come after me and the people that I care about. That made it personal. I'm never going to give up until the guilty verdict is announced in court with you being hauled away in chains," he said with the vision of her in an orange jumpsuit making him smile.

He was starting to see double and didn't even know what time it was. Being inside the secluded and secure storage unit made his sleep cycle somewhat distorted. He sometimes fell asleep with the caffeine still running rampant through his veins.

This wasn't like his other cases. The motives for the crimes usually revolved around revenge or love. Miss Fletcher was a different sort of criminal. She wasn't going to crack under pressure. The hot white lights in her face did very little to curb her lust for vengeance.

It was a game, and she knew how to play many parts with the help of those loyal to her including Reeves. The man was internal affairs through and through. He had the ear of his superiors. They would listen until he laid out all the facts before making a decision that was a consensus.

They had given him a long-range and very little oversight. It meant his reputation preceded him. They had no idea his strings were being pulled by Fletcher. Maybe it was time for them to know the unfiltered truth.

Jack had heard the chief of police was a creature of habit. That made him susceptible especially when he didn't have anybody to watch his back.

It was about time Jack and chief of police Peter Ames got better acquainted. He could at least set the record straight and let the chips fall where they may. It was an interesting American colloquialism.

He always shook his head when he heard somebody saying something he didn't understand. It must've been what foreigners felt like when they heard him speaking in his Australian native lingo.

He still had the accent, but he was trying to acclimate to his surroundings.

Today was a good day to have a conversation with someone sticking his head in the sand.

Peter was supposedly a good man, but that was merely public perception. He didn't know what he was going to find when he finally got an audience with him.

He checked his watch with a few hours to kill before daybreak. He would try to get some rest in the hopes of being in full control of his faculties. He didn't want to lose his composure when he sat down to breakfast with Peter at his favorite haunt.

It was going to be an expensive proposition. The price tag was extravagant but he wouldn't expect anything less from the restaurant at the bottom of the Rockefeller Centre.

He always did want to watch the kids skating with their parents watching diligently from the sidelines.

He would just catch some zzz's before introducing himself to one of the biggest players on the chessboard of justice. He wasn't the king but his power could be felt whenever he spoke into a microphone.

*****

Danielle was up early with a cup of coffee to see the sunset. She sat by the window listening to the humdrum of those about to start their day. She enjoyed this one moment to really listen to her inner voice.

She had her feet curled underneath her Grateful Dead T-shirt.

It was the only way she could keep from going insane when everything around her was falling apart. She was now standing in the shoes of her new partner on the precipice of losing her career.

It was all thanks to Kellie Fletcher. She had no doubt in her mind Reeves was a consummate professional most of the time. Ms. Fletcher was using him as a puppet by using something hanging over his head.

"Are you prepared for this evening?" She asked with her chin in her hand.

"I'm a big boy. This isn't my first date," Anderson answered over the speakerphone.

"Have you ever noticed how we don't take the time to smell the roses? Everybody is in a rush to get somewhere. They have priorities and commitments. We only get this one life to live. I've taken things for granted for too long," she sighed deeply with that pent-up frustration building almost to a breaking point.

"What are you going on about? Just don't tell me you found religion. That would be the ultimate cliché," he stated with a bit of a giggle.

He could be easily heard through the speaker.

She touched the window with the tip of her finger. "It's nothing like that. I've been through a lot but I'm still standing. That's more than you can say for some people. I count myself one of the lucky ones."

"We all have something to feel grateful for. Just waking up is a blessing. Nobody knows when their time is up. We all are born with an expiration date but we have no idea when it is. Would we live life to the fullest if we knew when that time was? That's not an easy thing to answer for most of us," he waxed poetic.

"I think I'm going to take some time off after this case is put to bed. My daughter and I need some time to get to know each other again. Maybe a camping trip to Arizona. Perhaps a spa day to be pampered by professionals. It's something I'm going to have to think about. A couple of months stress-free sounds like heaven," she said with a deep breath.

"I can't remember the last time I had a vacation. The job gets underneath your skin," Anderson responded.

"Tell me about it. It's not like we are irreplaceable. Crime is always going to be there even after we are gone. Why do we take it so personally?" She asked without expecting an answer.

"That's what makes us good at the job. We don't become complacent like those just sitting and waiting for retirement. People need us to protect them. We are the last line of defence. It's not a perfect system, but it's the only one we have," Anderson said with melancholy in his voice.

"How many times have we seen the injustice of somebody getting off on a technicality only to commit another crime? It's not biblical times. We can't just dispense justice without thinking about the consequences. It's not an eye for an eye," she said before reaching for the newspaper.

She was happy to see that her face didn't adorn the front page.

"I'll stop by later tonight after the date. We can compare notes. Let's hope Jack decides to stay off the radar. We can't afford for him to be messing around where he doesn't belong." Anderson closed the communication with a steady beep until she touched the button to bring a sense of quiet to the chaos.

She didn't bother looking at the headlines and went directly to the sports page. It and the funny papers were the only part of the newspaper that made her feel like the world made sense.

She had her daughter to take care of during a tumultuous time in her life. It was a struggle, and she was constantly juggling her career over her responsibility as a parent.

It wasn't making anything better that her life was now underneath a microscope. She should probably tell her daughter but she wanted to shield her from the worst of it until it was necessary to give her a heads up.

She could only hope the day would never come but that would depend on many factors including convincing those looking to nail her to the wall she was innocent.

CHAPTER 45

It wasn't easy going incognito after leaving the storage unit. The time was rapidly closing in, with very little chance to change his mind. It wasn't like he had anything to lose.

Jack had decided a pre-emptive strike was necessary. It involved getting to the restaurant a half hour before the arrival of the eminent chief of police.

The man was bigger than life when he walked in the door wearing a long tan trench coat. He took off his black scarf and followed the hostess to his reserved table in the back, where he wasn't going to be disturbed.

Jack had already staked out the place to make sure he had the best vantage point. There was no sign of an entourage. Nobody accompanied him. This was a man of strength and character, but also a man with the desire for some privacy before he started his day.

Jack took off his hat and placed it in his hand in a gesture of respect. He walked slowly to the table in the back. The other patrons were busy with their own conversations to notice him standing out of the crowd.

He was dressed impeccably in a dark blue suit. It cost more than his annual salary. His credit card was going to be a shocking revelation when he got the bill in the mail. It was a necessary expenditure, one that he hoped was going to pay off big dividends.

He sat down with his cup of coffee to get a read on the man from afar. He wasn't the most approachable person. His door was not always open. His policy had always been if you needed to talk to him, it better be damn important or else heads were going to roll.

This was all conjecture and things Jack had heard in passing. It was easy to get people to talk about what was wrong with the justice system. They always had an opinion and were happy to share it with somebody that showed an interest.

He had on a pair of glasses, but it wasn't prescription strength. The lenses had been removed after he procured them from a local pharmacy. They were mainly used for reading, but still strong enough to give him a headache. It wasn't like anybody was looking at him closely to discover his glasses had no lenses.

"I don't care. You tell him it comes from me. Don't take no for an answer. He has to learn to play the game. We all have some skin in the game. Remind him we have other investors to answer to," Peter said, while fiddling with the fork in a nervous habit when his anger got the best of him.

He was over 6 feet tall and 250 pounds of solid muscle. He enjoyed a steak dinner from time to time, but was always watching his cholesterol. He didn't even notice the man standing at his table until he looked up into the eyes of somebody familiar to him.

"Do you mind? You're in my light," he stated with his hand over his phone.

"I need to talk to you. It's a matter of some importance," Jack said with a glance over his shoulder.

"That's what they all say. Make an appointment with my secretary. I should be able to see you in a couple of weeks when things settle down. I don't have time for this," Peter said before his mind grabbed onto the face and put a name to it.

He looked at him for a very long time without saying anything. "Just get it done. I have to go." He hung up using an old-fashioned flip phone.

It was something without any data or the bells and whistles the other phones came with.

"I'm going to sit down now. Don't make a scene. This can go one of two ways. Look under the table very casually," Jack addressed with the snub-nosed revolver underneath the tablecloth.

It was relatively easy to get an unlicensed firearm in New York City. He just had to walk down the street until he found what he was looking for.

The man was selling out of his car. A few words were exchanged before cold, hard cash became the issue. It cost him $300 of his hard-earned money, but it was worth every penny to steal a few minutes of the Chief of police's precious time.

Peter followed his advice but didn't show any emotion when he saw the gun pointed at him under the table. "There's no need for the theatrics. You obviously have something you want to discuss. Get on with it, Detective Creed."

"I'm at the end of my rope. Reeves is working for Kellie Fletcher. I see from your expression you recognize the names. I don't have any evidence. It's just my gut instinct. You of all people know how important those instincts are to a police officer," he referred to Peter's limited tenure on the street, pounding a beat.

"I know exactly what you're talking about. It's not something easily taught in the academy. We are the last of the old guard, Detective Creed. Can I call you Jack?"

"Only if I can call you, Peter." Jack leaned forward until there was a file on the table between them.

"Jack, these are very serious allegations you are making against someone that I have full trust in. Let me see what you have. You wouldn't have come to me unless you didn't have any other options," Peter stated before reaching for the folder, only to meet some resistance.

Jack was hanging onto it with his eyes, staring at two police officers coming into the restaurant. He hadn't prepared for this eventuality, but he was going to have to wing it.

The morning had started with Danielle trying to put on a brave face. A second interview was conducted informally at her house.

She wasn't very happy to see Detective Robert Engler standing at her door, looking around impatiently. There was no other recourse. He made it quite clear with his expression that they could either talk in private or take it down to the station where everybody would be privy to what was going on.

"Let's go over this one more time. Start at the beginning and don't leave anything out. We wouldn't want you to be caught in a lie. That could be disastrous for your career and possible freedom," Robert threatened in a backhanded way.

She turned and placed a finger against his chest. "You're not coming in here until you tell me why you have it out for me. Don't give me those innocent eyes. We both know there has been a cold reception every time we are in the same room. Don't tell me it was because I turned you down the one time you asked me out two days after my husband died."

"I don't hold grudges. I do make it my business to understand the people I work with. I'm sorry for what happened to your husband. It's a police officer's worst nightmare. You must've known going into it that the possibility existed before one of you would not make it to retirement. It's in all of the statistics," he said, still standing at the front door feeling a little conspicuous.

"I think we all know love is deaf and blind. Those feelings can't be controlled, even if you know it's wrong. The one thing I promised myself was to never get involved with a police officer. I couldn't keep the promise," she said before moving out of the way for him to come in out of the cold.

"We have more important things to discuss. New information has come to light. We combed the neighborhood and found video footage. Do you want to guess what is on it? Robert stared at her with the question becoming this ominous dark cloud.

"I haven't the foggiest idea," she lied without even blinking, already expecting the other shoe to drop.

"Harboring a fugitive is a crime. It's a good thing Jack Creed isn't number one on the hit parade. The brass is looking for him, but a warrant for his arrest has not gone out. It's in your best interest to tell me where he is. We wouldn't want something bad to happen to him," he said with a forced smile.

"What are you trying to say?" She asked, pretending to be shocked by the possibility Jack was somehow inside her home.

"That's very good. It almost convinced me. Get ahead of this thing before you are buried underneath it. There's no doubt in my mind Jack is going to lose his job. You might be able to salvage what is left of your career by cooperating with me," he said with a hand extended until he was informally touching her knee.

"Take your hands off of my mother," Jessica said with her voice raised enough to get the man's attention.

He removed his hand as if somebody had poured hot water on him. "I'm conducting an unofficial interview. I wasn't. I mean, I wouldn't," he said, flummoxed by the interruption.

The young girl was dressed in black tights and a short white top that left very little to the imagination. He had to force himself to look directly into her eyes without appearing to be some kind of pervert.

"Detective Engler, I would like you to meet my daughter, Jessica. She's supposed to be in her room doing her homework. You'll have to forgive her. She's always protecting me even though I'm the parent and it should be the other way around," she said with a smile behind his back.

Jessica stood with her arms crossed and her eyes staring daggers. The Mickey Mouse logo on her T-shirt did nothing to make her seem sweet and innocent. She was understandably suspicious of police officers showing up unexpectedly after what happened with her father.

"I'm just having a friendly conversation with your mother. It is not for impressionable ears," Robert pushed his chair away with his hands in plain sight on his knees.

"If it's friendly, then you won't mind me staying close. Don't make any sudden movements. I'll be watching," Jessica stated before going up the stairs and sitting down where she could see them quite clearly from where she was.

"Can you do something about this?" he asked while leaning forward.

"I wish I could. She doesn't listen to me. Just be careful to keep your tone neutral."

The tension was thick enough to cut with a knife.

CHAPTER 46

They shared knowing looks when the two police officers came in without looking directly at them situated in the corner.

"Take it easy, Detective. I didn't call them. Just stay calm and look directly at me. The last thing we need is a tense standoff. The publicity alone would tarnish my image. I could be the last friend you have. Just keep it together," Peter advised when watching the two officers over his shoulder.

"I'm a little wired tight these days. I get that way when I feel the noose around my neck getting tighter. Nobody wants to listen to me. They only want to see me hang," Jack whispered with his finger tapping on the folder between them.

Peter was trying to be understanding, however, he was losing his patience. This man wasn't someone he talked about with glowing recommendations. His transfer was a little mysterious under a cloud of misinformation.

"Contrary to popular belief, not everybody is out to get you. It's perfectly natural to feel like the walls are closing in on you. As far as I know, you haven't been charged with a crime. The

261

worst that might happen is they will take your shield away from you. You could always start over someplace else, but you will never be a police officer again," Peter said in an effort to lay out the facts the way that he knew them.

"I've grown rather attached to the badge. I came here for a fresh start. My family is going to join me, but not until everything is settled. I'd like to hear what you have to say," Jack said with a motion with one hand and a nod of his head.

Peter was able to get into his possession of the file between them.

He opened it and found little to indicate Jack was being framed. He did use excessive force when he arrested Miss Fletcher. That was all documented with first-hand accounts and video evidence procured from the press through a duly warranted search and seizure.

He had to admit Reeves had become somewhat like a pit bull. It did appear the man was taking it personally from every account.

"I'm not sure what you want me to do. There's nothing here to indicate they have a past connection. You expect me to stick my neck out for you, but you're not giving me anything in return," he said with both hands, pushing the file back to where it was between them.

"That seems inconceivable that you would want something in return for doing your damn job." Jack hit the table with his fist.

"You know how things are done. One hand washes the other. Give me one good reason why I should open an investigation on Reeves. He has done tremendous work to weed out those police officers playing by their own rules. Cowboys are no longer going to be tolerated," Peter informed him.

"You're the second person to call me a cowboy. From your point of view, it might look like that. I don't cross the line," he defended himself.

"I'm sure you believe that, but that's not how it is projected to the public. We have to be very careful these days. Again, at the risk of repeating myself, what exactly can you do for me in return?"

"Peter, what you need more than anything is friends in the Department. I will grant you one favor. You can ask me to do anything, no questions asked. One time. One time only," he said with a finger raised to illustrate his point.

"That's very interesting to me. You'll get a phone call one night when you least expect it. This could come tomorrow or three years from now. I will forget this conversation even happened. Leave and don't bother me again." He waved his hand in a dismissive gesture.

Jack didn't like doing it and felt dirty for even considering having to owe him anything.

Peter was a necessary evil, but it would remain to be seen how much he could do with the little information he had.

There was no promise of things turning out in his favor. He would owe him just for looking into it.

That was a slippery slope.

*****

No bodies showing up in the last 48 hours was supposed to be a good thing. Anderson was getting ready for his date. The reservations had been made at a discrete table where nobody was going to see him pull out all of his tricks.

He was considered a ladies' man, but he never took things too far.

Ms. Fletcher was the exception. He had gotten the results back from the glass. It was inconclusive.

It meant that there could've been something added to his drink, but it wasn't anything that showed up in the toxicology report. Inconclusive was the formality of finding nothing useful to point a finger at Ms. Fletcher for trying to drug him.

It didn't surprise him to learn she had taken steps to make sure nothing was going to come back to bite her. Did she really sleep with him? He couldn't remember a damn thing other than flashes that didn't make much sense.

She hadn't bothered to come back after leaving his home. The woman was a little perturbed and slightly deranged, but she didn't leave any incriminating evidence on her phone.

There were no footprints in the metaphorical sand.

The call history didn't amount to anything other than more questions on top of the ones they already had. This date could prove to be the icing on the cake, but he could also be barking up the wrong tree.

He laid out his wardrobe, paying particular attention to the cologne. He always wore it during a date in the hopes of capturing them in the snare of the pheromones. He had no intention of sleeping with her, but things happened out of his control when his libido was talking to him.

He had the day and night off after changing shifts with one of the other officers. Jack had turned into a good friend. He still wasn't quite sure about him. There was a mutual respect to go both ways.

Being young and promoted to detective had been strangely rewarding. It also came with hurt feelings from those that had been wallowing in the gutter waiting to be noticed. It wasn't his fault that he was in the right place at the right time to bring closure to a kidnapping case nobody else could solve.

He was reprimanded for going off the reservation, but he was also praised for his due diligence in the same breath. He had gotten the attention of those in a position to make all of his dreams come true.

He spent most of the day getting himself acquainted with the details of his date. The woman didn't have any skeletons. He couldn't use her past against her when she was squeaky clean.

There wasn't even a speeding ticket. Christine followed the letter of the law to the best of her ability. She had one blemish, but it was barely worth mentioning.

It was during her teenage years when she was a little more promiscuous. She had been caught with the windows steamed up, getting a little hot and heavy with a high school quarterback.

It meant she wasn't as straight-laced as she pretended to be.

He had an early lunch with a few slices of apple and a small pizza from down the block. It was all about location. His place was perfect for those late-night cravings. He wasn't in the heart of the city, but he had chosen wisely to be close to amenities.

A small deduction from his rent was given when he revealed he was a police detective during the initial interview stage. They liked the idea of instant security. He didn't let them know he would primarily be using his residence for sleeping and nothing more.

It had the open concept he had been looking for with a small but functional living room. He enjoyed entertaining when time permitted. Young ladies could easily be persuaded to take a tour of the premises.

He did very little to encourage their affections, other than small whispers of appreciation. His dimples had opened a lot of doors, especially with the older generation. He was old enough to understand the power he had over them.

He continued to think about Miss Fletcher and those missing hours in her company. He invited her to dinner to get her to open up to him. She must've used the opening to pursue her own agenda.

Anderson wasn't sure what he would do if they came face-to-face again. He wanted to believe that he would let her down gently, but something about the evening stuck with him. It wasn't anything tangible other than this inescapable need to be with her again, despite his misgivings.

He had never felt the pull to be with another woman as strong as he did with her. It was no wonder men had become playthings for her. The woman was a black widow capable of cold-blooded murder. She also exuded raw sexuality no man was able to resist, including him.

Was it wrong that he wanted to remember the evening? He'd gone through the motions to have the glass tested. He really didn't want to find anything incriminating. Her guilt or innocence didn't concern him.

That was the first time he had admitted it. It made him feel better, but also worse at the same time. He didn't want the anchor around his neck. The only way to get her out of his life was to put her behind bars. It would kill him to do it, but it was best for everybody.

Anderson checked the messages on his answering service. She was running a little late and would require an hour before he could pick her up. It was a little old-fashioned, but he understood the need to put on a show for her.

He actually enjoyed parading himself in front of the female gender in a suit and tie. He projected something of a father figure. He also made them believe there were some good ones left that weren't gay or married.

Her off hours were spent at home watching television or going to a book club. She had a collection of different authors. The one she was currently reading was a thriller by Stephen King called The Cell.

It was on her desk when he came to the office. He noticed her in the corner, practically invisible.

She also looked up abruptly when he mentioned Ms. Kellie Fletcher.

CHAPTER 47

She was overwhelmed by how easily they had gotten the footage of Jack leaving her place. It was impossible to make the connection between him and her.

"What do you make of this? You just finished telling me you haven't seen Detective Creed. Do you care to amend your story?" Robert sat with his pen poised on the notebook in his lap.

"I didn't know he was here. It looks like I left the back door open. He didn't exactly break and enter. He must've been looking for me to provide him with some insight into the investigation ongoing against him. He wasn't going to get anything from me. Maybe that's the reason why he decided to take a different tactic," she said, pointing to the screen on the image of him walking away with his head on a swivel.

He slapped the notebook closed. "You expect me to believe you had no idea he was in your house? This was about the time Reeves showed up with a search warrant. Finding those drugs was awfully convenient. He must've had an anonymous call."

"You're not suggesting Detective Creed set me up to take the heat off of himself?"

"You said it. I didn't." Peter sat away from her while her daughter was standing at the top of the stairs watching the interaction.

Jessica pointed to her eyes and then back down at Peter to indicate she was taking an interest in what was taking place.

He couldn't make any false moves. Having an audience gave him a good reason to tread carefully on thin ice.

"I've answered your questions. I'm going to say this one time only. You can go back and tell him I had no knowledge he was in my house. That whatever he was doing had nothing to do with me. I'm not his friend. I do want to see him come in, but I'm not his keeper," she said before standing up to give him a good idea the interview had come to an end.

"This isn't over. The next time will be down at the station when you will be formally arrested for being in possession of a controlled substance. Are you sure this is the way you want to handle this?" Robert swallowed when he heard the stairs creaking.

The presence of the little girl loomed above him.

Danielle opened the door and watched as Robert walked away. He didn't get what he was after, and was going to have to slink back with his tail between his legs. That wasn't going to make Reeves happy. There was no telling what his next move was going to be.

"I appreciate you standing up for me, but it wasn't necessary. I did enjoy how you made him squirm while you were watching from the top of the stairs. The apple doesn't fall far from the tree," Danielle stated while continuing to watch Robert through the curtain until he drove away in a cloud of black exhaust.

"I got a bad feeling from him. There was no way I was going to leave you alone with him. The baseball bat you gave me for Christmas is right there by the door," she indicated with a nod of her head.

"It is good to know you are prepared for the worst. Men are notorious liars. You have to be able to read between the lines. Body language can tell you everything without them even saying a word. I'll teach you what you need to know when you're old enough to date," she said with a smile.

"I can't hear you," Jessica said with her fingers in her ears while running up the stairs singing a horrible song with screeching lyrics.

There was no accounting for taste. She had the same argument with her mother. It was a debate as old as time. She was getting a taste of her own medicine when she was blasting her stereo in her bedroom at Jessica's age.

It was a sign of rebellion and perfectly natural for them to be butting heads, but at least, they knew they had each other's backs despite their taste in music.

Danielle was very proud of the young lady she was becoming. Her father would be the first to smile and give her hand a squeeze for a job well done in raising her. She could still be obstinate and become a holy terror when she didn't get her way.

Her door slammed to keep her from having a discussion about dating. It was all a little too familiar. She now understood what her mother had gone through.

She could only hope Jessica wouldn't be as reckless as she was. It was a bridge she was going to have to cross eventually.

*****

Jack had never felt more alone in his life. He wanted to reach out to somebody. A lifeline was needed to give him that sense of being connected. Danielle had been a little put off by the assignment to take him on as her partner.

He was equally hesitant when he learned of how many partners she had gone through in the past couple of years. It turned out they were the problem. She had explained in depth how they were constantly putting the moves on her.

She shut them down, but they continued to pester until she broke the golden rule of turning the other cheek. The woman was a firecracker, and he admired her restraint when she broke one of their noses in an altercation after a few drinks at a bar.

It didn't take very long for him to knock down those walls until they were on the same page. It was widely known he was only saddled with her to make his life a living hell.

It was supposed to be trial by fire. Some kind of initiation.

He wanted more than anything to contact her, but he had already caused her more grief. If he was going to contact her, he would have to do it in the right way.

Miss Fletcher wouldn't have targeted her unless she thought she was in league with Jack.

That was a bitter pill to swallow, but nothing compared to being ostracized by those he considered colleagues in the trenches. Nobody would give him the time of day. He had to basically hand over his firstborn for any reconciliation with the Department.

Peter would do what he could with the wheels spinning slowly. He couldn't wait that long and had decided to be a little more proactive. It meant getting some necessary provisions, including supplies, to make him blend into his surroundings literally and figuratively.

The proprietor of the shop was very accommodating. He showed him the latest in hunting accessories. He looked like he was going on a weekend expedition when he finally left after forking out hundreds of dollars.

He had convinced the owner to rent his truck to him for the weekend. It wasn't anything to write home about. The truck was ugly brown with the rusted fenders staying together with some kind of hardened wire. The side mirrors were broken with one a kaleidoscope of different reflections looking back at him.

Everything was about attention to detail.

His police-issued weapon was under the seat, out of sight and out of mind. He had the rifle in plain sight hanging behind him. The orange vest and hat ensemble had been stashed.

He elected for the camouflage with everything hinging on what he would be able to uncover by going a little out of his comfort zone.

His next stop was an electronic store. He browsed through the many different items before finding exactly what he was looking for. He went next door to an army surplus store and was rewarded with a device that would come in handy.

Nothing of what he was doing was considered illegal. He was through being the ghost in the machine. A couple of colleagues had promised to get back to him, but he didn't want to wait around twiddling his thumbs.

He dialled the digits by memory until he heard the sleepy response. "I don't know who this is, but it better not be Robert Engler. You're the last person I want to speak to."

"It's your uncle Ramirez," Jack stated with his voice somewhat distorted by the crackle of static.

There was a moment of silence, but he could hear her breathing on the other end of the line. "I'm sure you have a good reason to call me at this hour of the night."

"I just wanted to remind you about our annual trip to Yosemite. It might have to be postponed for a couple of weeks. You know how I love to hunt. I don't find anything a challenge around here. Maybe I will have better luck outside of the city limits. Perhaps the island of Manhattan," he said, hinting to give her a blueprint of his whereabouts without having to come out and say it.

"The reception is terrible. Just be careful. You're not exactly as young as you used to be. I would hate to hear about you being mauled by a bear or some other wild animal," she warned.

Jack understood this was her way of letting him know he was out on a limb on his own. She couldn't offer any kind of assistance when she was being monitored. That much was obvious when he drove by on his way out of town.

"I have taken down bigger animals in the past. You never have to worry about me, little one. We will see each other soon. I expect this won't take very long. Maybe a couple of days. I wish you could come with me, but I know how you feel about hunting," he hinted about bending the law for his own selfish purposes.

"I'm not going to judge you. It would be hypocritical of me since I do enjoy the fruits of your labor. Stay safe and warm out there. Be careful about other hunters. Announce yourself. They can be highly unpredictable," she warned him about his prey.

He had a clear idea of what he was attempting to accomplish. Staying out of sight was paramount. The reports had pointed him in the right direction.

The veteran down on his luck he had met earlier had come through when he called upon his services.

The tracker had led him to an oasis for the rich and influential. The truck was parked in the bushes when he reached for the green bag he had gotten from the surplus store.

He didn't know why Warren had decided to come out here, but he was going to find out. He had everything to make him invisible to the naked eye. He painted his face with black shoe polish and put on the camouflage knit cap to go along with the jacket and pants.

"... A hunting we will go..." He whispered the melody underneath his breath while carrying his weight in gold over his shoulder.

CHAPTER 48

It was a gated community.

Jack had followed the tracker he had arranged to put on Warren without his knowledge during an accidental meeting. He was quite impressed by the veteran. He didn't even ask for much money, saying that he had been missing the thrill of doing something clandestine.

Jack understood the importance of keeping his memory alive after he was gone. He had every intention of sitting down with him and chronicling his life for the next generation to live vicariously through.

He moved closer to the location until he was hidden on a bluff. There was nobody around. The patrols from the private guards in the area didn't go any further than the property line.

He unwrapped a couple of sandwiches. Turkey salad was becoming fast, one of his favorites. It had a creamy and crunchy texture with little bits of celery mixed. A few energy bars and a protein powder added to his water would keep him alert.

He brought the scope up to his eye to verify Warren was nearby. It took a moment to adjust the parameters until the vision became clearer.

It wasn't just Warren. He was with a woman, but her back was toward him. He didn't want to move at the risk of somebody seeing something out of their peripheral vision.

He consulted the photos of Warren and his wife.

This woman didn't have the same build and was slightly shorter. Warren seemed like a family guy with no interest in straying. Something was bothering him. It couldn't be, but it was the only explanation.

His heart was beating quicker.

Warren was somewhat buzzed with his eyes glazed over, but he was far from being unable to make the distinction between right and wrong. There had to be a reason for their impromptu picnic on the beach at midnight.

He scanned the area for potential targets using the night vision scope. The houses all looked alike from his vantage point. They had set up their picnic near three summer homes. It was a bit chilly but nothing that a good sweater couldn't cure.

He wanted to hear what they were saying and had the means to do so with the device he had procured from the Army surplus store. It was handheld with a directional mic easily adapted, considering the terrain was nothing more than them alone on the beach, speaking quietly to one another.

He turned it on and put on the headphones while watching them intently from his perch high above. It thrilled him beyond words to finally be one step ahead of her.

She hadn't turned, but he was reasonably sure Ms. Fletcher had brought her accomplice to stake out another target. It made him angry to think of how easily they had manipulated the system.

It was possible he could catch them in the act of trying to kill whoever was next on their list. He didn't believe his luck would be that good, but a guy could hope.

He made a note of the three houses in the area. It wouldn't take much to dig into the property records. He could get the owners' names to figure out what connection one of them had to Kellie Fletcher.

His phone was buzzing, and he found himself somewhat intrigued. He carefully extracted it from his pocket while continuing to watch them very closely. It took him a few moments to juggle it and the scope. Multi-tasking wasn't easy for him.

Ms. Fletcher was actually feeding him grapes. It was a sickening display to trick those around them into believing they were star-crossed lovers.

He could see her face clearly. It was the bitch.

The message scrolled across the screen. It made him do a double take. There was no mention of this particular piece of information coming to light before this. It did add a new dynamic.

That could prove useful.

He had to wonder what was going on with Anderson. He had heard about his date with a certain someone from a little birdie whispering into his ear.

They were corresponding by burner phone.

He didn't know how long Warren and Kellie had been there. She was cautious, but he did catch her looking toward those three houses with a pair of camouflage binoculars. The girl was up to something and he couldn't stand to think of another person falling victim to her sociopathic ways.

*****

Anderson had picked up his date. She was in a white chiffon dress. It was very tasteful with not much skin showing. It was almost a tease for him to get his hands on her but he had to remind himself this wasn't a normal courtship.

He probably wouldn't have given this woman a second look of interest. She did look better out of the office. Her dark hair was pulled back away from her porcelain neck.

Idle chitchat wasn't exactly her strong suit but he could work with that by using a tried and true tactic of getting her to open up.

"I hope you don't think I'm being too presumptuous. It is a little late for a date. I convinced the owner of the restaurant to stay open just for us. The chef is a good friend and promises to treat us like royalty. He's making a special menu." He turned slightly to see the makings of a smile on the corners of her mouth.

The little mole on her right cheek was cute. She was so innocent. She reminded him of an untouched flower. An unspoiled piece of perfection.

She smoothed her dress down over her knees. "What's on the menu? I can't eat anything with dairy."

"I have no idea but I will be sure to have a private conversation with the chef when we arrive to address your issues. I'm sure that he can be accommodating," Anderson answered with visions of Ms. Fletcher replacing the dainty little flower next to him.

He could easily envision what she might do in the confines of the car. The woman was not exactly shy about extending the intimacy. Walking out of his bathroom in nothing but the towel had certainly gotten his attention under the sheets.

"Can I ask you a personal question?" she asked with her glasses pushed up to the bridge of her nose.

"You can ask me anything. I'm an open book," he expressed while signalling to move into the other lane.

She was nervously touching the strap of her purse. "Are the rumors about you true?"

"That depends. What have you heard?" He inquired with a bit of curiosity to see what gossip was becoming mainstream conversation around the water cooler.

She cleared her throat with her hand up to her mouth. "I've heard stories. I'm a big believer that the truth is subjective. They say you love them and leave them. If that's true, then you can turn this car right around and take me home. I would like to give you a chance to tell me your side of the story," she addressed.

Christine wasn't like the other ladies in his life. He couldn't expect her to become amorous before they reached the restaurant. The challenge was to keep it in his pants.

That wasn't easy when his reputation preceded him.

"I'm going to be perfectly honest with you. That was the past. My future is unwritten and I'm looking to add a different chapter to the story," Anderson explained with his eyes on the rear-view mirror.

"I'm not going to sleep with you. Not today and maybe not tomorrow. Trusting men has been a problem for me in the past. This time I want things to go slowly for us to get to know each other," she said with a slight tilt of her head to look at him with an unbiased eye.

She had to admit he was handsome and could easily convince most women to turn the date into breakfast in the morning served in bed. It didn't mean she couldn't fantasize about the possibilities.

Anderson hit the brakes hard. His hand came across the seat with an ingrained instinct to protect his passenger. She gasped in response with her cheeks turning a different kind of red until it was spreading down into the dress where he couldn't see it.

"Are you alright?" he asked with one eye on the mirror.

She moved her hands over her body with a stunned expression on her face. "I think so. What was that all about?"

"I thought I was going to run over a cat. It turns out it was an empty plastic bag. My night vision isn't very good. I should probably think about getting glasses for driving," he lied with his eyes confirming his suspicion there was somebody following him.

That in itself wasn't surprising considering how Reeves was pressuring him. He wouldn't put it past him to have somebody loyal to the cause watching from afar. It bothered him to think of how easily he might've let down his guard.

He drove the rest of the way to the restaurant with the pair of headlights disappearing. It reappeared when he stood outside with his hand draped over her shoulder innocently.

He saw the same pair of headlights with one dimmer than the other. It parked down the block. He didn't know how to handle it but he figured the best way was to keep things casual. Nothing good came from raising the alarm.

Anderson wasn't going to let his peeping Tom get the best of him. The midnight moon promised romance, and that was exactly what Christine was going to get.

Taking on a defensive posture wasn't going to work. He had to ply her with compliments and a few stiff drinks to loosen her tongue to speak freely.

CHAPTER 49

Danielle had become a night owl after losing her husband. She prowled the hallways under the cover of darkness. Stepping out to get a breath of fresh air gave her the chance to think about the psychology of a pathological liar and psychological torturer.

Ms. Fletcher had been getting off on making them look like idiots. She started her campaign against Creed. That wasn't enough for her. She must've found out Danielle was keeping Jack abreast of further developments.

It could've been anyone including those that had seen her around Boston. She tried to remain anonymous but a dead body in the restaurant made for some interesting public scrutiny.

Somebody could've gotten a picture of her at the crime scene being questioned by the police.

It could've been bad timing but it could also have been premeditated. It wasn't like anybody knew she had left the comfort of the hectic streets of New York.

Boston gave her a chance to unwind but also question those closest to Ms. Fletcher during her impromptu walk down the aisle two times in the same town.

It wasn't hard to find out she had benefited from their untimely demise. She was the sole beneficiary of both wills in the number of millions. She was no longer letting anybody run roughshod over her.

A car door slammed. She thought for a moment Anderson was stopping by to give her a progress report. It would be interesting to find out what kind of information he could get out of Christine.

She had learned Christine was a tough nut to crack. She was a stickler for details. Getting her to do anything illegal would take an amazing amount of skill. A few drinks would be preferable. It was unfortunate she was a recovering alcoholic.

"I was going to knock, but you saved me the trouble," Reeves stated while he was rubbing his hands together.

"Don't come any closer. You're the last person I want to see. Leave before I get my gun and fire off a few rounds over your head as a warning. It would be fun to make you squirm," she said with one hand reaching into the open doorway for the gun next to the door.

"I just came by to give you a chance to clear up any misunderstandings. Jack Creed is a loose cannon. He doesn't deserve to wear the shield. His time has come and gone." Reeves stood with his back against a plain white van with no lettering on it.

She had seen it before and had suspected she was under surveillance. There was most likely a two-man team inside watching her every move.

"You might be right. He is an old dog but amazingly, he can learn some new tricks. I'm as surprised as you are. He took me for a man stuck in his ways unable to bend to convention," she explained with her hand still inside the doorway poised to take action if he decided to invade her personal space.

"I find that hard to believe. You would know better than I would. He hasn't made any friends in the Department. Most of the other officers want to see him drummed out of the force. The others have a fantasy of seeing him in jail with those he put away," he said with a quick smile before it faded.

"I wouldn't bet against him. The man is very resourceful and quite capable of handling his own business. The last thing you should've done was rattle his cage. You can't undo what has been done. The storm is coming. It is best to get out of his way." Danielle watched him closely to see a crack in his armor.

"Are you threatening me? I might be the last friend you have. It wouldn't be a good idea to bite my hand metaphorically speaking," he said with that right hand waving back and forth in front of her face.

Danielle felt like a neutered dog. She wanted to hurt him physically but had to contend with hurting him financially.

Her day had not been wasted. Productive was a good way to describe her trip down to City Hall.

It was on a whim but she felt empowered to do something on Jack's behalf. He did encourage loyalty. He never asked anybody to do something that he wasn't willing to do himself.

"I'm just telling you the facts as I know them. Don't get bent out of shape over nothing," she answered while fingering the handle of the weapon.

"It sounds to me like Detective Creed is unstable. Maybe I should rethink firing him. A mandatory evaluation by a psychiatrist will help him sort out his issues. He might get lucky and receive a reprimand. He will never be out in the field again. That would be poetic justice," Reeves stated before smacking his hand on the sliding door of the van.

Danielle knew this was some sort of signal for those inside to continue monitoring the situation. He was tying her hands to keep her on the sidelines where she could barely breathe without somebody reporting back to him.

Reeves stopped at his car. It was a white Lexus with very expensive rims.

His hand was on the door. "There is one other thing. The drugs found in your apartment was ordinary icing sugar. You're off the hook. It must have been very traumatizing. You need a few days of paid leave before you come back ready to tackle another assignment."

Danielle was no longer considered a pariah. Her record was expunged. There was no further action against her. It struck her as odd; he would want to keep her in dry dock when there was no shortage of homicides in New York.

*****

Anderson couldn't relax when he knew somebody was conducting an unofficial surveillance on him. His movements were now being recorded for posterity.

"You seem a little distracted. Maybe this wasn't a good idea," Christine fretted while moving her fingers around the rim of the champagne glass.

"Nonsense. You know it's a good idea to leave work in the office but it's not always that easy. I'm sure you've had your fair share of troubled cases to keep you up at night wringing your hands with worry. I find what you do very fascinating," he fibbed.

"There have been days I didn't want to get out of bed. I'm sure everybody goes through some form of depression working for the government. It would explain all of those disgruntled postal workers going off the handle and shooting anything that moved," she said with her fingers gradually closing in around the fragile white linen napkin.

"Let's stop talking shop. We came here to relax. The chef gave me his assurance there is no dairy on the menu. We are starting with a chicken stuffed with a substitute for cheese and ham cut from a recently barbecued pig smoked to perfection," he said while kissing two of his fingers with a universal sign of delicious.

"I wanted to mention a phone call I got this morning after you left. Low and behold, it was the woman in the news claiming to be harassed by the police. I believe her name is Kellie Fletcher."

A violin was playing with a young lady pressuring him to buy a Rose for Christine. He gave in and placed the pristine flower next to her plate.

She smiled sweetly and brought the petals up to her nose. Her eyes were closed when she smelled the fragrance. She was not accustomed to the finer things and felt completely like a fish out of water.

"I have to wonder how a girl like that slips through the crack of society. Let me see your phone. I want you to have my phone number whenever you want to reach out and touch someone," he propositioned and was surprised by how easily she relinquished her phone into his custody.

"She has been a topic of conversation lately in the news. Let me be perfectly clear. Whatever she has done is none of my business. Getting involved is out of the question," she stated with her fingers tightly gripping the champagne glass.

Anderson really didn't need her to do anything. Just having her phone was more than enough. He pretended to type in his digits but this was an exercise to get a program installed.

"I'm a little nervous. I don't want to do anything to ruin our evening." He said with one hand shaking and the other typing with some degree of difficulty with just his thumb.

The program would eavesdrop on her conversations. It would gain access to her email accounts where he immediately spied a list of codes including the one used in the office to access personal records from the cloud.

"I think I did it but I can't be entirely sure. You might want to take a look to make sure I did it the right way," he advised while passing her back her phone with a direct link to whoever she was going to call.

Accessing the files would have to wait until he got back home to log into his personal computer.

It was a new bit of technology the government was using to monitor the activities of people on the terrorist watch list. It was a prototype, but he had only good things to say when the program was user-friendly. Expertise with a computer wasn't necessary.

The meal started with bacon-wrapped scallops in a white wine sauce. There were five of them arranged in a circle with a sprig of mint in the middle. Every bite gave them a taste sensation. They raved about the food with one course following the next until they got to the dessert.

Chef Raymond came to the table to put on a show by setting fire to the pan to caramelize the cherries. He was very entertaining.

He noticed two things on her phone which were immediately sent to the email of one Danielle Rodriguez. The code would make it easier for her to break into the office.

CHAPTER 50

Danielle was flirting with the guard at the child welfare building in the center of New York. Always keeping her hand in.

There were people on the street in Times Square when she rolled by in a truck donated by a neighbor without his knowledge.

She would make sure to fill the gas and leave $100 bill on the seat. No questions would be asked. Money was a good motivator to keep his mouth shut.

"I'm sorry to put you on the spot. We've had some problems in the last few days. You've been very kind about your evaluation of my service. Just sign right here. I hope this will result in a raise. I could certainly use the money," Timothy Baker stated while moving the hat on his head until it was angled away from the tattoo on his skull of a naked lady.

"Can't we all? We try to set a budget and we always break it the first chance we get. Don't you think monogamy is a crime?" She questioned abruptly.

"I'm a happily married man with children. Being with her is my pleasure but there are times when I think about the one that got away," he said with a billy club swinging in an arc while they walked down the corridor into the bowels of the building.

"Give me the code and I will punch it in," he advised until she rattled off the four-digit number.

It opened on the first try.

"I hope you're not going to get into any trouble over this. My boss is on my ass for this report by morning. I don't have access to my office computer at home. He expects me to burn the midnight oil but doesn't leave word that I'm going to show up unexpectedly at all hours of the day and night." Danielle stated with her mind occupied with what her daughter was going to find when she woke up.

Stepping out unannounced with the lights off and the drapes drawn gave her the best chance of getting past her tail. The van was quiet and nobody came rushing out to greet her when she drove away in the truck she had borrowed creatively.

"Stay as long as you need. We all have bosses asking for the unreasonable. I'll stop by later with a cup of coffee and we can talk about this concept of monogamy," he teased with the tip of his hat making those piercing blue eyes disappear underneath the cap.

It was a good thing she didn't have to show him her identification. A few words were all that it took to reveal he was new to the job. One week to be exact.

Claiming to be Christine was a white lie. That was what Danielle convinced herself of when she opened up the locked doors of the filing cabinet with a bobby pin. She skimmed through the names with a flashlight stuck between her teeth.

It was a very important moment where anything could happen. The excitement of the guard catching her going through the files forced her to hasten her approach.

She almost gave up when she felt a little resistance. A little extra tug revealed the file in the back of the cabinet.

The sealed juvenile document was now ready to peruse. It was a good thing Anderson had gotten the code to the office. The same one worked on Christine's computer. The lack of security to those authorized documents was astounding.

It could've been worse. The codes could've been found taped to the bottom of the keyboard or under the desk. This was a world where nobody could keep their thoughts straight.

Kellie's file had been misplaced under the leather G. Somebody had gone to a lot of trouble to make sure finding it was impossible.

She opened it and found that her youthful indiscretions were rather tame compared to what she was doing today. Smoke bombs, lighting up in the laboratory, and speaking with insubordination to her teachers was just the tip of the iceberg.

She had threatened students and teachers alike. There was a notation from her caseworker. Christine's name was signed on the dotted line. She had taken a personal interest in the case and was now monitoring Kellie.

The man's name was illegible on the documents transferring Kellie to a juvenile facility. She spent some time getting her head straight before she was released as a productive member of society.

Her disappearance baffled her caseworker. Christine had made some inquiries but nobody got back to her.

Spencer was his name. He later retired without following up. The file remained in mothballs gathering dust until Christine came along and found herself drawn to the woman's story.

Danielle jotted down two very important facts including the reason why Kellie had disappeared for almost 4 years. She literally fell off the earth but somehow Christine had gotten to the bottom of the mystery. It wasn't as damning as she hoped but the last piece fell into place when she came across a recent marriage license.

The ink was still dry on the document from a few months ago.

*****

Nobody could dispute Jack had a vendetta to pursue. Finding out that Ms. Fletcher was really Mrs. Palmer had certainly made for some interesting reading, even though she had a relationship with Vince Daniels. Maybe Vince was too slow on the marriage uptake or he was just a smoke screen. Kellie was one complicated, self-serving, bitch. He was able to track down a huge story in the New York Post about their wedding.

He was nowhere to be seen. There were no pictures of him in her place. No wedding photos and certainly no adventurous pictures of their honeymoon.

John Palmer was a megastar with his money made from soccer endorsements in the United Kingdom.

He had parlayed his athletic prowess on the soccer field into a brand name. The man was notorious for sleeping around. What made him settle down with the likes of Ms. Fletcher?

He had to know about her past and the unfortunate events surrounding those men caught in the web of betrayal.

Jack had been watching both suspects play the part of dutiful lovers. Nobody interrupted them. Loving looks and carefully orchestrated romantic gestures made him sick to his stomach.

There had to be a reason why Ms. Fletcher was keeping her marriage a secret. She wasn't even wearing a wedding ring. There was no mention of them living together.

He was traipsing around the globe promoting his brand of new sneakers made by Nike. It was a lucrative arrangement but required a lengthy promotion tour. He was hitting the entertainment circuit by sitting down with any journalist worth their salt.

They were packing up to leave. It was a little disappointing but at least, he had a semblance of a target they were going after. It was more than he had an hour ago.

"We can't be seen together. I think I mentioned something about taking your wife and children to a fancy restaurant. You make the reservations. Then we just have to arrange for the press to get wind of it. I'll take care of that. Just act surprised when they ambush you coming out of the restaurant," Miss Fletcher said.

"We have some final preparations to make. What exactly will you be doing while I am painting the picture of a good family man?" Warren inquired.

Jack could hear every word until there was some kind of feedback. He lost the connection and almost punctured his eardrums with the squeal emanating through the speakers.

He had to drop them on the ground where he could still hear them making the most ungodly noise.

A plane flew overhead which would explain the interruption. The plane's electronics messed with the device. There were still some wrinkles to iron out. It was just one of the many things the device fell short of doing.

The ambient noise of the water was bad enough. He wasn't going to get what he came for but at least, he would know where Warren was. He would have to stop by at a known corner to have a brief conversation with the veteran down on his luck.

He made the mistake of conducting the surveillance unofficially. It would make it look like he was harassing the suspect. He would have to pawn the job off on the veteran. The man was destitute but his instincts were still on par.

That was far better than those that came back with a chip on their shoulders.

His next stop would be to track down the ownership of those three summer homes. It would've been nice to narrow down the field a little more but three houses was a cakewalk compared to 100.

The fact she was married made him smile. The possibility still existed there were skeletons in her closet. The husband had been away for quite some time. His itinerary had him coming back to town in a couple of days.

His social media accounts gave him everything he needed.

John Palmer wasn't exactly an angel. His record made for some interesting reading. He had to admit his two allies had certainly gone above and beyond the call of duty. He expected no less from Danielle but Anderson was another story.

Jack wanted to know Ms. Fletcher through her husband's eyes and the best way to do that was to befriend him behind her back. He could arrange for an accidental meeting similar to the one the veteran had with Warren.

This time there was not going to be a tracking device necessary.

They could never meet for supper with his wife and he would have to use an assumed name. Everybody had a daily routine.

A little old-fashioned investigative work would make it easier to find the best way to approach John Palmer.

CHAPTER 51

Anderson hadn't slept with Christine but he was tempted. He didn't understand why she was alone. Maybe it was because of two disastrous relationships. She was gun-shy unable to pull the trigger thinking the same thing was going to happen all over again.

He was strangely drawn to her. She wasn't as boring as she appeared to be in the office. They took a walk to get some fresh air after dinner. They found a nice park well-lit and sat talking for hours on a bench.

It wasn't long before they shared their first kiss. It was soft and tender very exciting in different ways but more than enough for him to want another encounter.

It was the first time he didn't land in bed with a woman. She didn't invite him in for a nightcap.

He walked around in a fog trying to make sense of the tingling sensation on his lips. That didn't happen with Kellie. She would've been a nice distraction for a month but he was starting to think about a long-term solution to his many nights sitting in front of the television falling asleep with nobody there to put a blanket over him with a kiss on his cheek.

It seemed unfathomable for him to even consider making that kind of commitment.

*****

"I'm not sure what is going on with you. I thought I made myself clear," Reeves said with his pen pressed into the desk.

"I'm through being a lackey. There are files on my desk waiting to be solved. I don't have time for your personal vendetta. Stop pretending you care about my career advancement. Leave me out of it." Anderson stood there facing him down with the sleeves of his blue Armani shirt rolled up to the elbows.

Reeves was beside himself. Nobody had talked to him in that manner. He wanted to make an example of the young police Detective. It was his show and everybody was considered bit players.

"You are dangerously close to insubordination. Don't ever speak to me like that again unless you like the graveyard shift," he threatened with all of his teeth showing.

"I'm unionized. Think about that before you start throwing around threats. One call to my representative and he will be up your ass. You'll feel like you've had a colonoscopy without lubrication," Anderson stated with his hands on the edge of the man's desk getting increasingly agitated.

He had to admit the feeling was euphoric. He might've been new but there was a time when you had to speak up for yourself.

Christine had given him the courage to show the animal within instead of kowtowing to a superior.

Reeves was frustrated and had no further use for a man that wasn't going to jump when he told him to. He was reminded there were other young impressionable detectives ready to do his bidding.

He didn't need the headache of trying to turn Anderson into a carbon copy of himself.

He dismissed Anderson with a callous wave before turning his back and swivelling his chair to the window. Ms. Fletcher wasn't going to be happy but he could spin it in his favor. It was what he had always done and would always do to make him look competent in her eyes.

The alternative of disappointing her made him cringe with a cold chill running down his spine. She could make a lot of trouble for him. How she had found out made him wonder about his close associates.

The inner circle was his safe place with like-minded individuals looking to become powerful and influential. It was a select club, and the members were vetted extensively with a background check.

You could speak candidly.

Anderson had said his peace and decided to leave but he was not done. He had spied the briefcase with his monogram on it in gold italics lying next to the desk. It wasn't handcuffed to his wrist.

The locking mechanism would be simple to bypass.

The biggest obstacle was getting him out of the office. Whatever Ms. Fletcher had on him would be found there within his reach. If he could get a look, then maybe he could find a way to take the leverage from Miss Fletcher. Maybe then Reeves would no longer be a neutered puppy waiting for his mistress to give him his orders.

He would need time to come up with a suitable plan of attack. The idea of first consulting with Danielle was appealing. He just didn't want to go running to her every time. He had to do it on his own without oversight.

He could always ask for forgiveness after the fact. Reeves had to have a weakness. Something that kept him up at night. It wasn't a lover. He hadn't seen a picture of a woman or a man, for that matter, on his desk.

There were no children at least none he mentioned in passing during several of their interactions.

He had a light bulb moment when he remembered the keys to his pride and joy dangling from a hook behind his desk.

That was just the ticket to get him out of the office. It would have to be arranged through a proxy. He couldn't afford to be spotted vandalizing his car in broad daylight. It didn't mean he couldn't source it out.

He just had to make one phone call to get the ball rolling.

Jack knew getting an audience with John Palmer wasn't going to be easy. He was a busy man and had appointments around the globe. He tried the customary route by calling his secretary only to be informed he would be unable to see him.

Jack mentioned he was a good friend and wanted to surprise him.

That didn't sway the woman on the phone. She never deviated but did make mention he had a standing golf game every Friday afternoon like clockwork.

She did pencil him in a month from today under the assumed name of Jackson Crane. It was a pseudonym. He came up with it while standing in line to get his next fix of caffeine.

Jack carefully scrutinized those around him. It was in the middle of nowhere. He half expected a police officer to tap him on the shoulder. He wouldn't be arrested but they would want to bring him down to the station for further questioning.

He knew his badge was in jeopardy. The only way to prevent his career from flushing down the toilet was to take Kellie Fletcher into custody.

He had three houses to research in the local vicinity of where they were having their picnic on the beach. The internet provided no answers.

His next stop was going to be to property records.

Danielle had convinced him to let her take care of it. She asked him to stand down. He had exhausted every avenue by going over the cases. None of his former colleagues had reached out as requested.

Going stir-crazy made him want to lash out at the first person to look at him sideways. He wasn't stupid. The car across the street followed him. It didn't matter how they found him.

He had to remain calm and pretend he wasn't being tailed by a professional. The person was good. He drove a nondescript dark sedan.

It was hard to spot except for that one broken headlight on the right.

It must have been an oversight and certainly gave him a way to differentiate it from the other vehicles on the street. Biding his time took a lot of patience. He was known to wait for the right time but he had to show some restraint.

He found a table at the back after retrieving his black coffee. He sat down to find a newspaper folded at the corner.

Jack glanced around; however, nobody was showing any signs they had left it for him.

He ripped off the edge where the writing was legible. Directions would lead him to the person who had written the cryptic note. He didn't like scavenger hunts. He hated being led around by the nose.

It could've been the man across the street. That didn't seem likely considering he hadn't moved from his original spot. The vehicle was nestled between two delivery vans. One of them could've been surveillance but he wouldn't know unless he was able to get a look inside.

He not only had the man watching him to worry about but now he was going to have to play a dangerous game. The location written down was a few blocks away. He could make it in plenty of time to make the meeting in less than 30 minutes according to the little clock above the location.

He took the precaution of eating the piece of paper. He washed it down with the caffeine sending a jolt of adrenaline through his body. He flipped through the pages of the newspaper print. He looked for any pertinent information about what was happening back home.

It appeared his story was still getting a few soundbites. A novice journalist had taken an avid interest. She was spouting rhetoric about police brutality running rampant in New York City.

Racial profiling had become big news.

He waited until the afternoon rush hour for dinner to make a strategic move. It wasn't going to be easy to shake his tail. The best way to accomplish any sleight-of-hand was by making the other person see what they wanted to see.

He made his way to the bathroom while eyeing the exit sign at the back.

CHAPTER 52

Danielle worried herself sick about the publicity surrounding her recent detainment. It didn't seem to have any adverse effects on her daughter. She was old enough to understand without having to sugar-coat it.

She paced back and forth with her daughter sitting there and playing with her phone somewhat distracted. The girl giggled while kicking her feet back and forth barely able to touch the floor with her feet.

"Can you please put that down for one minute? I swear you're on that thing every second of every day. We need to have a serious conversation. It can't go any further than this room. You have to promise me. I'm doing my best to treat you like an adult but you're not making it easy," she stated with a wagging finger in her face.

"You have to learn to chill. Take a breath," her daughter placated her.

"I'm sorry. I didn't mean to raise my voice." She took a breath and turned toward the window to see the same damn surveillance van mocking her from across the street.

They would have earned a few brownie points for originality if they had bothered to change the lettering on the van. It had to be somebody beholden to Reeves. That would explain why they were limited to using one van.

"This better be important. The one day I have off and you want to have one of your 'talks'," she said with her two hands making air quotes in the air.

"I hate it when you do that. I think you do it to see how far you can push me. That's not a good idea when I'm this close to losing it," she said with her finger and thumb moved back a fraction of an inch.

Her daughter finally put down the phone long enough to glare at her. "Are you happy? What is so damn important? I already hear the rumors. I'm not the only child of a police officer in school. You more than adequately told me what was going on. What more could you add?"

She had to admit her pride was overflowing. The way she had handled Reeves amazed her. She intimidated him with one look. The man was not comfortable around children.

"I'm making some enemies. You already met the one making all the waves for me at work. He is putting pressure on me. They're using dirty tactics including trying to frame me for drugs found on the premises. They were planted but you already know that. He won't stop there. I just want you to be aware of your surroundings at all times," she said with her hands clasped together.

"What do you think is going to happen to me? It's not like I'm going to be kidnapped for ransom. That only happens in the movies," she answered flippantly.

"This isn't a joke. What you don't know is that there was a bag of the same drugs in your room underneath your mattress next to your diary. He has no problem using you to get to me," Danielle explained.

She kept looking at her watch wondering when the next shift was going to be at the property records office. She knew one by name. He was a timid young man with horn-rimmed glasses and a pocket protector.

Benjamin would be putty in her hand once she laid on the charm.

"You just finished telling me to be on guard and then you look at your watch in the same breath. Do you have some place better to be? I do. Are we finished?" She asked perturbed with her chin touching her chest.

The girl grew up before her eyes.

The way she dressed made her anxious.

The tight black pants and a revealing blue top were the fashion of the day. Everybody wore their sexuality on their sleeves practically calling attention to their bodies.

Her mother would've grabbed her by the ear if she had attempted to walk out of the house wearing something like that back in the day.

"As a matter of fact, I do have a pressing engagement. Take this. Use this button if you ever feel threatened. It is a high decibel personal alarm. Wear it around your neck. It is quite fashionable with a small dog engraved on the device. The button on the back has to be pressed for more than five seconds to activate it," she said while showing her the small locket capable of rendering a man speechless and on his knees clutching his ears.

Her daughter took the device and put it around her neck. "It's nice. I have better stuff in my jewellery box upstairs. You have nothing to worry about. I know that's not going to stop you from calling me every chance you get."

Danielle grabbed her and hugged her with all of her might. The girl struggled, but she didn't want to let go until the last possible second. It did give her some peace of mind to know she could use the device.

"I know. You did teach me a few basic moves to defend myself. That was what you were going to mention. It's almost as if I can read your mind. Speaking of which. Don't bother trying to crack into my diary. I don't use it. I haven't since I was five," she said before bounding out of the house while struggling with her jacket on the way out.

She wanted to follow from a discrete distance to make sure nobody thought it was a good idea to go after her daughter. She had to trust it wasn't going to be an issue.

The clock chimed noon. The young man at the records office would be there having lunch as usual.

He brought it with him in a plain brown bag. He was probably a virgin, but she wasn't going to make assumptions.

*****

Anderson stood in the alley with his back against the brick wall. His informant was late, but he was never the most punctual person in his Rolodex. He had to convince the kid to do something illegal without getting caught.

The trashcan in front of him was overflowing with leftover cartons of fast food.

Three cats were fighting over the scraps. It looked like the black one had become the alpha of the group. He swiped his claws back and forth to keep them from getting any closer.

It was interesting to see their dynamic. He enjoyed the nature channel. It was not something he advertised to his friends on the force. They were always talking about baseball games or hockey games.

He would nod along with no idea which player pitched and which player stood in front of a net trying to block a rubber puck from getting in.

Anderson tried his damnedest to fit in. Most people would consider him to be Metro-sexual. He liked to dress to impress and enjoyed testing the fragrances of colognes in the department store. He loved lavender and so did the ladies.

Somebody cleared their throat, and he looked to see a young man with dirty blond hair.

He wore a dark hooded sweatshirt with no discernible logo on either side. The baggy jeans looked like they were going to fall off. He constantly pulled them back up over his slim almost non-existent hips.

"You're late. The day you are early, I'm probably going to have a heart attack," Anderson jested.

The man looked around nervously fidgeting with his cuffs. "I can't just drop everything and come running whenever you call. This has got to stop."

"We could always revisit the drug possession. I'm sure your mother would be very proud to learn you are following in your older brother's footsteps. Let's skip puffing your chest and get down to business," Anderson enforced while showing him the handcuffs attached to his belt.

"You've made yourself very clear. What do you want this time? I don't know anything about a shipment of pure heroin," he stated with a deep breath.

"I never mentioned anything about a shipment. You obviously know something. Nobody will ever know you told me. Tell me. I know you're dying to," Anderson pressed almost forgetting about the reason why he had called him.

"I shouldn't be doing this. I'm not a snitch. You look pretty damn happy. You really like putting the screws to me. The meeting is at midnight." He grabbed Anderson's hand and scribbled down the address on his palm in blue ink.

New York was a port city with many deliveries from around the globe including those that were not considered legal. Pure heroin would be a catastrophe. It would most likely be cut with Fentanyl to make it more addictive to the first-time buyer.

"I almost forgot the reason why I called you. Do you see the expensive car across the street? You can't miss it," he said with a pointed thumb over his shoulder.

The kid took a cursory look and nodded his head. "What about it? Don't tell me you brought me down here to brag about buying a sports car. That is the dictionary meaning of a midlife crisis."

"It's not mine. I want you to break into it. Steal whatever you can get your hands on but make sure you break the window. Don't stick around. This should be right up your alley if you pardon the pun," he referred to where they were standing next to a pack of cats still fighting for the leftover lasagne in one of the cartons.

"Let me get this straight. You catch me with a dime bag about a year ago. I remember you stressing the importance of cleaning up my act. Now you want me to vandalize a car in broad daylight where anybody can see me. Why didn't you say so?" He asked with a grin before producing a black bar from underneath the sweater.

"I don't even want to know why you have that. Make it noisy. The alarm has to go off. I can't stress that enough. Do this for me and you will be one step closer to having your life back," he lied already knowing the kid was going to be a font of information going forward.

He had saved him from becoming just another statistic. The only thing he asked was to keep his eyes and ears open. It was nice to have the inside track, but he was very careful to keep his informant from becoming a footnote in history.

"Let's just say somebody else rubbed me the wrong way. It's not anything he can't afford. It made me feel better. This is going to be fun. It makes up for giving you the information about the shipment. That bust is going to cause a lot of trouble for a lot of people," he mentioned while palming the black metal bar.

Anderson took one final look at where the shipment was going to come in. He had just enough time to organize a raid. The boys in the drug enforcement division were going to shit themselves when he gave them the information to break the heroin trade wide open.

He walked across the street with his head turning from side to side to make sure he wasn't going to become somebody's hood ornament.

He just had to wait for his informant to do what he promised.

CHAPTER 53

Jack watched the reflection of the glass in several different stores on his way to the meeting.

He had no idea what was waiting for him. It could be a trap yet he really didn't have much of a choice. He grasped at straws.

The man following him had gotten out of his car before blending into the crowd. He wasn't fooled when he went to the bathroom and didn't return.

Jack only noticed him by the green shoes on his feet. It appeared he had stepped into some sort of paint making him stand out from the crowd. It made it easier to keep tabs on him.

He weaved through the throngs of people before ditching his jacket when he turned the corner. He rolled up the sleeves of his white shirt and pulled the collar high on his neck.

His gait changed to somewhat of a shuffle no longer in the same posture with his back bent and his shoulders slouched.

He went around another corner and grabbed a jacket lying on a bench. The owner was arguing with a black man about a woman named Desiree. He put on the Brown bomber jacket and placed his hands in the pockets.

The final piece of the puzzle came with a green English cap from an old man busily wiping his glasses while waiting for the bus.

The disguise probably wouldn't trick him for long. It didn't have to.

He just had to keep moving while casually looking over his shoulder. His adrenaline pumped through his veins in no small part to the caffeine. The excitement of staying one step ahead of his adversary made it a game in his eyes.

He ducked down a side road and came out on the other side. He didn't bother waiting for the light to change. He made sure the coast was clear before advancing across oncoming traffic.

"You have to get up pretty early in the morning to follow me. I was trained by the best in the art of counter-surveillance. I've already done the important part. I no longer look like the subject you are looking for," he whispered to himself in a type of pep talk.

It was something that his coaches gave him when he was rattled on the field.

Rugby was a man sport. There was no padding. The danger of getting hurt was real.

He had broken a few bones but had returned the favor twice over. His mother screamed when he came home with a broken nose or limping.

She couldn't understand why he was smiling with blood coating his teeth. He had made his bones with his teammates. Being one of the younger ones and a little smaller gave them a license to try to hurt him.

He showed his courage several times under fire. The game toughened him up and gave him a thick skin.

He enjoyed the competitive nature of the sport. It prepared him for life with his body transforming into something the girls were now taking a second glance at.

He heard the honking, and it brought him back to the present. He slapped his hand down on the hood of a Lincoln Continental completely black with tinted windows. The owner must've thought he was important enough to warrant anonymity.

It was out of place in a small town. He must have been compensating for something lacking.

He got to the next block and stopped next to a display of suits in a window. It made him look like he was doing a little window shopping. He checked out his surroundings without being too obvious.

The hat was tight, and he had lowered it almost until it was over his eyes.

The man had got lost in the shuffle. The town was small. The location of the meeting was a few blocks away. It made him anxious but also hesitant. He didn't want to make the same mistake he had made with Ms. Fletcher by underestimating his opponent.

Nobody was looking around frantically trying to find him. The man had probably given up. Giving him the slip gave Jack a reason to smile. He had been to several crime scenes and had taken down suspects with extreme prejudice.

Being proactive sent a jolt of electricity through his body. He walked slowly down the sidewalk. A man washed the front entrance of his shop with a hose. A dog was tied up to a fire hydrant. It was one of those huskies with two different colored eyes.

Jack hadn't had a chance to explore the town. He came in for provisions and left shortly after. This was the America he knew and loved. People worked hard in their jobs and enjoyed several pastimes including going on annual vacations.

He envied their carefree lifestyle.

Having a family made him understand the importance of keeping them safe. He received word from them through the anonymous email of a Gmail account. They were understandably upset, but they knew how important it was for them to remain hidden for as long as it took to bring closure to the case.

He found the place after circling around to make sure there were no unwanted pests. He didn't want to show his hand.

He backtracked several times until he was certain the man following him had no idea where he was.

The place for the meeting was a building with a brick exterior and three names on the plaque on the door. They were all lawyers paid extremely well for their discretion. One name stood out from the rest.

He ran his finger over to make sure he wasn't hallucinating.

Palmer and Associates.

*****

Danielle attempted flattery with the young man behind the desk. He blushed fiercely and tried to look away. She made it difficult for him when she wore her sexuality in white.

The white cashmere sweater with no bra put her assets on full display.

"You have to go through proper channels," he repeated from the rule book.

"Are you sure that I can't take a teensy little look at the books?" Danielle asked with the point of her manicured nail sliding along his index finger.

He looked behind him to see if anybody noticed the shameless flirting going on between them.

Danielle moved closer until she leaned over the desk to give him a better view. His eyes widened, and he shifted nervously in the high-backed metal chair.

"You don't play fair," he protested.

"All's fair in love and war," she said with just the tip of her tongue sweeping across her lips.

"I can give you a few minutes. You'll find what you're looking for upstairs in the archives. The homes you mentioned are classified," Benjamin whispered with his hand up to his mouth in the hopes he wasn't going to be overheard.

"This would go a lot faster with your help. Do you think that I can pull you away from the desk for a few minutes to give me a hand?" She asked with a seductive drawl to her request.

"I don't see why that would be a problem. There's nobody here. They went out to lunch. Let me put the sign on the door indicating that I will be back in 15 minutes. That should give us plenty of time to track down the owners of those homes. It's all a shell game," he said enthused about helping a police officer in the course of her duties.

It didn't hurt for her to look like a wet dream come true in his eyes.

He walked ahead of her and she stayed a few steps behind to make sure nobody was going to interrupt them. He used a jangle of keys until he found the right one for the door in question upstairs.

It wasn't locked and opened before he even gave it a good turn. It didn't look like anybody had been there in weeks. A fresh layer of dust covered everything.

Danielle coughed into her hand seized by the airborne allergies floating around. She hadn't felt that way since she was a kid.

"I believe those records are around here somewhere. I just did the inventory the other day and I recall a file folder lost behind one of the cabinets. There it is. Just where I left it. You have less than 10 minutes," he said before backing away to give her room to breathe.

The room was dusty, but the table was immaculate. Three chairs were arranged around it tucked in to preserve the space needed for people to get around.

She sat down with several files dedicated to those with more money than brains. They made sure to have their assets hidden by using company names instead of their birth names.

She brought out the black book and began to write down the business names associated with those properties. It took her a few moments to get acclimated. She found the three properties using the local area as a starting point.

Jack had pointed her in the right direction.

The kid left her alone while she poured over the documents completely engrossed. It took her a few minutes to realize the kid hadn't returned. 50 minutes had gone by.

There was no noise out in the hallway. She strained to listen but could only ascertain something scraping on the floor outside the door. A shadow could be seen standing motionless.

Somebody out there was making her skin crawl.

She had her police-issued weapon. She released it from the holster and had her hand on the handle.

The small comfort made her breathe easier. She fingered the weapon and prepared herself for a possible confrontation with somebody that wasn't too keen on her learning the identity of the people in possession of those homes.

She pushed away from the table without scratching the legs against the floor. She held the gun while studying it intently. It laid on the table pointing at the door.

She didn't want to use a weapon violently to take somebody's life.

The shadow stood there before the door handle began to jiggle. It moved back and forth. There was no lock impeding their progress. They could've easily come in to confront her but they were purposely trying to get a rise out of her.

The time to panic had come and gone. She had no way of knowing what happened to the kid. Did her research get him killed? She hoped for the best but prepared herself for the worst.

Danielle didn't approach the door and stayed well away to give her more than ample opportunity to send a message of her own. The gun felt heavy in her hands. She couldn't remember the last time she had fired the weapon outside of the targeting range.

The lights flickered and went off.

CHAPTER 54

Jack took a look around to make sure he wasn't walking into a trap set by none other than Reeves. He really did want to make an example out of him for others to live by.

What he had done still made him shake his head. The press was there to record his shameful display. The woman was capable of getting him hot under the collar until he said something he was going to regret.

Her outburst about police brutality gave the press and the public something to feed on. They rallied around Ms. Fletcher, believing that she was the injured party. They couldn't know she was a Machiavellian genius.

He came around to the front and looked at the double black doors. He checked and found it unlocked. He opened the door gingerly. His hand touched his hip where there should've been a gun. He blindly went inside without a weapon to defend himself.

He looked back over his shoulder before entering. It had the similar fragrance of an old courtroom. The clock on the top remained still. It probably hadn't functioned in quite some time.

It was a unique feature, and preserving it was important to the townsfolk.

He stopped with his foot poised to climb to the next level. A door opened, and a man stood there wearing dark suspenders and a white shirt. There was no tie.

"You're right on time, Detective Creed. Actually, you are a little late but I guess I can understand you need to take precautions after everything you're been through. It doesn't look like you are armed. The metal detector would have gone off if that were the case. My name is Patrick Peters. I'm one of the associates." He backed into the doorway and disappeared.

Jack had never felt more perplexed in his life. He could've walked away, but it wasn't in his nature to shy away from the unknown.

He climbed the stairs, using the black metal railing to navigate the steep steps one at a time. He kept looking over his shoulder to make sure nobody caught him unaware.

It would've been nice to have a weapon, but they would have detected it the moment he entered. He would've been asked to relinquish it, and he wasn't sure that he could do that without feeling vulnerable.

The door at the top opened into an office space. The architecture was from a time long ago when things were simple. The preservation necessary to keep the original design must've been a painstaking effort.

There was a desk.

It was something of an antique sitting at the front when he turned the corner. A woman dressed in a dark blazer and a quite fetching yellow canary blouse spoke quietly into a microphone attached to her ear.

She didn't even bother to introduce herself and continued with her conversation as if he wasn't standing there waiting to be noticed. He gave her a careful once over before continuing down the hall.

The doors were closed except for one at the very end. He held his breath and slowly pushed the door open with his foot.

The man he had seen at the top of the stairs stood at the window overlooking the courtyard. It was a panoramic view of a pavilion. It looked like a stage had been erected in the centre, most likely to incorporate local bands in the area.

The place had all the charm of old school meeting new school.

"There used to be a swimming pool there before it was relocated. There was a time when gasoline didn't cost an arm and a leg. You could get candy for a penny from a local vendor peddling his wares. I imagine a man selling candy out of his home to children wouldn't look very good these days," the man stated with his hands behind his back.

"Forgive me, but I fail to understand what this has to do with me. I gather someone from this office proffered the invitation to come here. I'm at a loss for the reason, but I'm more than a little curious," Jack said quizzically.

"It's really something when you think about it. Time continues to be the one constant in our lives we can't control. That and death and taxes. We see the advancement of technology all around us. The town isn't what it used to be, but it has grown to become a mecca for young urban professionals looking to settle down with a family and a white picket fence in the yard," the man continued without addressing Jack.

"Am I missing something? You didn't bring me here to talk about urban development. What exactly is this about and why should I give a damn?" Jack said with a bit more force than necessary.

Peters watched his childhood and smiled despite the interruption from going down memory lane. He lived in the town for most of his life. He left primarily to get a better education, but came back to put his shingle on the door.

"What do you see out there, Jack? I'll tell you what I see. Economy getting a boost from those with money to burn. Real estate is at an all-time premium for those that can afford it. You and I are the last of a dying breed. We see things differently," Peters enthused, with a hand touching the glass.

"This is getting old quickly. I'm a police detective with the New York City Police Department," he announced when his blood ran cold at the mere presence of somebody behind him.

*****

Anderson sat at his desk doing his job. The cases were getting cold with every passing second. He'd already compiled a few leads.

The one domestic call resulting in the death of the woman could easily lead back to the disgruntled husband after he lost his job.

He claimed to be innocent, but he was covered in her blood and holding the knife when they found him at the scene, begging for somebody to save her life. It was an argument that got out of hand and turned deadly in a hurry, to the chagrin of their nosy neighbors.

Anderson looked at the clock to see that 15 minutes had gone by since he had met his informant. It was just like him to wait. He probably enjoyed making him sweat a little.

It did give him time to contact the drug enforcement agency.

They were appreciative of the tip and agreed for him to join them on the raid as a courtesy. He would be mentioned in the official report and take centre stage to answer any questions when everything was said and done.

It would be a real shot in his arm to be recognized again for his professionalism and ability to come up with information nobody else had. He did know how to cultivate sources better than most, thanks to his father.

Anderson exploited witnesses for his own gain. The game had different rules, but he was playing in a different league.

He had a few interviews to conduct before he was able to put some of the cases to bed. It would be easy to close one. It was a suicide, plain and simple. There was no sign of foul play.

He worked tirelessly for another hour, vaguely aware of people coming and going. Nobody stopped to talk to him. They were most likely bitter about his promotion. He didn't let that bother him when he knew he deserved the accolades.

He jumped back when several more folders dropped on his desk. "he said to give them to you. Don't kill the messenger." The officer backed away with his hands in plain sight.

Anderson understood immediately how vindictive Reeves could be. He had made the mistake of speaking his mind. He blamed Christine. She made him a better man, no longer in a position of taking crap off of anybody.

The three files on his desk would need to be solved in triplicate. The red tape drowned him in indecision.

He wanted to wipe the smug look off of his face. The idea of being the one to hold the Damocles sword swinging over his head made him smile.

His informant took his sweet time.

Benjamin could've easily been lost in the shuffle with other inner-city kids. His mother convinced him to give the kid another chance. She was so damn nice and offered him a piece of cake. He couldn't bring himself to lay any charges against Benjamin.

He did wonder if the child's mother would understand. He didn't exactly reveal her little boy was an informant. The kid was crafty and could easily blend into any conversation without them even being aware he was there.

That had to be his superpower.

Becoming wallpaper didn't sound like much, but it did give him the inside track.

Anderson used it to selfishly promote himself. Finding the information about the kidnapping came courtesy of his informant.

He made some physical notations in the pen before scratching them out. One particularly unnerving case had him going over the evidence, scrutinizing every detail until he came to one painful conclusion. There was no clear-cut perpetrator in the crime.

The alarm went off out front.

It took less than five seconds for Reeves to come out holding on to the key to his prized possession. He ran past without even looking at him.

A sideways glance confirmed the door was open, and he had left his briefcase behind.

Anderson carefully pushed the chair away from the desk. He stood up and looked at the other officers in the bullpen.

They weren't looking at him.

CHAPTER 55

Danielle seized the moment to think about her daughter and what would happen to her if something happened to her. She didn't want to think about that and put it away for a rainy day when she could come up with a few emergency contact names.

The emergency lighting did very little to lighten her mood.

The door opened a crack with a black-gloved hand appearing in the crack of the door.

She acted on instinct when she jumped over the table and slid across the surface. She landed on her feet with her foot extended until she jammed the hand in between the door hard enough to make the damage quite extensive.

She pressed her shoulder against the door. Those fingers wiggled and somebody was grunting, but she didn't recognize the voice.

"You are one cold-hearted bitch," somebody whispered in pain.

"Give me one good reason why I shouldn't arrest you," she pressed.

"I have information pertinent to your case," he said with a grimace.

"That doesn't explain why the lights went out. Do you want to be seen as some sort of Deep Throat? I'm not at liberty to give you immunity." She grabbed the gloved hand and pulled it free to see an ornate ring adorning one of the fingers.

The class ring could easily be seen with the help of the emergency lighting.

"I had a feeling you were going to say that. I don't want to get involved in matters above my pay grade. Could you ease off a little? I think you might've broken my wrist," he protested, with his fingers moving a little.

She lessened the pressure on the door just a little. "Tell me what this is about."

"I think you already know. Do you think you're the only one targeted by Miss Fletcher? There is a list as long as my arm. We all want to see her pay," he said, using the plural form of the word.

"What is this, some sort of club I don't know about? If there is, I would gladly pay the dues," she joked.

"There are a select few of us. We've been watching and waiting. She hasn't made a mistake, but it's just a matter of time. The one thing you should never do is turn your back on her. She will have no problem stabbing you repeatedly without mercy until you are begging at her feet to stop. Metaphorically speaking," the man grunted and was able to pull his hand out from where she had it pinned.

She opened it but could barely make out his face. It took a moment to register. He had a Nixon mask to hide his features. The temptation to take it off of his face was almost too much for her to bear.

"You don't have to worry about your daughter. I have somebody trailing her discreetly. It's not the first time Miss Fletcher has used children to get what she wants and it won't be the last. You did the right thing by giving her the device. We just don't like to take chances," he said before stepping back with his gloved left hand, massaging the one revealing the Harvard class ring of 69.

"What do you know about my daughter? How could you possibly know about the device? Answer my questions and maybe I will show you some leniency," Danielle interrogated with her hands, taking a hold of his lapels.

"Easy there, Detective. I'm on your side. We know a lot about you. We make it our business to know those we might consider an ally against Ms. Fletcher. Damn, that hurt," he groaned when he touched his wrist with his thumb.

"Stop being a baby. You're lucky I didn't shoot you between the eyes. I would say it's a good day when you don't find yourself on a slab in the morgue with a toe tag affixed to your feet." she stood back and leveled the gun until he raised his hands.

"As I said, we are on your side. We might've gotten off on the wrong foot," the man stated, with Nixon looking back and forth down the hallway.

"What happened to the kid at the desk? You better not have hurt him," Danielle addressed.

"Perish the thought. He's going to wake up with a headache. That happens when you use a little too much chloroform. We are pacifists working behind the scenes to shine a light on her activities. We almost had her a month ago," he said with his back against the wall.

She slammed him heavily against the white brick exterior. He was dressed entirely in black.

"What happened?" She asked with her curiosity prickling.

"She found a way to make all the evidence disappear against her again. We are patient, but we have grown tired of the chase. We heard about you and Detective Creed through the unofficial grapevine. We have a network dedicated to bringing her down, but we refuse to be one of her victims. She already cost us more than you are privy to," he sighed deeply with his hot breath curling her nose in the scent of overpowering garlic.

"Jesus Christ, take a breath mint. You could melt wallpaper," she said while fanning her face.

"That's the garlic fingers talking back. It's delicious but comes at a cost. It is a good thing I'm not dating anybody regularly. Can we dispense with all of this? Don't ask me to take off the mask. I have a reputation to uphold. Nobody can know I'm involved," he stressed, with his hand digging into his pocket until he came out with a key.

"What's that for?" She asked with her hand extended palm up.

He dropped it in her hand. "I think it belongs to a safe deposit box under her married name of Palmer. We can't get a look at it, but maybe you can. This is where you can reach us. Type in the website and log in under Ms. Fletcher sucks." He said with one hand, offering her a card with a black snake embossed on the front.

"I don't like talking to faceless people. It makes you look like a coward. Don't you think it's time for you to stop hiding behind Nixon?" she blasted with the gun down by her side, still with the safety off.

"I suppose you're right. We can't let her have all the power," he answered before taking off the mask to reveal the face behind it.

The shock radiated through her face.

*****

Jack narrowed his eyes with his body tense.

"I would like you to meet John Palmer. He came here in hopes of meeting you. It was only fair, considering you have been looking for him. He called me and paid me extremely well to bring you here without anybody knowing," Peter said.

"You really don't know how to take no for an answer. My secretary was somewhat concerned for my safety. Let's get down to brass tacks. What does this have to do with my wife?" John mentioned from behind him.

A slight nudge made him move out of the way. The man was shockingly gray to the roots. John wore his wealth with his clothing and jewellery, including a $4000 watch. The Rolex logo was proudly displayed when he purposely showed him.

"You are a hard man to track down. I have one important question before we begin. Why did you secretly marry? There was only a small article dedicated to it before it got lost in the funny pages," Jack said.

"I'm not sure why that is any of your business. I'll play along. It wasn't my idea. I wanted to shout it from the rooftops, but she begged me to keep it as quiet as possible. I got ahead of it by calling a friend at the post. He buried the headline at my request," John said before sitting down with his leg crossed over the other.

He motioned Jack to take the other seat at the front of the desk, where Peters was still standing at the window, looking at the scenery.

"You haven't even spent that much time together since the wedding. You don't live together. The lifestyle you lead isn't conducive to a happy relationship. The private plane is always on the go, never staying in one place for too long," Jack rattled on until he was comfortably sitting in a chair made of the softest Corinthian leather money could buy.

"You've done your homework, but so have I. You have a grudge against my wife. She is an acquired taste. I have to admit there is some merit to what you say. We have what is described in the lifestyle as an open relationship. I have other lovers in a variety of different ports around the globe. She's the only one that demanded a ring on her finger," he stated while toying with the Rolex until he was making it glitter in the fluorescent light above them.

"You're not exactly an open book. Why would you agree to marry her on paper? Don't you know that gives her access to all of your money?" he stopped when John raised a hand to object.

"All the money that she knows about. I haven't gotten where I am today by leaving anything to chance. She refused to sign a prenuptial agreement. If she is plotting to kill me without my knowledge, then that's news to me," he said with a wave of his hand.

"I'm guessing from your reference you know about her other two husbands. Doesn't that at least concern you a little? I know I would be keeping one eye open and a baseball bat beside the bed," Jack inferred.

"You're a funny guy, Jack. We hardly see each other. You don't want to mess with her. Keeping her happy is a full-time job, but not even I can do the impossible. There is no doubt in my mind she's capable of everything you have accused her of. I think I might like the bad girl," he snickered until he was coughing up blood.

Jack took note of the way that he tried to cover it up with a monogrammed handkerchief.

CHAPTER 56

Anderson knew the window of opportunity was going to close fast.

He silently approached the door with some trepidation. The alarm was very loud. It had attracted the attention of those at their desks. Nobody seemed to notice him at all, which was exactly the way he wanted it.

The light was still on. It made it easier for him to make his way to the desk.

He lifted the briefcase and fiddled with the lock. He thought turning the dial to zero would do the trick.

It didn't.

He kept listening, but nobody interrupted him. He found a paperclip and understood the mechanics of the briefcase better than most.

His father used to have one similar. It took some trial and error to get inside with those grisly photos, making him regret seeing it up close and personal.

His father was notorious for bringing his work home at night, never leaving it at the office where it belonged. That was a contention between him and his wife. Arguments ensued when she found him in his office.

He angled the paperclip in a certain way by bending it. His tongue stuck out of his mouth while he concentrated on the task at hand. He finally heard the distinguishable click.

He placed the case gingerly on the edge of the desk while holding his breath. He opened it to find a pack of nicotine gum in one of the slots. He moved his fingers through the papers without disturbing anything.

He didn't want Reeves to know somebody had invaded his personal space.

Nothing could be found incriminating against him. It could be he had it safely tucked away some place else. He almost gave up when he noticed a small flap with a Velcro enclosure.

He pulled it back slowly with the fabric of the Velcro ripping. He ground his teeth together. Nobody came to investigate.

The photos were somewhat disturbing from a layman's point of view. He had seen worse but never imagined in his wildest nightmares this was what his so-called superior was into behind closed doors.

The whips and chains were nothing compared to the baby scenario. The embarrassment would make him a laughingstock in the Department. He would lose all credibility and nobody would ever take him seriously again.

He should've been more careful. It was one thing to enact a fantasy, but another thing to have photographic evidence lying around.

He remembered some of his reckless encounters and shook his head at the memory.

He took a few photos and took them over to the copier machine. It came to life with the press of a button. He made copies of all the photos. He absconded with one negative. It would prove none of the photos were doctored.

He returned them to exactly where they were. He closed the Velcro enclosure. He snapped it shut and then placed it where it was next to the desk.

He walked out to find Christine at his desk, tapping one of his pencils. "I hope I'm not disturbing you. I figured I would take the initiative and come over to invite you to lunch. Everybody has to eat."

"That was very kind of you. Let's go this way." He motioned with his hand for her to follow him down the hallway to the red-painted exit door.

They stepped out in time to see Reeves chasing his informant.

"What's that all about?" She asked nervously, tugging at the hem of her skirt.

He noticed immediately how she was trying to get his undivided attention.

"I don't have the foggiest idea," he said before escorting her to the other side of the street.

They stood together with her arms wrapped around his waist. He had learned about her fascination with Mexican cuisine during their last date. He didn't worry about his informant. The kid was fast and resourceful.

"You remembered. That is so sweet," she said with a pointed finger while bouncing up and down on her heels enthusiastically.

"It's not a big deal." Anderson worked his way down the menu until he found a certain item to strike his fancy.

"It is a big deal. Don't sell yourself so short. A man that listens is a keeper. That's what my mother says every time I come over for Sunday dinner. I think she'll like you, but I don't want to put any pressure on you," she said, still vibrating with her eyes drawn to a fish taco with special seasoning.

"Why would I feel any pressure? Just because you came down to my work and dragged me away from my desk. How should I take that?" He said nervously, biting his cuticle.

"Wait a minute. Hold your horses. I didn't come down here to ambush you. This isn't a social call. I'm sorry you got the wrong impression. This isn't me stalking you," she said with her ire raised.

He found it hard to believe her until she fished around in her handbag for something hidden within.

*****

The coughing fit lasted more than a minute, with Peters gently patting his back. It dawned on Jack that maybe his condition could have something to do with the black widow.

"You're dying, but I think you only know that. I'm betting your new bride understands that you have 1 foot in the grave and the other one on a banana peel. She's waiting for you to kick the bucket." Jack grabbed a stapler and threw it at the wall in frustration.

"You don't know what you're talking about," John protested with a dab of his napkin to the small drop of blood on the corner of his mouth.

"I think I do," Jack responded.

"She didn't know about my condition when we first met. It was at one of those boring functions. She caught my eye from across the room and the rest is history," John sighed and fell back in his chair with his ribs aching.

Jack slapped his hands together. "You've got to be kidding me. She probably orchestrated the meeting. This time, she doesn't have to do a damn thing. Waiting to see you take your last breath must be killing her inside. How long did they give you?"

"I have six months, but I've been taking experimental treatments. It's the reason why I have been spending a lot of time in Europe. They say the treatments have not been tested on humans. The trials are promising. They expect to prolong my life by five years and they say that's conservative. It's good enough for me," he stated.

"Can I be there when you tell her? I want to see the change in her demeanor. Forget I said that. Don't tell her a damn thing. You don't have to believe me, but the moment you utter anything relating to prolonging your condition is when you are going to sign your death certificate. There is a way to prove me wrong," Jack hinted.

John put his handkerchief back in his pocket, stained with his own blood. "I've always been a betting man. What are you proposing?"

"You also have your doubts about her. We can put all of this behind us with one simple test. Tell her about the experimental treatments and see how she reacts. She might not be too obvious. That's fine. You'll be the bait and I will be there with the handcuffs when she finally shows her true colors. If I'm wrong, I will eat my hat with a nice Chardonnay," he joked.

"That gives me a good idea. I'm willing to play along. You might be right, but you might be wrong. I can have the house equipped with monitors and cameras, unbeknownst to my blushing bride. We can watch her every move. We can finally dispense with this notion she is some sort of black widow. The only question that remains is what I'm going to get when you lose this little wager?" John pondered while stroking the black shadow of his moustache.

"What do you want? Name your price." Jack regretted saying it the moment it came out of his mouth, but there was no taking it back.

"I'm taking a huge risk by putting my head on a chopping block. If you lose, I take everything you own. That includes prized mementos and things that you consider priceless. You will be penniless without a pot to piss in. What do you say? Are you a gambling man, Detective Creed?" John asked with the expectation he was going to back down.

Jack thought long and hard before he decided to leap off the cliff without a parachute. "Draw up the papers and make it official. Isn't it fortuitous we have a lawyer present? It couldn't have worked out better even if I planned it. You have yourself a bet."

CHAPTER 57

It took Danielle a few seconds to adjust. She was looking at a ghost. The theatrics behind the scenes had to have cost a fortune.

"You're going to have to start at the beginning. This is just freaky," Danielle reached out with a hand to make sure what she was seeing wasn't some sort of optical illusion.

She almost jumped back when she felt the warmth of his cheek against her fingers.

Chase Adams was alive.

She remembered with explicit clarity the production inside the café. The question that remained was why he had gone to the extreme of faking his death.

"I made the mistake of crossing Kellie Fletcher. She didn't like me poking around in her past. The woman is certifiably insane. She finds a weakness and pulls on that thread until the entire story unravels. It was my bad luck to push her into a corner. You know what they say about an animal with nothing to lose?" Chase sighed deeply with the mask hanging from his fingertips.

"This better be legit. You're not exactly unbiased." She waved at the flash drive.

"You don't understand," he said before turning his back with the mask falling from his fingers to the floor.

"Make me understand," she pressed for more details.

"That woman took everything from me, including my best friend. His death was suspicious, but nobody could put two and two together. She was that good at covering up her tracks, but I don't think I have to tell you that." He plucked a cigarette from his pocket and placed it between his lips without lighting the tip.

"Let me guess. You're trying to quit cold turkey. I can tell you from experience it doesn't work," Danielle recalled her own addiction when it came to nicotine and the sweet sensation of drawing the smoke into her lungs and back out again.

She lived vicariously through others by placing herself in situations where smokers congregated. It usually meant spending time outdoors next to office buildings and restaurants.

"I have to get this monkey off my back. The one thing good to come out of meeting her was the need to better myself. I'm not proud of some of the things I've done to get ahead in life. It usually didn't bother me until the shoe was on the other foot," he expressed with his eyes staring right through her.

"Snap out of it." She snapped her fingers to see him blink her back into focus.

Chase looked around nervously with the cigarette still dangling from his lips. "The only way to stop her was to fake by death. The plan was already in the works long before you contacted me. I figured I could kill two birds with one stone. Give you just enough information to go after her and then make it plausible by having you as a witness to my demise. It couldn't have worked out better."

"I have to admit, it was pretty convincing. The paramedics were a nice touch. One of them probably gave you something to slow down your heartbeat. I was at a huge risk. I understand why you had to do it. What did she have on you and don't tell me nothing?" She asked with the flash drive creating an indentation in her hand.

"She wanted me to back off. When I refused, things got a little dicey. My wife left me when photographs showed up of an extramarital affair I didn't have with a man. There was no way to reason with her when the photographic evidence spoke volumes. Then I lost the backing for a huge investment. It left me scrambling to get out from underneath the debt. Let's just say my death solved a lot of problems for me." He held the cigarette and moved it away from his mouth.

He let out air as if he was actually enjoying a puff.

"The group you got involved with is very interesting. You all have one thing in common. A deep-seated hatred for Ms.

Fletcher. She had to know one day somebody was going to fight back. I'm glad to be a small part of this unusual fan club," she said with a smile.

"Where do we go from here? Faking my death is a crime. I wouldn't last very long in jail. I would be considered fresh meat. I don't even have calluses on my hands," he said with one hand moving in the air to prove his point.

She pointed the flash drive at him with a grin stretching across her face. "I'm not interested in you. This thing is bigger than both of us. She has ruined many lives. It's time for all of us to pool our resources. What are you going to do now that you are free of her?"

"I'm going to wait until she is behind bars. My plan is to find someplace where nobody knows my name and start over from scratch. The group will help fund my new enterprise for a piece of the profits. They will be my silent investors. Each one brings a different skill to the group. We expect big things from you. The noose is closing around her neck," Chase mentioned with his eyes lighting up like the Fourth of July.

"I'll be in touch. Don't leave town. This thing with her isn't over. She hasn't made any mistakes. It's her arrogance that is going to trip her up. This will hopefully fill in the blanks," she said before she pocketed the flash drive somewhat anxious to get a look at it.

She turned around to find him gone. She didn't even hear him leave.

*****

They were locked and loaded ready to storm the metaphorical castle of steel and girders. Each one wore a bulletproof vest along with the insignia of the DEA stencilled on the blue windbreaker.

"It looks like the gang's all here. They are just unloading the shipment. We've already arrested the guard on duty at the gate. She was very chatty when we got him into a vacant room with threats of incarceration. We know exactly when they are going to leave. A few of my men are slowly taking out those individuals hiding while they unload the shipment." Agent Trevino said with 1 foot on a suspect lying on the ground unconscious handcuffed and gagged.

"I'm grateful you allowed me to tag along. It was after all my tip that led you to the biggest bust of your career. This will help me. The only thing I asked was to make the announcement. Most of the credit will go to you. It benefits us both," Anderson said with his gun drawn and the safety off with a flick of his thumb.

"Don't go getting carried away. We've been monitoring these people for quite some time without your help. They keep moving the location of the shipment at the last minute. Let's do this thing. Stay frosty," he said with a raised fist before they moved out in single file around the guard tower to take up their positions.

They could feel the vibration of the truck coming toward the entrance. The big engine under the hood carried millions of dollars of illegal drugs. They no longer had a contingent of soldiers watching their back.

The truck stopped at the gate with the driver behind the wheel somewhat confused with his hands lifted. He got out and approached the gate.

The agents swarmed in and had him on the ground before he was able to utter a word. The others worked seamlessly to pull the passenger out of the truck until he was in a similar position on his back on the pavement.

They surrounded the truck with weapons ready. Those inside under the green flap had no idea what was going on. They found out in a hurry when the agents took them by surprise.

Three trained agents converged.

No shots were reported and there were no injuries during the take-down. The tip provided by Anderson and his informant had prevented unnecessary bloodshed. Nobody lifted a finger in retaliation when they realized the numbers were against them.

"This is only the beginning. We'll get them talking and there's no telling what other players will come out of the woodwork. Deals will be made to get our hands on the bigger fish. You should be proud of yourself. This will prevent thousands of people from overdosing this year alone." Agent Trevino patted him on the back.

"I would like to be there when you question them separately in different rooms. Let me conduct one of the interrogations. That will go a long way to prove to my superiors we can work together when there is a good reason to. We could call it a professional courtesy. We don't cooperate with each other enough. Look what happens when we do," he said with a motion of his hand to those that were being loaded into the back of a van for transport to a local facility in the area.

"You didn't get this information on your own. Those kinds of connections are useful to us. We have an opening in our department. It's a special division of the DEA. We don't have the same red tape as other agencies. I'm usually a good judge of character," agent Trevino said with a small comb he was using to make sure his moustache didn't curl.

"Are you offering me a job?"

"Detective Anderson, I'm offering you career advancement. They don't come around often. We need good people like you in this fight. You'll be my second in command groomed to take over when I retire in one year. What do you say? Are you ready to play in the big leagues?" The agent asked.

"This is happening so fast. I'm not sure what to say. Give me some time to think about it," Anderson proposed.

"I can give you 24 hours. Things move fast around here. I have a raid in Mexico I would love to have you join us. It will bring down a huge cartel but we both know another one will pop up. There is never an end to the drug trade but we chip away hoping that one day the streets will be clean. Make a real difference. You'll finally have a purpose," Trevino suggested.

Anderson was completely floored and couldn't fathom leaving for greener pastures. It was a plum assignment but it would mean being away from the woman he was falling for.

He wanted to believe Christine would be able to handle a long-distance relationship. It would get him out from underneath Reeves. He already had what he needed to back him down. He could easily cut off his balls with one phone call.

It was a phone call he was very excited to make. A piece of her vast network would no longer be there to pull her fat out of the fire. It was nothing more than a Band-Aid solution but would make him feel better to give Reeves a taste of his own medicine.

They packed everything up and it didn't even look like anything had happened when they left. No shots were fired and nobody was being escorted to the hospital under guard.

It was a good day, and it was only going to get better.

CHAPTER 58

Jack had commandeered a surveillance van by calling in a marker. He was always good at making people beholden to him. He couldn't convince anybody to join him when they thought he was on the last leg of his career.

John Palmer had helped significantly. He was about to lower the boom. Jack held back his enthusiasm when he adjusted the cameras previously installed in the past 24 hours.

Every room in the house including the bathroom was being monitored for activity and sound. He had everything he needed at his fingertips. The deal he had made was a small price to pay to finally see all of his hard work pay off.

"She should be here any time. We get together once a month like clockwork. It's an arrangement that works for both of us. I love her but I will never be monogamous. We only get this one life to live. Why should I be tied down to one woman when I can play the field?" John Palmer said holding a glass of cognac and looking into the fire crackling under the mantel of white brick.

"Do you want to go over this one more time?" Jack asked using the toggle to zoom in on the black leather couch connected by sections around a glass coffee table.

"You don't know her like I do. She's misunderstood and damaged. She has shared with me many of her secrets which I'm not at liberty to talk about. She has never confessed to cold-blooded murder. That is a line not even I will cross to get what I want," John Palmer said with his fingers playing along the chilled glass.

The door slammed and Miss Fletcher stepped through the doors looking like she was going to explode.

She didn't even bother to address her husband sitting with his legs crossed on the couch looking relaxed and focused on the fire in front of him.

"I am surrounded by incompetence. Today was not a good day to get out of bed. Everything that could go wrong did go wrong. You don't want to hear about my problems. We only get one day a month to be together. I don't want to be selfish and take away the limited time you have left," she said with her hand behind her.

She unzipped the black leather skirt hugging her hips.

"We have to talk. Sit down with me. I might just have something to brighten up your day," John said with his naivete on display by the way he was anxiously bouncing his right foot up and down.

"I could use some good news right about now." She said with the zipper halfway down before she sat on the couch next to him with her hand on his knee.

"I didn't want to jinx things until I knew something for certain. Money does open doors to research never before completed. It was about finding the right doctor. Nobody has made any advancements concerning the disease ravaging my body until now," he said with a deep breath with his fingers holding the glass tightly.

Jack was watching and listening from a mile down the road where he wasn't going to be spotted. The van wouldn't show up on any requisition order. It was relatively new with that new van smell. It wasn't scheduled to be used until the next week.

He moved closer to the screen and turned up the volume.

"What are you trying to say?" Kellie asked.

"I haven't exactly been honest with you. You know about my illness. It's primarily hereditary. I've been having experimental treatments done for the past little while. They didn't hold out much hope and were surprised by the changes in me." He said before he reached into his pocket to place an unopened bottle of painkillers on the table.

"I'm so happy for you. It must be a load off of your mind that you don't have to continue taking those pills. Pain management is important. You can live the rest of your days without being drugged out of your mind. I never did like that far away look in your eyes," she said with her hand touching his face gently.

"I didn't hold out much hope, but I was willing to pay anything for the chance to live longer than my father. This is big. Life-changing. I no longer have six months to live," John swallowed hard with his head bowed.

"I'm sorry. This is no reason to be sad. You should be celebrating. Let's go upstairs." She reached out to him and held his hand lovingly with one finger moving across the back of his hand.

"I gave you the wrong idea. I didn't mean to give you the impression that I was dying quicker. It's the exact opposite. These tears are not sadness. They are happy tears," he stated when he looked at her in the eyes to see the confusion.

Jack had a ringside seat. He couldn't believe what was going to happen, but it was her reaction to the news that was going to make him smile from ear to ear.

"I'm not sure I understand. I guess I just assumed the treatments had an unusual side effect. I'm grateful you no longer have to pop those pills like skittles. You should be made as comfortable as possible during these last days," Kellie lamented with tears streaming down her face.

"I never want to see you unhappy. It kills me to know that you stuck with me through all of this thinking that I was going to leave you in the next week or two. It's the reason why I reached out to a variety of research and development companies small and large," he said with the underlining meaning of his words slowly sinking in.

"It sounds like you're trying to tell me something important but you don't know how to put it into words. You don't have to worry about me. I knew this day was coming. I have prepared myself as best as anybody can under the circumstances." She moved to her knees with her head in his lap.

He stroked her hair. "I'm still going to die but you're not going to get rid of me that easy. I might not be as healthy as a horse, however, the treatments have prolonged my life," he stopped and waited to see how she was going to respond.

Jack was beside himself with his hands rubbing together. He was as giddy as a schoolgirl on Christmas morning when she went downstairs to open up her presents.

This was going to be his Christmas and birthday, all rolled into one.

*****

Danielle opened the flash drive in her car with the use of her laptop plugged into the cigarette lighter. It was too important to let even a few minutes pass by without learning more about Kellie Fletcher.

She shook her head at how easily Chase Adams had fooled everybody into believing he was dead. That included her. She didn't exactly feel like she had been bamboozled. It was actually clever to be able to work behind the scenes without Ms. Fletcher interfering.

She found several files.

One had digital transactions from several high-profile individuals including the internal affairs investigator. Reeves was a sick puppy with a fetish for baby talk. It was not something she needed to know about him but it certainly explained why he was going out of his way to help Ms. Fletcher.

The same thing could be said for three politicians including the governor.

He appeared to suffer from the affliction of a leather and whip fetish. It involved payments to a high-priced Mistress willing to give him the punishment he deserved while wearing a leather mask during their sessions. It happened in his office.

They were all being blackmailed in one form or another to keep their secrets from becoming public domain. The information on the flash drive was going to save them a helluva lot of legwork. She was just going to have to get in touch with them discreetly to discuss their willingness to testify against their blackmailers.

She was going to need some help to navigate the minefield. They wouldn't want their dirty laundry aired in public. She needed to touch base with Anderson. The best way to attack this thing was from two different angles.

They couldn't afford those with power to exercise their right to talk to a lawyer. It was her guess they would want to keep their secrets close to their vests.

Lawyer and client confidentiality was a hurdle she didn't want to encounter. The best way to avoid the ambulance chasers was to ambush the clients. They could have a civil conversation and maybe come up with a plan of attack for them to get ahead of the accusations of their predilections.

She dialed the number with each digit getting her closer to contacting Anderson. She expected his voicemail but received an unexpected surprise when he answered on the third ring.

"I figured I would be hearing from you sooner than later. We shouldn't talk on the phone. Let's meet up at our usual spot in about an hour. I'm guessing this phone call means you haven't exactly been sitting on your hands." Anderson said with the background noise of some kind of celebration going on.

"What's going on?" she asked when she could specifically hear the sound of champagne flowing freely.

"I'll explain everything when I see you. Let's just say a certain person is in for a rude awakening. You know exactly who I'm talking about without saying her name. We are getting close to the finish line. We can't let our guard down," Anderson replied.

"I don't know if I can wait an hour. We've been a few steps behind her this entire time. This thing has taken on a life of its own. We need to play things very carefully and not jump the gun until we have concrete evidence," Danielle said.

"You took the words right out of my mouth. She has made a laughingstock of the department. We can't let that go unanswered. She is going to pay for her crimes. I have a good feeling but I'm not going to get my hopes up. We should loop him in on the investigation," he referred to Detective Creed without being too obvious.

Danielle disconnected and was drawn back to the folders on the flash drive. She found certain pieces of information including a man by the first name of James. There was no last name.

She didn't know why but the name didn't sound dangerous yet she was consciously looking over her shoulder afraid somebody was watching her.

She had every reason to want to have our eyes in the back of her head.

CHAPTER 59

Kellie Fletcher had fleeced her fair share of extremely rich benefactors over the years. She enjoyed the research before she finally got her hooks into her next victim.

The money was gone to pay for the lifestyle she was accustomed to. Jet setting across the globe and living the life of leisure took an extremely hard toll on the pocketbook.

She lavished herself with riches and spent her vacations in the luxury of a Hawaiian tropical paradise.

She learned a long time ago to enjoy life to the fullest. It didn't stop her from plotting against those that had done her wrong. She squandered her wealth and came back just to find her next fortune by going after those vulnerable to her advances.

It was fortuitous to be in the hospital at the time John Palmer was having a spirited debate with his doctor behind closed doors. He was flamboyant and loud but he had every right to want to scream at the injustice of it all.

She accidentally bumped into him on purpose to strike up a conversation in the hospital cafeteria. It wasn't long before he was inviting her to dinner. Thinking that he was dying made him susceptible to a night of debauchery to leave a smile on both of their faces.

She was brought back to the present when she heard the grandfather clock down the hall chiming 7 o'clock with one bell after the other.

"Did you hear me? That's great news. I'll be able to spend more time with you. Five years doesn't sound like much but it's a lifetime to me. We can do all the things we talked about," John Palmer said enthusiastically.

Kellie had heard every word with her thoughts going back to the days she had targeted him. She wasn't going to have to lift a finger. He was understandably upset when she refused to sign a prenuptial agreement but that didn't stop him from putting a ring on it.

"This is amazing. You really do know how to sweep a girl off of her feet. You must be so happy. It sounds like you have plans for these five years," she said, a little shell-shocked by the news.

"I have been giving it a lot of thought. My relationship with my daughter comes first over everything else. I need to reconcile with her. I haven't been the greatest father but I want to make up for the time wasted. I'm leaving tonight and I want you to come with me to meet her," he said with his hand on her chin.

She looked up at him, completely at a loss for words.

There was no way she could leave when she had too many things going on. Warren was laying the groundwork for his alibi. He was a chessboard pawn in her game and easily sacrificed when the time came.

"The best I can do is join you later. You know how important my humanitarian work is on your behalf. I'll have to start interviewing somebody to take over my job in my absence. I have a couple of candidates in mind," she lied when there was no foundation.

She had taken the money earmarked for the foundation consisting of nothing more than a name on paper and deposited the funds in an undisclosed bank account. The money would be released upon a certain condition.

She was reminded how accidents could happen at any time at any place. It was a known fact bathtubs were dangerous. So many things could go wrong including electronic devices accidentally falling in.

She was ready to put an end to the farce of a marriage to a man she despised. It had always been something in the back of her mind. She had to bide her time, but he was leaving a little earlier than expected.

What she thought was going to be a pleasurable three hours of uninterrupted pleasure was now shaping up to be his imminent demise. She just had to convince him to postpone his trip. A good argument would be undressing before his eyes.

John Palmer watched his wife with his mind focused on the delectable treat being unwrapped.

She took his hand, and he never hesitated to follow her naked form to the stairs leading to the master bedroom where the magic happened.

*****

Jack wasn't expecting the woman he hated to show compassion. He might have been wrong about her, but everything he had learned had led him to the belief she always had something cooking up her sleeve.

The buzzing of his phone made him look at it with one eyebrow raised. It was from Danielle. She was requesting his presence at the disclosed location. There was no way he could leave when he was close to getting everything, he wanted on a silver platter.

He didn't know how she was going to do it but time was of the essence. It couldn't have worked out better. His idea of reconciling with his daughter came out of the blue. He was leaving soon and wasn't leaving anything to chance.

His invitation for her to join him to get to know his daughter made him punch his fist in frustration.

John Palmer wasn't following the script they had come up with. That would be enough to renege on the deal. It was a handshake and didn't mean much in the grand scheme of things.

Jack was an honorable man, and his word was his bond.

He sent a message to Danielle with his fingers furiously moving across the tiny keyboard of his newly acquired flip phone. He didn't need the bells and whistles. Anything he wanted to look up on the Internet he could do it on his personal computer.

"I'm sorry but I'm a little busy at the moment. Link me into the conversation when Anderson arrives. I won't be there in person. We do have to compare notes. It's been quite some time and I'm sure we have learned a lot we need to share with one another," He pressed sent and turned toward the monitors.

He was sickened by the display of her undressing him slowly in the bathroom. How she kissed each piece of exposed skin until she was on her knees. He couldn't see exactly what she was doing but the expression on John Palmer's face was priceless.

"Enjoy it while you can. The only way you're going to see her in prison is during conjugal visits. That's assuming you want to see her at all. Why is she being so nice?" Jack asked while squeezing his fists with his upper lip twitching.

He was a one-man show against a homicidal maniac. She was unpredictable and could easily turn the tables on him. He had to account for every variable.

Jack played over different scenarios in his head with one outcome predominately making him laugh out loud.

He could almost taste the sweet texture of victory on the tip of his tongue. It was better than any drug including his daily influx of caffeine.

"You've never been squeamish about my scars. Other women look away," John referred to the injuries inflicted during a fire when he was younger.

"I've been looking for you all of my life. Why should it matter that you have a few blemishes? Nobody's perfect. I have some scars but you can't see them. I've been through a lot in my life. People have always told me I was never good enough. I've done everything I can in my power to prove to them how they have underestimated me," she stated while escorting him into the tub filled with steaming hot water and bubbles.

Jack didn't enjoy being a peeping Tom. It was unconscionable to see them in this way without acquiring some sort of warrant. He wasn't going to use anything he saw against her in an open courtroom.

John had promised to leave the front door unlocked. There would be no need to bust down the door. He could walk in unannounced at any time without probable cause since he was invited by the owner.

"I saw you the first day, and I knew we were meant to be together. I'm not sure what brought us together. It had to be some sort of higher power at work. I've never been a big believer in God but I found religion when I was diagnosed," John mentioned while moving his hands around in the bubbles.

Kellie took a washcloth and moved it over his shoulders until his eyes were closed to the soothing touch of her hands.

"You held me and listened to me when I needed you to. I couldn't ask for a more caring and loving husband. It's an open relationship, but it works for us. Sex and love are not the same thing. I'm glad you understand that better than most in your position," Kellie said with those same hands moving down his broad back.

He sighed deeply. "You always do know what to say to make me feel better. I'm glad we don't have to say goodbye right away. Five years is more than I could hope for in my wildest imagination. I would've made a deal with the devil. Maybe I already have and I don't know it."

Kellie looked around the room. "I don't see anybody with a pitchfork and tail. It's just the two of us. You have been the only man who has ever understood me. I've tried to leave a legacy behind. Let's just say I took a page from your book when I learned how fragile life was when you revealed to me that first night why you didn't want to come in for a nightcap."

"I didn't want to lead you on since I knew it couldn't go anywhere. You opened my eyes. It was the crowning achievement of my life when we walked down the aisle in front of the Justice of the Peace. The moment you said I do, my heart beat a little bit quicker," John laid it on thick.

Jack stuck his finger in his mouth, pretending to gag. It could've been a harlequin romance novel playing out with the visual aid of them getting closer to one another.

"The last few months have been the happiest of my life. You have always given me the benefit of the doubt when you probably shouldn't have. I'm not what you think I am. Dammit. This is hard. I can't afford this sentimental drivel," she said with her back turned still holding onto the washcloth.

Jack had one hand on the seat and the other one on the sliding door handle. He didn't know how she was going to do it. The fact remained she would have to wait five years to get her hands on his money.

It didn't matter how much she cared for him.

His death was the only answer to a problem she didn't even know existed until he told her about prolonging his life by five years at the bare minimum.

She had him wrapped around her little finger, but that wasn't going to be enough for her.

CHAPTER 60

She was promised heaven too many times to count. Men were notorious for telling women what they wanted to hear. The rare ones were looking to settle down and have children with a white picket fence.

Danielle had found her man. It was a time she never wanted to take for granted. It was short and sweet, but she was left with a precocious young lady to raise on her own. He wouldn't be there for some of the milestones of their daughter.

Anderson came through the door and scanned the area until he spotted her. She waved with a motion similar to a pageant queen addressing her audience.

"It looks like you are way ahead of me by at least a couple of cups of coffee. Do you want to get right into it? Where's Jack? He's not coming...is he?" Anderson asked with a shake of his head.

"I'm here but I don't have a lot of time to chit chat. What have the two of you learned about our suspect? That's exactly what she is. Don't forget how she has manipulated the system at every turn," Jack said tersely through the speakerphone which was between both Anderson and Danielle.

"Christine gave me something of a surprise. Ms. Fletcher is a card-carrying psychopath. I hate to make that generalization but her past does speak for her. Those incidents made somebody nervous enough to ship her out of sight and out of mind. I found out she had a child. His birth name was Walter. There was no designation for the father," Anderson repeated what he had written down on the pad in front of him and flipped to that certain page.

"Why do I recognize that name?" Jack pondered with the silence quite deafening even when patrons were busy talking among themselves in the coffee shop.

"I learned what dirt she has on certain high-profile officials. She won't be able to call them for reinforcements. Most of them have agreed to a joint press conference. They're going to come clean tonight in exactly 20 minutes. It will cost them dearly but other politicians have weathered worse scenarios," she told them the names written down for posterity in a similar notebook.

"Her latest victim is working with me. He doesn't believe Kellie is a cold-blooded killer. He's willing to put his money where his mouth is. I believe that is an American thing I heard in passing somewhere. He was going to die in a few days; however, modern medicine is prolonging his life by at least five years. He just finished filling her in," Jack stated.

"I'm not even going to ask how you know that. You're probably breaking several laws as we speak. It is better for me to have plausible deniability. The DEA will do an in-depth evaluation of my previous cases, including this one. I don't need the headache. This is where I get off the merry-go-round," Anderson expressed.

"I can't blame you for having doubts. She's very slippery and has people in her pocket but I have those names. We can stop her together. What does this have to do with the DEA?" Danielle asked.

She didn't look up from her laptop once again, perusing a few of those files. A name popped up. She stared at it for quite some time before she had a moment of clarity.

"I hate to cut this short but there is something I need to look into immediately. Jack, stay in touch. Don't do anything foolish. The last thing you need is for your case to unravel if you do something that won't be looked at favorably in court." Danielle touched the screen with her finger highlighting the name.

"I'm being careful, Mom. Everything has to be done by the book. Anything else will have her walking out a free woman again. She does know how to hire the best lawyers. We all saw what she did for Warren. Wouldn't it be nice to be able to tie this up in a nice bow? I guess that would be too much to ask for," Jack said before ending the conversation with the line going dead.

"You have the look," Anderson addressed with his finger waving above the laptop.

"What would that be?" she asked without looking up.

"Forget it. I haven't known you for very long. It's too bad. I'm sure we can be friends, but it won't go beyond that. I know you're going to find this hard to believe. I found somebody," he confessed, with this look of relief coming over his strong features.

"Christine is a lucky woman," she replied, still completely engrossed in the name, almost jumping out of the screen.

"How did you know? Did she say something? What did she say? How did she sound when she said it? For God's sake, don't leave me in suspense," he said with one hand closing the laptop, almost catching her finger.

"She didn't have to say a thing. It's the way you look at each other when you're in the same room. Men are oblivious. Women know those subtle cues. It wasn't like you were trying to hide it. Hide it. That's it. I've got to go," she said, frantically picking up her laptop and tucking it underneath her arm.

"Don't worry, I will pick up the bill," he called out to her sarcastically while fishing out a $10 bill more than enough to compensate for the two coffees with a generous tip on top.

Danielle barely heard him as she opened the door with the bell over the top ringing upon her exit. It was right there in front of her the entire time and she didn't see it.

The property was located near the river exactly where Jack had staked out the previous night. It couldn't have been a coincidence.

The man who had shipped her off to parts unknown when she was younger was none other than the owner of one of the houses.

She had an airtight alibi.

She would be nowhere in the vicinity if something happened to Dr. Michael Long. He was her psychiatrist and a good friend of her father. She spent a year under his care and had the baby while institutionalised.

It was no wonder she held a grudge, but she didn't want the crime to come back to her. It would stand to reason; Warren was once again going to be her fall guy. She had a feeling his alibi wasn't as solid as his co-conspirator's.

She rushed to her car, swung the door open, and jumped inside with the key in the ignition. It turned over on the first try. She put it into gear and drove with the lights flashing when she knew today was the anniversary of Miss Fletcher's time abroad hidden away from the rest of the world.

*****

Jack felt the same thrill he got when he was about to collar a suspect. His fingers were itching and the hairs on the back of his neck were standing up.

He watched the way she looked at the hairdryer plugged in on the counter. Jack almost ran from the van, expecting to hear John Palmer cry out when he was electrocuted.

She touched the cord and pulled the hairdryer closer to the edge of the counter. It dangled precariously. One last tug would give John an electrifying experience. She stopped while still holding onto the cord when she looked directly at him.

Jack lost his breath and felt his chest constrict. She couldn't see him, but it felt like they were looking into each other's eyes. He backed away from the console with his hands in plain sight.

John had his eyes closed to notice anything out of the ordinary.

"I know you have obligations. I admire what you have done with the foundation. I'm glad that I could be a small part of your success. They say money doesn't grow on trees. I can't believe how stupid some people are. Real estate is where I made my fortune. Lumber is at an all-time high due to inflation. It's all relative when you think about it," John stated with his head back against the tiles.

A washcloth covered his eyes.

Jack could only imagine what it felt like to be pampered by someone you love. He thought about his wife and what he had to go through to protect her from something from his past. It haunted him to know that he was responsible for his family hiding some place off the grid where there were no electronics.

"I'm only as good as the people I surround myself with. They have been an integral part of the success of the foundation.

Each one deserves a medal for putting up with me." Ms. Fletcher stood up until she was moving closer to the door.

"I have heard you have been called Attila the Hun. You demand perfection and you won't accept anything less. That's another thing we have in common. I can't stand insubordination. It bothers me when somebody thinks they can talk back. They find out in a hurry my patience only goes so far," John said with a deep breath causing the water to rise a few inches without going over the edge.

It was a claw-footed tub made in the same fashion as those of Victorian times. There was a skylight bringing in some natural illumination. The night sky was speckled with a blanket of stars and the moon winking from above through the cloud coverage.

"That sounds good but we both know you're lying. What about Walter? You used him and spit him out. I can't forget that," she stated.

Jack sweated heavily with beads trickling down his hairline. He knew something was wrong.

She could've gotten away with murder and claimed it was an accident. That would've been the final nail in her coffin. The video footage would ruin his career, but the damning evidence would finally put the conniving bitch behind bars where she belonged.

Losing his job was a small price to pay, in his opinion.

She was somehow in a blind spot.

Jack moved through every camera installed in the house. He had instant access by utilizing a password given to him by John Palmer. There was no sign of her.

"You probably don't know this and I've never told anybody. Money isn't everything when you don't have somebody special to spend it on. I want to give you the world. I don't care who you sleep with but I don't want to know the details. The last thing I need is a visual," John continued completely unaware he was talking to thin air.

He didn't even hear the name Walter on her whispered lips.

Jack jumped, startled by his phone once again buzzing on the table next to him.

He picked it up and found some disturbing information being relayed. *"I don't know why I'm doing this for you after you left me high and dry. Nevertheless, I did some digging and found out her child had a nickname. He grew up in foster homes fighting for everything he could get his hands on. He hurt animals when he was younger. That behavior escalated until he became the serial killer known as Damien..."*

Jack remembered it like it was yesterday. His curiosity had always gotten him into trouble. He took a cold case and found a link to it with other similar murder scenes. It was a serial killer with his own special signature of leaving his initials carved into the left arm of his victims.

They tracked the weapon back to a tattoo artist in high demand. He was found with his latest victim. Damien a.k.a. Walter never showed any remorse in court.

He was her son.

He was sent away to a special institution for the criminally insane. He had died one night after the lights went out. No suspects were ever found. He did recall his roommate. He was mute and didn't speak a word. He was released a month later when they found his body dismembered with a certain part of his anatomy yet to be discovered.

It was all making sense to Jack. She was the boy's mother. That bond couldn't be broken no matter how far they were separated from each other. She blamed him for what happened to her son. It was a matter of nurture over nature as far as he was concerned.

He caught something out of his peripheral vision.

Ms. Fletcher was back in the bathroom and she stared at the camera above the door. She made a motion with some kind of instrument pointing at him in the van.

It took him a second to register what the instrument was.

It was a tattoo gun.

CHAPTER 61

Anderson felt better than he had in days. He was no longer associated with Danielle and Jack. The last thing he needed was for his career to fall short. The best thing he could do was distance himself from the situation.

It was too bad fate had other things in store for him, including a blatant slap to the face metaphorically speaking.

He was going over transcripts from conversations during interrogations. He wanted to make sure everything was aboveboard. He had to admit working with the group from the DEA gave him a reason to think his future was bright.

That was before he came across some grainy footage of surveillance a few months ago during a raid that didn't go exactly as planned. He rummaged around in the desk until he found an old-fashioned hand-held magnifying glass.

He was alone in the office with only the ticking of the clock behind him as a reminder that he was burning the candle at both ends. He avoided Christine. Every phone call went to voicemail. He couldn't exactly tell her about his future career plans over the phone.

That sort of thing had to be done in person where he could look her in the eyes and tell her how important it was for him to have her in his corner.

He never thought Cupid's arrow was going to find him.

The magnifying glass did little to clear up the image.

He flipped through some of the transcripts. Those low on the totem pole decided to speak candidly without a lawyer present. They pretty much described the same person with only a slight variance.

It had to be Kellie Fletcher.

"You should've stopped but you are a dog with a bone." The voice was followed by the feel of a cold muzzle against the back of his head.

He dropped the magnifying glass with his heart in his throat. "Let's not do anything foolish." Anderson slowly reached across the desk when he felt the gun nudging with more conviction. "You can see my hands. I'm not armed."

"I thought this was going to be an easy assignment. Imagine my surprise when I begin tailing police officers. It didn't bother me when I knocked out Detective Creed and took all the incriminating evidence with me. I'm afraid you have become a liability," he cocked the weapon with his finger on the trigger.

"We can talk about this. You obviously have some misgivings. Think about what will happen if you kill me. The blue brotherhood will never stop hunting you. You'll always have to have eyes in the back of your head. It's not a matter of them finding you. It's a matter of when. It could be tomorrow or the next day. Rest assured, one day you will look over your shoulder and see a sea of blue uniforms pointing their guns at you. You take me for the kind of man that won't go down without a fight. You might think you will be famous but they will forget about you when something better comes along," Anderson rattled on.

"You do make a valid point. I'm getting too old for this. Maybe it's time to look for another line of work. I can only do that if you make sure Fletcher and Reeves are taken care of. You've already proven to be quite resourceful," James stated without wavering in his commitment to fire one into his brainpan.

"We are working on it. Disappear while you have the chance. Don't come back to New York. You haven't done anything you can't come back from. Ordering you to kill me makes Reeves look desperate. You must see that," Anderson debated while looking around for something to level the playing field and finding nothing.

He had to find a way to defuse the situation. His words seem to be swaying his would-be assassin. The man behind him was an enigma. He had scruples. He also had a moral compass pointing toward what was considered right and wrong.

"Count to 100," James said with his eyes scanning over his shoulder toward the exit down the hall.

He had let things get too far and wanted no part of assassinating a police officer. He could hurt people in different ways including financially. He never had to resort to using a silencer. That was a line he had learned recently he didn't want to cross.

"No offense but I hope I never see you again. Make sure you follow up on your promise. Reeves will want to come after me but he won't be able to do that from jail. Anybody in his pocket won't give him the time of day." James backed up still with Detective Anderson's head in his targeting cross-hairs.

"You've been following me for quite some time. That's not easy to do. I counted at least five times when I felt somebody was watching me. You did a good job of staying out of sight. Rest easy knowing this is going to end very soon. I'm going to forget this happened," Anderson called out over his shoulder.

There was no answer.

He swung around in his chair with his gun drawn from the holster strapped over his shoulder. He saw the door closing and moved to cut him off at the pass.

He slammed into the door leading with his shoulder. The back alley was silent.

A homeless hunched over a garbage can rummaging through discarded cartons of fast food delights.

"Did you see where he went?" Anderson inquired.

"I don't get paid to watch other people. He just told me to keep my eye on you. Jack is one of the good ones. You did the right thing by talking him down. It's been a long time since I have fired a gun. I might be a little rusty. You won't see him again," the veteran whistled with his tattered sleeves dragging over his knuckles.

Anderson was in disbelief. Jack had been monitoring him to make sure he didn't get in over his head. Utilizing someone down on his luck was pretty damn smart.

Transients were invisible.

He was about to tell the man to shove off, but he was probably doing him a favor.

He went to the street and checked for anybody trying to run away from the scene of the crime. Nobody stood out from the crowd. It wasn't like he knew what the man looked like.

Then he remembered the camera over the back of the door.

He rushed back to the authorized-personnel only room. He used his key to get in to access the footage before it was erased in 24 hours. He scrolled through the camera over the door. It would've taken longer, except it was only activated through motion.

He found him leaving, but unfortunately, he was wearing a mask. He didn't have to zoom in to know he was also wearing gloves. This was a professional. He was someone used to taking chances, but killing was the invisible line in the sand.

He had almost died and was grateful to be alive.

Thanks to Jack. Damn him.

*****

Danielle screamed through the streets with her siren blaring until she was five blocks away.

She turned off the lights and slowed down her speed so there was no chance of some over-anxious police cadet pulling her car over for a traffic infraction.

She found the house with the lights on. Somebody was home.

She held her gun to her side and walked with deliberate steps toward the gate. It was open, with one guard unconscious bleeding from the top of his head. She applied pressure and heard him moaning, indicating he was somewhat confused but still breathing.

"You might have a concussion. Stay here and call 911. I'm going in for a closer look," Danielle advised, before continuing down the cobbled red stone walkway to the front entrance left ajar.

She pushed it open with her foot until she was in a wide-open entrance way. Voices came from the left.

"Calm down. Take a breath. I'm not going to resist you. Take whatever you want and leave. I'll even open the safe for you. Money is nothing if I'm not around to enjoy it," Dr. long stated in a neutral voice.

"Stop talking. I need to think for a moment," Warren said while pacing back and forth in front of the chair the good doctor was restrained to.

Danielle poked her head around the side. It was a tense situation, and it was only going to get worse when Warren heard the sirens approaching. She had to act fast, but she needed to use the element of surprise.

"You can still walk away from this. Take the consolation prize of $100,000 and call it a day," the doctor negotiated for his freedom.

"She said she was going to be here. I'm such a fool to believe anything she tells me. I need to revaluate my options. I have nothing against you. She wants you dead. Why the hell am I doing her dirty work again? Do I have stupid tattooed on my head?" Warren asked with the gun tapping his forehead.

"It's not your fault. Some people are easily manipulated. She made you believe in yourself. That you could do anything with a few encouraging words. That is classic sociopath behavior." The doctor struggled against his bonds.

"You should know. She confided in me how you made her life a living hell. You're no better than she is. The only difference is that you have a degree on the wall. I could do the world a favor by pulling the trigger. You shattered her psyche," Warren explained.

"You're talking about Kellie Fletcher. I tried to help her, but she didn't want to listen to me. The only thing she could think about was revenge. She was a tough nut to crack. Pardon the pun. I should've known she would come for me eventually," the doctor stammered through his dry lips.

He caught movement in the corner of his eye and he turned in time to receive 2 feet planted in his face.

He whirled back with his hands flailing in the air until the gun came loose and skittered across the floor out of his reach.

An arm came across his neck, with his feet coming out from underneath him.

He was twisted like a pretzel and handcuffed. His last thought was the very idea of telling them everything he knew about Miss Fletcher. She would soon join him in prison or in hell. Whichever came first.

CHAPTER 62

Jack could only stare at the monitor completely frozen in time. She had just said without saying a word her intention was to kill John Palmer. She didn't seem to care he was watching from a distance.

He ran from the van, almost tripping over his own feet in the process. He had no idea he was capable of sprinting that fast down the street.

He leaped over a hedge when he saw two police cars converging on his location.

He checked the door and found it locked. He tried to kick his way in yet the door was reinforced to keep trespassers from getting inside.

"I'm going around back. Get the battering ram and go through the front door," he said with a wave of his badge.

He made his way around to the back of the house looking for any opening he could use.

There was a window in the basement slightly open with an encasement of chicken wire around the frame.

He removed his knife and cut through the wire slowly. He finally removed the wire weakened with age. It wasn't much of an opening. He had to hold in his stomach and squeeze through going in headfirst with no way of knowing what he was going to come across.

His jacket snagged on the exposed wire.

He wiggled free of it until he fell to the hard pavement on his hands and knees. It temporarily knocked the wind out of him but he was back on his feet bounding up the stairs.

He flung open the door when he realized he had left his gun in the van. It was biting into his hip and he relieved the pressure by removing the holster. There was no time to go back and retrieve it.

He heard the officers at the front door banging repeatedly with the battering ram. He didn't know what brought them out on a night like this but he wasn't going to quibble over details.

There had to be a break in the case he didn't know about.

"You're too late. I can finally rest. This has been a long time coming. I know you were just doing your job, but that doesn't negate what happened to my little boy when you put him in the system. I never trusted men, and they never gave me a reason to." Ms. Fletcher sighed, with no visible weapon in her hand.

"The kid was nutty for Cocoa puffs. I guess the apple doesn't fall far from the tree," Jack said while trying to open the door, only to find there was something jammed underneath it.

"That's an interesting choice of words. Not exactly clinical. You have one chance. Leave me here and get out the same way you came in. You really don't want to be around for what happens next," she said with her head held high and her eyes closed while inhaling something sickeningly sweet.

He didn't notice, but now he was well aware of the gas filling the room. One spark was all that it was going to take.

She looked wild-eyed at the door.

He realized the metal piece at the bottom was definitely capable of causing a spark.

He made a split-second decision with the sound of the battering ram hitting the door repeatedly in cycles of 20 seconds apart. He pointed at her, but there was no further discussion.

He wasn't going to make it back to the basement.

He could feel his feet slapping heavily against the parquet floors in the living room. He didn't even slow down when he hit the bay window. He felt the glass cutting into his cheek and shoulder when he was suddenly propelled by a gust of hot air.

The heat stripped away his clothing until he felt like he was burning alive.

*****

390

Danielle held his bandaged hand while looking at the machines beeping incessantly for the past 48 hours. She had found him lying prone on the ground when she arrived. His shirt was on fire.

She suffocated the flames with her suit jacket. It had become a casualty of a case that brought them closer together and tore them further apart at the same time.

It was touch and go but the doctor told her he was going to need plenty of rehabilitation. He was expected to make a full recovery.

Jack's family were on their way to the States to join him.

They had found two bodies after the fire died down. Dental records confirmed both Kellie and John had succumbed to the blaze. Warren was waiting for his day in court, but this time, he didn't have Kellie's resources behind him.

A lot of very powerful people, including Reeves, had resigned from their positions after revealing their unusual carnal desires to the public.

Reeves went to jail for hiring a hit man. They couldn't find the man he hired. He became a ghost. His text messages and finances were more than enough to convict.

Danielle felt Jack's fingers tighten, and then his eyes opened.

"It's over," he whispered.

She placed his badge on his chest. "We are just getting started, Partner.

Crime doesn't stop in the city that never sleeps."

ABOUT THE AUTHOR

C T Mitchell is regarded as one of Australia's most prolific mystery thriller writers having written 45 short read books and novels in his first eight years as an author.

His love for crime stems from his appetite for Agatha Christie novels and his devouring of British whodunit television series including Morse, Touch of Frost and Midsomer Murders.

After attending a lunch with James Patterson in Sydney 2015, Mitchell worked heavily on connecting with his audience by building a 40,000 + social media presence and a 10,000-email list of veracious readers.

C T Mitchell's books have enjoyed Amazon bestseller status many times; often in the company of Ann Cleeves, Jeffrey Archer and Peter James.

In 2019 his novel Murder Secret, published by traditional UK publisher Austin Macauley, was short listed to be made into a film through the Queensland Writers Centre, Adaptable program.

While this book was not successful, the Detective Jack Creed series was pitched to Amazon Prime and Netflix as a potential television series with some interest shown.

Mitchell has a strong distribution deal with India's Juggernaut Books; perhaps Bollywood might be calling soon.

C T Mitchell's production team is a global enterprise with formatters in the Ukraine, cover designers in US and editors in Australia and America.

To date most of his books are produced by imprint company Wood Duck Media, but Mitchell is not averse to looking at other publishing options.

His books are set in the Northern Rivers NSW where towns like Kingscliff, Cabarita Beach, Pottsville, Hastings Point, Byron Bay and Bangalow feature prominently.

This new series, Jack Creed New York series, is a move out of Australia, after Mitchell fell in love with New York after attending his son's 2017 wedding in Central Park.

Australia is C T Mitchell's home – expect more books to have an Aussie flavor in the future.

https://CTMitchellBooks.com

FREE DOWNLOAD

Grab two free downloads at
<ins>https://CTMitchellBooks.com</ins>